D1351303

OTHER BOOKS BY
CATHERINE COOKSON

NOVELS   Kate Hannigan
          The Fifteen Streets
          Colour Blind
          Maggie Rowan
          Rooney
          The Menagerie
          Slinky Jane
          Fanny McBride
          Fenwick Houses
          The Garment
          The Blind Miller
          Hannah Massey
          The Long Corridor
          The Unbaited Trap
          Katie Mulholland
          The Round Tower
          The Nice Bloke
          The Glass Virgin
          The Invitation
          The Dwelling Place
          Feathers in the Fire
          Pure as the Lily
          The Mallen Streak
          The Mallen Girl
          The Mallen Litter
          The Invisible Cord
          The Gambling Man
          Miss Martha Mary Crawford

The Tide of Life
The Slow Awakening
The Iron Façade
The Girl
The Cinder Path
The Man Who Cried
Tilly Trotter
Tilly Trotter Wed
Tilly Trotter Widowed
The Whip
Hamilton
The Black Velvet Gown
Goodbye Hamilton
A Dinner of Herbs
Harold
The Moth
Bill Bailey
The Parson's Daughter
Bill Bailey's Lot
The Cultured Handmaiden
Bill Bailey's Daughter
The Harrogate Secret
The Black Candle
The Wingless Bird
The Gillyvors
My Beloved Son
The Rag Nymph

THE MARY ANN STORIES
          A Grand Man
          The Lord and Mary Ann
          The Devil and Mary Ann
          Love and Mary Ann

Life and Mary Ann
Marriage and Mary Ann
Mary Ann's Angels
Mary Ann and Bill

FOR CHILDREN
          Matty Doolin
          Joe and the Gladiator
          The Nipper
          Blue Baccy
          Our John Willie

Mrs Flannagan's Trumpet
Go Tell It To Mrs Golightly
Lanky Jones
Nancy Nutall and the Mongrel
Bill and the Mary Ann Shaughnes

AUTOBIOGRAPHY
          Our Kate
          Let Me Make Myself Plain

Catherine Cookson Country

WRITING AS CATHERINE MARCHANT
          House' of Men
          The Fen Tiger

Heritage of Folly

CATHERINE COOKSON

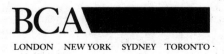

THE
House of Women

BCA

LONDON   NEW YORK   SYDNEY   TORONTO ·

This edition published 1992
by BCA
by arrangement with Bantam Press

CN 3873

Third reprint 1992

Printed and bound in Germany
by Graphischer Großbetrieb Pößneck GmbH
A member of the Mohndruck printing group

THE HOUSE OF WOMEN

PART ONE

1968

I

'Something wrong, Peggy?'

'No. What can be wrong?'

'Well, I haven't seen you sittin' in the park, not at this time. It's near on dark; they'll be closing up shortly.'

'Well, let them close up. Let them close up.'

'There is something the matter, isn't there?' The boy carrying the guitar case slowly sat down on the park seat beside the young girl and, holding the case between his knees, he folded his arms about it and hugged it to him as if embracing it. He did not immediately speak but made a slight rocking movement; presently, he said, 'It's Andrew Jones, isn't it?'

'Who said it was Andrew Jones? And you, Charlie Conway, you are always sticking your nose into somebody else's business.'

The boy did not turn towards her to counteract in any way this short tirade, but remained still, his arms tight around the guitar case, until she said in a small voice, 'I'm sorry, Charlie. Don't stick your nose in; it's . . . it's . . .'

When her voice broke he turned quickly towards her, saying, 'Come on home. Look; it's gettin' on dark.'

11

'No, no.' She shook her head.

'You frightened?'

She did not answer him, but turned her head away and blew her nose. When, however, he said, 'Can't you talk about it to somebody?' she rounded on him again: 'Talk about what!' she cried. 'What you meaning? Talk about what?'

'Well.' He allowed the case to slip between his knees until the bottom came to rest on the grass; then he said, 'Well, there's your mam and your gran and your great-gran; surely you can talk to one of them.'

'*About what?*'

He now turned on her, and in much the same vehement tone as hers, he answered, 'About what's troubling you, making you cry. Sittin' here on a park seat where I've never seen you sit before; you're always flying through here as if the devil was after you; no time to talk to anybody.'

Through the deepening twilight, they stared at each other, and in the silence that had fallen between them she bowed her head deeply on to her chest and her voice was almost a whimper now as she said, 'I'm frightened, Charlie. It's . . . it's Dad. I'm frightened of Dad.'

'He can't kill you.' His voice was as low as hers; and when she answered, 'He could,' he replied, 'He'd get over it. Da did with our Lucy.'

She almost reared back from him now, crying, 'Anyway she's married and got two children. I'm . . . I'm . . . ' She stopped; then bringing her head forward and glaring at him, she said, 'What are you insinuating?'

'Nothing. Nothing . . . only . . . '

'Yes; only?' Her head was nodding now.

He jerked himself to his feet, pulled the case up under his arm and said, 'They're talking. It's all over the school. Your dear friend Mary Fuller couldn't keep her mouth shut if it was glued.'

12

Seeing her face quiver and her shoulders droop, he said, 'Somebody wants to give Andy Jones a black eye; and that's not all. Look; come on home with me.'

She was bridling again. 'Why should I? I've got my own home to go to.'

'Then why don't you go to it and talk to your mother, or them?'

'Oh you! It's all right for you. Talk to my mother or them. You're so clever at working things out, the great mathematician. Great-gran said you were born old.'

She swung round from him, shaking her head wildly as if she were throwing something off, as she muttered, 'I'm sorry. I didn't mean that.'

'Oh, I don't mind. It's a sort of compliment. Coming from your great-gran an' all, yes, that was something; my mother's always saying she can cut you to pieces with a look when she likes. Look, Peggy.' He stood in front of her now. One hand holding the guitar case, he placed his other on her arm and said quietly, 'My mother knows how to deal with things. She'll go and talk to your mam on the quiet. Come on, else' – his voice lightened – 'we'll be thrown out.' The short laugh he emitted verged on a giggle. 'Fancy being thrown out of the park at our age. I used to make a point of it at one time . . . being thrown out of the park. I used to hide behind the bushes till old Mr Terence caught a glimpse of me, then let him see me on purpose and run, not out of the West gate but the far one.' He jerked his head backwards. 'I used to like to make the old fellow shout. He couldn't run: he was past it.'

Peggy Hammond raised her head to look at this boy whom she had known all her life: she could never imagine him teasing the park-keeper because he never seemed to do anything that would get him into trouble. He was what her mam called solid. She used to say, 'May'll never have

13

any trouble with him, he's too solid.' At times she would add, 'and dull'. Sometimes she thought her mam was jealous of Mrs Conway. Once she had referred to her as Auntie May and her father had barked at her.

When Charlie said, 'This one can run, so I think we should be slippy,' his broad plain face went into a smile and the thought passed through her mind that he looked like a man, not a boy, and when she stood up and started to walk by his side she changed the conversation by pointing to the guitar case and saying, 'Where were you going with that?'

'It's where I've been with that . . . it.' Again he swung the case up into his arms and he hugged it to him as he said, 'I've been for my first lesson.'

'You don't need lessons; you can play it.'

'That isn't playing it, that's just strumming. Anybody can strum. I'm going to learn it properly. He's a classical guitarist, Mr Reynolds.' He laughed now, saying, 'He hates groups. The tiddly pom-pom-poms, he calls them. He's very funny: he makes you laugh, that's until he starts the lesson.'

'Then you won't be going to the old people's sing-song or keeping in with the school group, because all that is tiddly pom-pom-pom, isn't it?'

He continued to walk on, the guitar case again being carried by the handle; and when he made no retort she muttered, 'I'm being bitchy; I don't seem to be able to help it these days. I . . . I . . . '

'Oh! Peggy, don't cry. Oh lord, don't cry. Look, we'll cross over to Hooker's field and go in the back way . . . '

'*No! No! Not that way.*' She had stopped abruptly, and he with her.

'Well, I just suggested it because it could be a short cut. All right, we'll keep to the road, but we can still go in the lane by the bottom way.'

14

They walked on in silence now, and five minutes later they entered the lower end of Bramble Lane, where bungalows had recently been built opposite the cemetery wall. Beyond the bungalows were older houses. These were detached, each with a quarter of an acre of land, some divided from their neighbours by tall cypress hedges that had grown twenty feet or more in the eighteen years since they were planted shortly after the houses were built.

The last house of this type in the long lane was Charlie Conway's home. It, too, was separated from its neighbour, which was Peggy Hammond's home. This house, however, had been built in 1913 when Bramble Lane was a real country lane; and it had taken its name from the lane and was called Bramble House. It was a much larger house than the superior dwellings that, apart from the bungalows, completely bordered one side of the lane. It stood in two and a half acres of its own grounds and was overlooked by no-one. Here, cypress trees had been planted along three of its four sides. The front side, facing east, looked directly on to cow and sheep pastures belonging to a farm which was the last bit of open agricultural land within Fellburn itself.

Naturally the occupants of Bramble House felt superior to the rest of the dwellers in the lane. Over the long years they had kept themselves to themselves. In a way, it was as though a concession had been granted to the forging of the friendship between Lizzie Hammond and May Conway. May, being forty-six, was the older by nine years, yet in spirit she was far younger than Peggy's mother. As she was apt to say to her husband Frank, 'Between Gran and Great-gran and Leonard Hammond, Lizzie has been nulled.' . . .

May Conway now looked from her son to young Peggy Hammond, and in her breezy fashion she said, 'What now, brown cow! What's up? You hit Peggy?' and she grinned as she looked at her son, and he, answering, said, 'Don't be daft, Ma.'

'Then why have you been crying, Peggy? Come and sit down. Have you had your tea? If not you can sit with us.'

'She hasn't been home yet, Ma.'

'Oh.' May turned and looked at the kitchen clock. 'Your mother'll be worrying. Where have you been?'

When Peggy still made no response Charlie said, 'She's been sitting in the park, Ma. She's worried; she wants to talk to you. I'm going up to me room.'

'Don't you want your tea first?'

'No; that can wait.'

'All right, sir. Very well, sir. I'll bring it up when you ring.'

'Aw! Ma.' The boy tossed his head as he laughed; then he glanced at Peggy, saying, 'She's daft at times, but not all the time.'

When the door closed on her son, May Conway pulled a kitchen chair out from under the table and, pointing to it, said quietly, 'Sit down, Peggy.'

When the girl was seated, she herself sat down opposite her and, placing her forearms on the table and joining her hands together, she said, 'Well, what's it all about?'

Peggy looked across the table into the kindly face of the woman whom her father considered common; but she couldn't bring herself to say the words that were terrifying her, yet when her lips moved in and out, and her eyes blinked, and the tears pressed from her lashes, she had no need to use words, and May Conway said, 'Aw! hinny, no.'

Peggy gave no answer, she just nodded her head a number of times; and when May Conway's hands came across the table and gripped hers she burst into a storm of tears. Immediately May was round the table and at her side, holding her and saying, 'There! now. There! now. Come

16

on. Come on. You're not the first and you won't be the last. But my God! what's he going to say? I mean, your father. I'm not worrying about your mother, or the other two, but him. Who is it? Do we know him?'

Still Peggy couldn't speak; all she could manage was a gulp in her throat to save herself from choking.

'Come over here and sit down in the old armchair; it's easy. Now, sit quiet, stop your crying. Try to relax. That's a daft thing to say, isn't it? try to relax. Why do people say such daft things. Look, I'll make you a cup of tea and perhaps you'll talk while I'm making it.'

She switched the electric kettle on. She made the tea; she poured it out; but still Peggy had not uttered one word until finally, the cup in her hand and rattling in the saucer, she whimpered, 'I'm . . . I'm frightened, Mrs Conway. I'm frightened.'

'Yes, of course you are, lass, you're bound to be; but believe me, you'll get used to the idea. How far have you gone?'

'I've . . . I've just missed my third period.'

'What! Three? Oh, my God, girl! You should have come clean before now. And to keep this to yourself all this time. When did it happen?'

'I . . . I don't rightly know.'

'You mean you went with him more than once?'

Peggy's head drooped again; and now she whimpered, 'He . . . he said it would be all right; he had used things.'

'Does he know?'

'No. He . . . he dropped me.'

'By God! he did an' all, he did drop you, lass. You mean he's given you the chuck? Since when?'

'Well, since I . . . I wouldn't go to the barn. Well . . . I mean, I wouldn't any more.'

'The old barn at the bottom of Hooker's field? Eeh! God Almighty! That place should be turned into a museum the way it's helped to swell the population. What's his name? How old is he?'

Again it was a mutter: 'Andy . . . Andrew Jones. He's . . . he's turned seventeen.'

'Still at school?'

'Yes.'

'Well now, drink that tea. I'm going to slip next door to your mother and have a word. But don't worry, what's done's done. And I'll tell you this: it isn't the first time a young lass has sat in that chair and told me the same story. But likely you've heard it from your gran or your great-gran. Thank God, though, in her case it turned out all right: she's married and has two bairns now and she's happy. Amazing that, she's happy, and him not worth two pennorth of copper. But it takes all types. Now sit quiet, and drink that tea, as I told you. I'll be back in a minute.'

From her kitchen door May walked along by the side of the house before crossing the strip of lawn, along a short path bordered by rowan trees, and towards a narrow wooden gate in the high brick wall that led into the garden of Bramble House. This she opened and made sure she closed before making her way knowingly through a dark strip of woodland. Coming out into the open she had to tread carefully through a bed of azaleas before crossing the lawn to the front of the red-brick, plain-faced house. This she quickly skirted, then crossed a broad courtyard that was bordered on one side by two garages which had at one time been stables and a number of outhouses. She was approaching the kitchen door when it opened and Lizzie Hammond emerged.

Lizzie was pulling on her coat and although she showed some surprise that May should be calling at this time of night, because she never came over when Leonard would be in, she didn't question her but said, 'Peggy hasn't come home yet. I've just realised there's no choir practice tonight. I don't know where she's got to.'

'Lizzie.' May put a tight hand on her friend's arm, saying, 'I know where she's got to: she's next door in the kitchen. Look; let's go back a minute.'

'What's she doing in your place? Why isn't . . . ?'

'I'll tell you everything in a minute. Get inside.' She almost pushed Lizzie into her own kitchen, only to bite hard on her lip as she saw Lizzie's mother, Mrs Pollock, sitting at the table peeling apples.

Victoria Pollock would be the last person to take this news quietly, and she was about to say to Lizzie, 'Will you come over to our place for a minute; I want your advice on something,' when the kitchen door opened and the matriarch of the house entered.

Mrs Emma Funnell was seventy-four. She was born in 1894 and she married Patrick Funnell, a builder, in 1913. She was then nineteen and Patrick had given her the house as a wedding present. It had always been her house, she had always been the mistress of it, and being determined to live to a hundred, she still had some way to go.

She was known never to waste words and this she proved when, looking at May, she said, 'What's the matter, May? You look white around the gills.'

May liked the old girl, as she thought of her, but there were times when she annoyed her; this was 1968 and the old madam acted as if she was still in the last century, with Victoria on the throne. So it was her manner now that caused May to say, 'Well, since you're here, Great-gran, and Gran is too, I may as well tell you.'

'Tell? Tell? Tell us what? Something we don't already know?'

'There wouldn't be any point in telling you otherwise, would there? Oh, blast! Come on, Lizzie; I can't talk here.'

'Look! Wait a minute, woman.'

Almost pushing Lizzie before her towards the open door, May turned to the old lady, saying, 'No; you wait a minute, Great-gran. And don't call me "woman",' she said, emphasising her words by nodding; then taking a reluctant Lizzie by the arm she drew her into the yard.

The air had turned chilly and she had come out without a coat and she shivered, and when Lizzie said, 'What on earth is it? What's the matter? Is . . . is it something to do with Peggy?'

May answered, 'Yes, it's something to do with Peggy, Lizzie. But I can't stand here; I'm freezing and you will be an' all. Come on.' And now taking her hand, she almost ran her up the yard, across the lawn, through the azalea bed and into the wood strip, where she slowed to a walk, but continued to pay no heed to Lizzie's questions and protests until they were at her own back door. And there, panting, she turned for a moment and peered at her friend in the light from her kitchen window, and in a low voice she said, 'This is going to be a testing time, Lizzie. The two witches over there' — she jerked her head in the direction of the house they had just left — 'they'll do enough squawking, or at least your mother will. But you have to remember it's your daughter you're dealing with.'

'*May.*' Lizzie was now clutching May's arms. 'What are you trying to tell me?'

'Well, I think you should have guessed by now.'

'Guessed what? *No, no. Dear God! You mean? Oh no!*'

'Be quiet!'

'It mustn't be. May, what are you saying? He'll . . . he'll go mad. He'll kill her.'

20

'He'll not, not if you stand on your hind legs. And if I know anything, you'll have Great-gran behind you, just to spite him, if nothing else. Anyway, remember she's just a bit of a lass; she's just escaped childhood.'

'Oh, May, *shut up! Shut up!* Just escaped . . .'

May was pushing the door open now, and when Lizzie entered the kitchen she looked across to where her daughter was sitting in the old leather chair, staring fixedly at her.

'Sit down.' May pushed a chair forward but Lizzie waved it abruptly aside and, looking at Peggy, said, 'What's this?'

'Oh, Mam. Mam.'

The sound was like the whimper of a child, but Lizzie came back harshly, saying, 'Don't "Oh Mam. Mam" me. What's this? Don't tell me . . . don't tell me you're pregnant. You're not, are you? You're not.'

'She is, and must be close on three months.'

Lizzie now turned on May, crying, 'How is it that you know all about it and I don't?'

'For the simple reason that your daughter was frightened to go home and Charlie brought her in here. I've just heard about it myself.'

Lizzie gulped, then took two steps towards her daughter, but seemed to find it impossible to approach her further. And now, from between clenched teeth, she said, 'Why have you done this, you of all people? How's he going to take it? What's he going to say, your father? Who was it?' Her voice was rising.

Quite slowly Peggy drew herself up from the chair and, confronting her mother, said to her, 'It was a young man, Mam . . . you know. It's always a young man.' Then, the unusual boldness quickly evaporating, she went on: 'I . . . I thought you'd be shocked, and . . . and Gran an' all, but I thought you'd understand.'

The push that her mother gave her knocked her back into the chair and she cried out as her head hit the wooden headrest, which brought May straight to her defence, crying, 'That's enough of that! And look, Lizzie: I thought you would be shocked – that's only natural – but not enough to lift your hand to her. She'll have enough of that from your dear, considerate husband.'

'Don't you interfere in this matter, May.'

The clock on the mantelpiece struck seven and they all heard each strike before May said with quiet dignity, 'Very well, Lizzie, I won't interfere in your business, but when you next want to come running, don't forget you made this statement. Now, if you'll take your daughter home and get on with your business I'll be obliged.'

'Oh, May, May, I'm sorry; but I'm . . . '

'If you don't mind, Lizzie' – May went towards the kitchen door and opened it – 'I have my own *business* to see to: Frank will be in in a moment and he likes his meal in peace.'

May now watched Lizzie march from the room; then she looked to where Peggy seemed to be having to drag herself up from the chair. And when the young girl came to pass her and muttered, 'Oh! Mrs Conway,' May put out her hand and patted the unhappy girl twice on the shoulder, then followed her to the door and closed it.

She returned to the table, sat down and was about to rest her head in her hand when the kitchen door opened and there entered her husband and son. Her husband, coming to her, bent over her from his long thin length and said, 'That's what you get for trying to help.' And she sniffed as she looked from one to the other and said, 'One of these days someone's going to blow on you from the other side of the keyhole.'

'Didn't need the keyhole, lass; we were standing up straight, both of us, weren't we?' He turned to his son, and

Charlie, looking at his mother, said, 'What'll happen now?'

But it was his father who answered: 'What'll happen now, lad, is that her kind, considerate and thoughtful dad will attempt to murder her because he won't be able to stand the disgrace.'

2

Although Bramble House had a plain exterior, its inside, by comparison, could be regarded as beautiful. All the rooms had high ceilings with ornamental cornices and matching centre-pieces. The hall struck the visitor immediately, being twenty-five feet long and twenty wide, with a broad, shallow-step, half-spiral staircase rising up from the middle of it.

To the left of the entrance was an iron-framed fireplace, the overmantel in wrought iron reaching half-way to the ceiling, and to the side of it a door led into a twenty-five foot drawing-room with two long windows on the left looking out on to the front of the house. At the end of the room a glass door led into a conservatory.

Also at the end of this side of the hall a passage led to a door and into what was known as the cottage annexe. This had been added at the early stage of the building of the house to accommodate Patrick Funnell's mother. It consisted of two medium-sized rooms and a kitchen downstairs and two bedrooms and an attic above.

At the far end of the hall a door gave on to a large kitchen with its accompanying pantries and storerooms. At the right-hand side, opposite the drawing-room, was the dining-room, and what had once been the breakfast-room but was now Mr Leonard Hammond's study.

On the first floor a narrow balcony gave way to a quite large landing, termed the upper hall, from which five bedrooms and a bathroom led. And above this there were five attic rooms, which at one time had been used as a nursery and servants' quarters.

But there were no sleeping-in servants now at Bramble House, for, as Emma Funnell was apt to say: There were three able-bodied women in the house, so what did they want with servants? Even at seventy-four she still considered herself included in the term 'able bodied'. And compared with her daughter, Victoria, she was certainly able bodied.

Leonard Hammond was thirty-seven years old, although no-one would believe it for he looked and acted like a man in his late forties. He was of medium height and broad, with a suggestion of a pot-belly. If he hadn't been a tee-totaller this protuberance could have been put down to drink; in his case, however, it had been created through over-eating. And he over-ate presumably as a defence against the frustration brought on through having to live in this house of women. Moreover, he had a grudge against life because it had cheated him, led him astray. Had it not dangled this house before his eyes, pointing out that it was a place he would never be able to acquire through his own initiative, bemoaning as an excuse that, coming from the lower end of the working class, he could see no way of ever attaining such a place as Bramble House and perhaps inheriting a car business like the Funnells, unless it be through marriage? And so, at eighteen and working as a junior car salesman, he set his sights on Lizzie Pollock, who was directly in line, as he saw it, to one day owning the lot. He wasn't twenty when he gently manipulated the line and caught the fish, and ran off with it. It was very romantic. What could her mother, or indeed her grandmother, do? He was to learn and quickly just what her grandmother could do.

Long before he was twenty-one his eyes had been opened to the situation inside the house and to the knowledge that Emma Funnell disliked him almost as much as he disliked her. But he still wasn't beaten. When his daughter was born he felt he had a handle, for what augured well was that the old bitch, as he termed her, took the child over as if she herself were the mother of it.

But as time went on he had to add to his learning the fact that nothing was changed and that the only hope he was left with was that Emma Funnell would make her demise at an early date. But now, at seventy-four, she continued to disappoint him because she was more alert than her daughter or even her granddaughter. His wife he considered to be spineless.

And here she was now, at this moment, facing him across his desk, and he greeted her in his usual fashion by saying, 'What is it now? I have work to do. Mine doesn't stop at five, you know.'

Lizzie said nothing, but she continued to stare down into the face that she had come to hate. In spite of the broadness of his body, his face was thin, his chin almost pointed. His hair was sandy and of the texture that couldn't be brushed flat: it sprang out from the back of his head and sometimes from above his ears, no matter how he plastered it down. She had soon become aware of his reason for marrying her; and in her own way she had gloated, and still did, over the fact that his plan had misfired and that his position today wasn't that of running the works, as he had expected it to be, for he was still in the showroom and sales department, with the glorified title of manager. The real managers of the business were Fred Cartwright and his assistant, Henry Brooker.

27

As she looked into his cold gaze she thought, as she had so often done, If only he had loved me a little, been kind. But he had no kindness in him. He had no real friends, not even amongst those at church, or at the youth club. The only reason he took that over was to give him a place to exercise his power. She wondered if he loved anyone but himself. But why was she asking that? He loved Peggy . . . well, if he had any feelings at all they were for his daughter. And now she closed her eyes and muttered to herself, Oh my God! How am I going to put this?

'*What's the matter with you?*'

'There's nothing the matter with me.' Her voice was as loud as his own; it was that bawling that did it. She could stand up to him when he bawled. She'd had to learn this defence or he would have bawled her down on every occasion. That was one part of him her granny had been unable to subdue, his voice. And now, for a moment, she felt a sort of pleasure touching on impish delight in contemplating the words she was about to deliver to him.

'I would hold tight on to something if I were you.'

He sat back in the chair.

'What's up with you?'

'Nothing's up with me, but there's something up with our daughter.'

He slowly rose to his feet, pushing the chair back with a thrust of his foot and, after staring at her for a moment, he said, 'You're taking a delight in this, whatever it is, aren't you?'

'Oh yes' – her head bobbed up and down – 'great delight, great delight; I've always wanted to be a grandmother: there's not enough of them in this house.'

His lower jaw was thrust out, his eyes narrowed. He turned his body slightly away to the side while still looking at her before he said, 'What are you saying?'

28

'Well, you're not dim, are you, Leonard? You've always pointed out to me how quick on the uptake you are, that you know what people are thinking before they open their mouths. It's a bone of contention with you that people don't understand how bright you are.'

It was she now who half turned from him; her mind was jumping to his defence: Why was she going for him like this? She knew what the news would do to him; and, in his own way, he certainly had something to put up with in this house.

As if in one movement he sprang round the desk and was now standing close to her, his face only inches from hers. Spittle on his lips, his nostrils wide, spluttering at her, he said, 'She isn't . . . she's not? She couldn't be! Not her.'

Her defence of him was gone. Her voice was even calm as she said, 'Why not? she's female.'

She watched his eyes widen, his brows lift; she saw his hand come up slowly past his face and his fingers raise the front of his hair until it matched the back. She thought he looked like a porcupine on the defensive. But the yell he now emitted showed that he certainly wasn't on the defensive but on the attack.

'Fetch her! Fetch her in here! My God! I'll . . . I'll . . . '

'Yes, what are you going to do? Kill her?'

'Fetch her! And shut that taunting mouth of yours.'

She was about to say, 'Why don't you come out into the hall or into the kitchen; there'll be more room there to knock her about,' but she thought better of it and walked purposely slowly from the room.

As she crossed the hall towards the stairs her mother and grandmother came from the dining-room, and her mother called to her, 'Did you move my indigestion tablets, Lizzie?' But before she could answer, her grandmother, on a laugh, said, 'I saw the cat running off with something,' and added,

29

'You and your indigestion tablets. If you did a little more bending you wouldn't have indigestion. That dining-room hasn't had a good polish for weeks. Now get at it tomorrow and you'll find you'll be able to eat your dinner without indigestion . . . tablets!' Mrs Funnell had moved from her daughter towards Lizzie and stopped her as she mounted the third stair, saying, 'Something the matter? You are as white as a sheet. You feeling bad?'

'No, Gran; I'm not feeling bad.'

'Well, what is it? What happened over at May's?'

'You'll know soon enough. Oh, yes, you'll know soon enough.'

'That isn't good enough for me; tell me now.'

'I won't tell you now, Gran, you'll wait. And you won't have to wait long if you stay there.' Lizzie now ran up the remainder of the stairs.

When she pushed open the bedroom door she saw her daughter sitting at the foot of the bed, and for a moment she wanted to rush to her and pull her into her arms because she didn't look a sixteen-year-old, but more like the child who had stood before her in her new school uniform, how many years ago? She was still in her school uniform, but she was pregnant, and before this year was over she'd be a mother. Oh dear Lord! Lord! Why had this to happen? And in this house. But it wouldn't happen in this house, she'd be married. Oh, yes, yes, her mind emphasised this. Whoever it was would be brought to book and she'd be married. If it was the last thing she did in her life, she'd see that she was married and had a place of her own. But where? Who would provide that? He was likely just a bit of a lad.

She sat down on the edge of the bed and, looking at the bowed head, she said, 'How old is he?'

'Seventeen.'

'And still at school?'

'Yes.'

'What's his name?'

'It doesn't matter.'

'It doesn't matter?'

The yell startled Peggy and the look on her mother's face frightened her, and she stammered, 'Andrew Jones.'

Lizzie drew in a long and calming breath and, putting out her hand, she jerked Peggy from the bed, saying, 'Come on downstairs. You've got to face him.'

'I'm . . . I'm frightened . . . Mam.'

'I'll be with you.' . . .

Lizzie wasn't at all surprised, when they reached the hall, to see her granny standing near the drawing-room door, but when she lifted her hand, finger wagging, saying plainly Wait, she saw surprise come over the old lady's face.

She had to push Peggy before her into the study, then she quickly closed the door behind her. And when she saw the look on her husband's face she said quickly, 'Don't you try any rough stuff.' Then, 'We're going to talk.'

'*Shut up!* And *you* come here.' His index finger formed a crook; but Peggy remained where she was by the side of her mother; only for a moment though, for in two lightning strides he had her by the shoulders, pulling her towards the middle of the room, crying as he did so, 'You dirty little slut! Whoring! Whoring! Who is he? Who was it?'

'Dad . . . Dad.' The words came out with each shake of her shoulders; and when Lizzie, gripping his arm, cried, 'Give over! Give over!' he kicked at her shins, causing her to let out a high yell and stumble backwards.

Just as his shaking hands moved over his daughter's shoulders towards her neck, Emma Funnell rushed in like a soldier on a bayonet charge, except that she didn't carry a gun but a walking stick. Quickly reversing her

31

hold from the handle to grip the bottom and, thrusting it wildly out, she did something she had wanted to do for years and used physical force on Leonard Hammond. But it was he who was clutching at his throat and trying to release himself from the handle of the walking stick. And when, stumbling sideways, he slid from its hold he dropped on to one knee, where he remained gasping and staring up at the formidable woman bending over him. Then he was on his feet, his fingers stroking his neck as he cried, 'What do you think you're doing, woman?'

'The same as you were doing to her.' Mrs Funnell pointed to where Peggy was leaning over the desk; then looking towards Lizzie, who was rubbing her shin, she demanded, 'Now tell me what this is all about.'

'Oh, you don't know?' Leonard Hammond was still fingering his neck. 'Fancy anything happening in this house that you don't know. Well, as I understand it, my daughter is pregnant.'

In the silence that followed this announcement, Mrs Funnell looked at the schoolgirl, and from deep inside herself she wanted to cry, 'Ah, no! no! Not Peggy. No!' She loved Peggy as she had never loved her own daughter, because Victoria had been a sickly specimen since birth, a whinging kind of child and then a more whinging woman. Victoria's daughter Lizzie had been different. She liked Lizzie, she was fond of Lizzie, but that was as far as it went: but where love was concerned she had given it to Lizzie's child.

She was brought to face Leonard Hammond once more for he was bawling again: 'Well! this is the finish. I'm putting my foot down. I've stood enough. She's not staying here. Whoever gave it to her can have the responsibility of her. She's not staying in my house!'

32

He knew immediately he had made a mistake, for the bark that Emma Funnell now let forth almost lifted them all up off their feet: '*Your* house! *Your* house!'

The word 'house' seemed to have come out of the top of her head and its echo floated away before she added, 'This is something new: *your* house. Let me tell you, you little insignificant nincompoop, this is *my* house. Always has been and always will be; even when I'm gone you'll have no share in it. I've seen to that. Now, as for warning your daughter to get out, your daughter stays here as long as she likes. But if you want to go and take your wife with you, you are quite welcome, any time. In fact, I think, after living rent free, and food free, all these years, it's about time you found a place for yourself, isn't it, Mr Hammond?'

Leonard Hammond stared back at the woman who topped him by inches and who at this moment he would have struck, even strangled, if only he dared. She meant what she said: she could put him out tomorrow. And what then? Probably a life in a council house with Lizzie.

He forced himself to turn away, to turn from her, to grope towards the desk, around it and into his chair, and there, placing his elbows on it he dropped his head into his hands. And from this position he did not see them leaving the room; he heard only the padding of their steps on the carpet. But with the clicking of the door he raised his head and looked towards it and then, taking the blotter in his hand, he slowly picked it to bits; he did not tear it, he just picked bits out of it as if he were plucking a chicken . . . alive.

3

'I don't want to go, Mam.'

'You've got to go. He's got to face up to his responsi-
bilities; he's got to marry you.'

Peggy flung round from the window, crying, 'I don't
want to marry him, Mam. I don't want to have anything
to do with him.'

'You should have thought of that before, girl, then we
wouldn't have had this trouble, would we? And it's no good
bowing your head like that. You've got to see him and his
people; they've got to take the responsibility.'

'I can take the responsibility. I can go out to work
and . . .'

'Don't be silly, girl. And anyway, I'm not thinking so much
of you now but of the child. Have you any idea what it's like
to have an illegitimate child? The proper name for one is a
bastard. D'you hear that? a bastard. There's one half-way
along this lane. She was made to feel different from when
she first went to school. And her mother is known as a bad
lot. Whether she is or not I don't know, but her neighbours
fight shy of her. Years ago they even tried to get her out of
the house. But her mother owned it and now she owns it,

and she defies them. Perhaps you've seen her strutting down this road dressed like a peacock. Her girl is eighteen now. They say she's very bright, but what's she doing? She's in the packing room at the factory. She's likely stamped because she can't have a proper birth certificate, though why they should want a birth certificate for that, I don't know. She'll find it difficult to get a decent man to marry her though.'

'Perhaps she doesn't want to marry. I don't want to marry anybody. Do you hear? I don't, Mam, never!'

'Don't talk stupid, girl.' Lizzie turned away, and pointing to the wardrobe, said, 'Get your hat and coat on.'

'I don't, Mam. Do you hear? I don't.'

Slowly Lizzie now turned about and looked at her white-faced, wide-eyed daughter, and she said quietly, 'You don't know what you're talking about. You haven't even started to live yet. You've tasted something that'll be a torment to you in a very short time, and without marriage you won't be able to have it, unless you become a loose woman. So shut up! girl.' Her voice had risen now, and she ended, 'No more talk. Get your things on and come downstairs.'

'I . . . I won't. I'll go and see Great-gran. She'll . . .'

'Huh!' Lizzie stood holding the door and looking sadly at her child as she interrupted her, saying ruefully, 'Your great-gran might be more up-to-date than next year's newspaper, but where respectability comes in, let me tell you, your dad doesn't hold a candle to her. If you want to know, it's her express wish that you get married and as quickly as possible.'

''T'isn't. She wouldn't, not . . . not Great-gran.'

'Yes, Great-gran. Go on, confront her with it' – she jerked her head to the side – 'I'm not stopping you. The only thing is, I don't want you to change your opinion of her because, as you are always saying, she's with it . . . Now, let's have no more of it.' And lowering her voice, she went on, 'You've

36

got to go and see this boy. If you don't, your father will go, and imagine what'll happen then. He's only staying his hand because I told him Gran's opinion, and that he had better leave it to me . . . '

They went out and down the stairs, and were crossing the hall making for the front door when Lizzie's mother appeared from the dining-room, saying, 'Oh, I've caught you. I thought you were gone. Look; would you call at the chemist and pick up my prescription? Just hang on a minute and I'll get it.'

'We are not going that way, Mother.'

Victoria Pollock stopped. Her mouth had gone into a grim line, and her hands now going on to her hips, her usual stance when annoyed, she said, 'Nobody's ever going that way when I want anything done. It's Mother this, Mother that, or it's Victoria, do this, Victoria, do that, but when Victoria wants anything done, nobody's going that way.'

Lizzie had paused but did not answer her mother; she just cast a side-long glance at her before nudging Peggy again towards the door, and she followed her out and down the three steps, on to the drive that curved between an avenue of trees to the main gate, and she immediately took in the fact that Peter Boyle, the part-time gardener, was mounting his bike.

She looked at her wrist-watch. It showed a quarter to five, and he wasn't supposed to finish until five. He wasn't a satisfactory man, not like old Herbert who had died last year; he would stay till all hours and not demand a penny extra. But then, what did it matter, what did anything matter but this present situation? She didn't know how she was going to face these people, or what their reactions would be. If she were to say to them half the things Gran had said they would likely turf her out into the street. She'd had quite a time stopping her Gran from accompanying them.

She glanced at her daughter. She was walking with her head well up, that defiant look on her face she had come to know more and more of late. She was a bonny girl; she would grow into a beautiful woman. Oh God! Why had this to happen to her? She should have spoken to her about things. She hadn't talked to her about personal matters since she started to menstruate. And that was three years ago. But she had seemed so level-headed, so sure of herself. What was she talking about? What was she thinking? Youth was never level-headed or sure of itself. Youth was a time of false values, false urges, wild desires that drove you to prove that your night longings could be eased by a piece of paper on which you wrote your name in front of a man. Youth gave you no inkling that you would regret it for the rest of your life. But oh! didn't you soon learn. Well, knowing this, why was she pressing her daughter into marriage?

No; this was a different kettle of fish altogether. She herself had hung on till she was married. But her daughter hadn't waited and there was a penalty to be paid for such haste: an illegitimate child.

It wasn't to be thought of. But then, there was a point: if she had liked the boy well enough to allow what had happened to happen, and not only once, then she would likely settle down with him and live a normal, happily married life. Were there any normal married couples?

Yes, yes. She nodded to herself. There was May and Frank next door. She'd always envied them their happiness. Then there had been her grandmother and grandfather. They had been close until the day he died. But what about her own mother and father? Well, could anybody be really happy with her mother? Her whining would get on anybody's nerves. From an early age she had both loved and pitied her father; as she grew older she had wondered why he stayed with her mother. Could he have loved her? Could a man love a woman who lives simply for her ailments, most of them imaginary? Her mother had had that one operation in her thirties and from then on had taken on a career of sickness.

Look at herself, too.

She couldn't bear to look at herself and the life she was leading, because it wasn't life.

'Mam. What if he won't marry me?'

Yes, what if he refused to marry her? Oh, she couldn't bear even to think of the result of that situation: her schoolgirl daughter with an illegitimate baby and having to live in such a house with four females, perhaps five, depending on the baby's sex, and Len. Oh, no! There had to be a solution to this situation, and the only one was marriage and getting them set up somewhere on their own.

She ignored her daughter's question.

As the bus took them past Bog's End, past the bottom of Brampton Hill and to the new council estate, she wished they had come by car; although her driving a car, she imagined, would have emphasised their superior position and so would preclude his understanding that he or his parents would have to support the child.

Peggy rose first to get off the bus, and as she followed her, Lizzie wondered how she and the boy had first met, because he would have gone to a school nearby, whereas Peggy went to Brixton Road Girls' High School. Of course there were the clubs and there was the school dance at Christmas. Here she recalled that Peggy had been very excited after the dance. She'd had a lovely time, she'd said. Yes, the school dance. She had invited Charlie to accompany her as her partner, but at no time had she become excited over Charlie, because she had been brought up with him, played with him since they were babies. There was, it seemed, nothing exciting about

Charlie. No, this was likely why the other one, whoever he was, appealed to her.

'What street is it?'

'It's . . . it's called Clover Close.'

Clover Close. Her chin jerked up. 'You know the number?'

'I . . . I think so. Seventeen.'

'You think so?'

'I'm sure.' The last words were almost a covered growl, and Lizzie answered in like manner, saying, 'Well, how have you come by being so sure of the address? Have you been here?'

'No, I haven't, but he wrote to me.'

'And you wrote back, I suppose?'

'Yes, I did.'

Number seventeen was in the middle of a row of identical houses. They were newish, and looked like a row of barracks. They stood before the door for a moment before Lizzie raised her hand and knocked.

It was opened by a young girl of about Peggy's own age. She looked from one to the other, then glanced back down a short passage as she enquired, 'Yes?'

'I am . . . I am Mrs Hammond. I would like to see your mother or father.'

'Hang on.' The girl did not actually close the door but pushed it a little forward, and they heard her running down the passage.

It was a full two minutes before the door was pulled open and a man in his shirt sleeves, black-haired and dark-eyed, aged about forty, looked at them, and he, too, said, 'Yes?'

Lizzie drew in a long breath before she said, 'You are Mr Jones, and I think you know why I'm here.'

'Come in.' He pulled the door wide and they passed him, and as he closed the door behind them they waited, then followed him down the passage and into what appeared

40

to be a kitchen-cum-living-room, for the table was set roughly for a meal.

Besides the girl, there was a woman in the room and the man said, 'This woman says we should know why she's here. Well, we didn't up till a few hours ago, did we?'

The woman wagged her head now, saying, 'No, we certainly didn't.'

'I told you last week, if you'd only listened,' at which interruption, the woman turned around and half raised her hand to the girl, saying, 'Shut your mouth! Minn.'

Not one of the three people was appealing to Lizzie. She wasn't class-conscious, she often told herself, but there were some and some and there were limits; and she would put these people just below the limit. Common was the word. But still there were many nice common people; in fact, she knew quite a few.

The man now said, 'Well, sit down; it'll cost you the same.' And then he added, 'And you, lass . . . two for the price of one.'

Oh, so there was a joker here. Lizzie took her seat but it was some seconds before Peggy slowly lowered herself down into a chair some distance from the table, and she watched the man and woman now seating themselves. But the young girl remained standing near the fireplace, her hand outstretched towards the mantel as if for support. And yet she didn't appear like a girl who needed support; she looked perky.

The man was staring hard at Peggy, and then he suddenly said to her, 'So you say my lad's got you into trouble, do you? That's what it's all about, isn't it?' His tone was no longer jocular.

Peggy stared back at him. She was unable to answer. Her throat was dry, her stomach was trembling. She had the desire to cry; at the same time she wanted to shout at him

41

and say, 'Yes, he did; but I don't want anything more to do with him.' But her mother was answering for her, at least she was asking the question: 'Has your son admitted to this?'

'No; why should he?' It was the woman speaking now, and Lizzie quickly answered her: 'Simply because, madam, he has given my daughter a child,' she said.

'We'll have less of the "madam"' — the woman was nodding at her — 'I'm Mrs Jones, if you please. And what if he says he hasn't been with her? It could be anybody; there's been others after her. There's a lad next door, I understand.'

'Nonsense! They are like brother and sister; they were brought up together. He's a different type.'

'Oh. Oh. A different type from what? Eh?' It was the woman on the attack again, the mother of the son defending her brood, and she half rose from the chair. 'You want to be careful what you say.'

Lizzie swallowed. 'Well,' she said, 'what I meant was, Charlie is a quiet kind of lad; he's never bothered with girls.'

'No; perhaps because he had one close at hand.'

'Shut up!'

All eyes in the room were immediately drawn to Peggy. She was sitting straight up on the edge of the chair. 'Charlie Conway *is* a different type from your son. It was your son Andrew who . . . who . . . well, he is the father. I have never known any other boy. I was never out with a boy until I met him last Christmas at the school dance. And from then he . . . he followed me. He came to the school and . . . and set me home time and time again.'

'He did, Ma. I saw him, I mean waiting at the school gate, and once I saw them going across the field to . . . ' interrupted Minn.

'Will you shut your mouth, our Minn!'

42

'Why should I? Because he's your bright-eyed boy? He couldn't do any wrong, could he, but me . . . '

'Be quiet! Minn.' It was her father speaking to her now; and the girl looked at him, her eyes blinking as if to ward off tears; but her voice held no tears when she said, 'You know what I'm saying is true. It's always been our Andrew, our Andrew, our Andrew. Our Andrew's going to the Grammar School . . . Our Andrew's been picked for this . . . Our Andrew's been picked for that.'

When the woman swung round in her chair her husband cried, 'Enough! Enough! And she's right. She always is, you know.' He grinned now, then, looking at Lizzie, he said, 'Families. Families. Well now, the thing to do is to get the lad in and confront him with this, isn't it?' He looked over his shoulder again to his daughter, saying, 'Go and fetch him. He'll be in the shed seeing to his bike.'

'I bet he isn't; I bet he's skipped.' Minn interjected.

A movement from her mother caused the girl to run from the room. And the father, sitting back in his chair and folding his arms, said, 'Nice kettle of fish. He was all set to go places, you know. He could have an' all; he's bright. Oh, he's bright. Good at art an' figures. I could see him being a draughtsman or an accountant. They're the blokes that make the money, the accountants. But if he's going to be lumbered with a bairn, well, that puts a different complexion on it, doesn't it? He won't be able to stay on at school.'

'He will!' His wife interposed now. Her lips pouting, she repeated, 'He will.'

'And who's going to support the child, eh?'

'What's the matter with you, man? You're taking it already that it's his.'

'Well, what d'you think?'

'Why should he support any child? They've got money.' She was looking at Lizzie now. 'Your people own the Funnell

43

garage and showrooms, don't they? off the market place, so you're not without a penny.'

'That is quite beside the point at the present moment' — Lizzie's voice was stiff — 'but what is very much to the point is that my daughter is not going to bear an illegitimate child; she must be married.'

The husband and wife looked at each other as if Lizzie's words had come as a shock to them, which apparently they had, because Mrs Jones, leaning slightly across the table now towards Lizzie, said, 'He's only seventeen; he's too young to take responsibility like that.'

Like a flash Lizzie came back. Her hand swinging round as though to embrace Peggy, she retorted, 'And so is my daughter too young to take the responsibility of a child without a father and the ensuing disgrace that child will have to bear all its life; not forgetting how people will look on its mother.'

It was at this moment that the door opened and Andrew Jones entered the room. He stopped just within the doorway, but a push from his sister, who wanted to get in, caused him to take two quick steps forward, and at the same time to turn an angry glance down on her. Then he was looking at Peggy.

He was a tall boy for his age. His hair was cut short but it was thick and dark. His eyebrows, too, were dark, as were the eyelashes; his blue eyes were large and set well apart. His nose was in proportion to the length of his face, which was longish and pale in comparison with his dark hair, and on first glance he could have appeared promisingly handsome, except that his mouth was full-lipped and slack. It hung now slightly open.

'Well!' His father was addressing him. 'No need to make any introductions, is there? I suppose you know why she's here?'

'No.'

'Come off it, our Andy,' and the interjection caused the mother to half rise from her chair. With her finger thrust out towards her daughter, she said, 'Another word from you and you know what you'll get. Anyway, go on! Get out of the room.'

When her daughter didn't move she turned and, almost glaring at Lizzie, she said, 'You know what I think? I think it's a damned cheek you coming here and blaming him . . .'

'Shut up! will you, Carrie.' The man now turned and, looking straight at his son, demanded, 'Have you been with this lass?'

The straight question obviously shook the boy: he blinked rapidly, pulled his mouth to one side and bit on his lip, and seemed about to speak when his father said, 'All right, that's evidence enough. The thing now is, what's to be done about it? You're a bloody fool. You know that? Your career's gone to blazes, whatever it was going to be, because the situation is this: if you don't marry her' – with a jerk of his head he indicated Peggy – 'they'll make you stump up, an' that means leavin' school and gettin' a job.'

'He's not going to.'

James Jones turned his head slowly and looked at his wife, then as slowly he turned again to look at his son and continued to speak to him: 'The choice is up to you. But at this stage what I think should be done is to let you two youngsters have a talk about it. I don't know whether the lass wants to marry but her mother seems intent on it.' He spoke as if neither Lizzie nor Peggy were in the room. Then, getting to his feet, he said, 'Now, take the lass into the front room.'

His wife, too, was quickly on her feet, saying, 'They can't go in there, it's in a mess.'

'Well, it shouldn't be in a mess, woman.' He was a tall man and, towering over her now, he ended, 'If you'd get off your

45

backside instead of looking at that bloody telly at night . . . Oh! what does it matter. Come on, you two.'

He walked to the kitchen door and pulled it open, then waited and watched Peggy slowly rise from her seat; but when Lizzie put in, 'I think I should be . . . ' he said, 'Stop thinkin', missis, at least for her. She's old enough. They've had a try and she's carryin' a bairn, so she should be able to think for herself. Come on.'

The impatient movement of his head seemed to jerk the two young people past him and out of the room, across the passage and into the sitting-room.

And Peggy saw straightaway that it really was in a mess, as her granny would have said, it had never seen a duster since they were made. There were papers on the floor, two ashtrays lying on a cheap coffee table were full of cigarette ends, and there was a smell in the room suggesting damp or lack of air.

After the door closed on them they stood well apart, not looking at each other, and as he walked towards the window she said in no small voice, 'We're supposed to talk this out, so let's get it over with.'

This brought him quickly about and, looking at her, he said very quietly, 'It wasn't all my fault; you were ready and willing.'

'I wasn't! You told me there was a horse there and a young neglected pony.'

'Well, there used to be.'

'There might have been, but they hadn't been there for a long time.'

'You . . . you didn't need much persuasion.'

She turned her head away from him and looked towards the brown-painted door. He was right, he was quite right; she had been curious, she had wanted to grow up. She'd had an unease in her for a long time, part of it brought about by

46

her wanting to get away from home and her father. Oh, she didn't like that man, she had never liked him. But after that first time with Andrew, when she had thought she would die, why had she gone back again? And then a second time? and a third and a fourth? Yes, why had she gone back again? And then he . . . he had dropped her and not only with a baby, he had just dropped her. She really had no intention of uttering the next words because they were common-sounding and she had heard her gran and great-gran say them, but now she heard herself speaking them: 'When you got what you wanted, you disappeared, you ran off,' she said.

She watched him now hunch his shoulders and jerk his chin to the side as he said, 'It wasn't like that, not the way you mean. Yes; yes, I ran off because I . . . I—' He now stretched his neck upwards and hissed at her, 'I was frightened of this happening, as it has now. You . . . you were so ready, so . . . so . . . Oh!' He turned from her and went to the window again.

Had she been all that ready? She looked at his back. It was narrow; he looked like a young boy, not seventeen, nearly eighteen. Had she ever dreamt about him at night and wanted to be with him? At this moment she didn't even like him. How was it she had let him touch her? . . . Touch her, did she say? More than touch, do what he did? How? She couldn't face up to the fact that the person she was now was someone entirely different from the girl she had been three months ago.

He had turned towards her again and, looking at him, she actually saw him as a young boy much less mature than she was. He had always given her the impression that he was grown up: it was his chatter, she supposed, his chatter that Charlie had once called 'his yap from his wide open gap'. Charlie had never liked him. He had met them once coming from the stable area and had straightaway endeavoured to ignore him, but Andrew had talked all the time and laughed and acted the goat. She had felt a little ashamed of him that day.

Why was she thinking of Charlie? She had to get this thing settled. Oh dear, dear Lord, she didn't want to get married, but there was no way out, she knew that.

He spoke her thoughts now: 'You don't want to get married, do you?' he said.

She didn't answer for a moment, and when she did her answer was a statement: 'I've got to.'

His whole body moved as if shrugging off his clothes. 'Well, where would we live? We couldn't live here,' he said.

'*Oh no!*' The words were emphatic.

'Well, you said before about your dad being . . . ' His voice trailed off, and she immediately brushed aside what she knew he was about to say: 'He's got nothing to do with it, the house I mean. It's Great-gran's house. There's a sort of annexe. It's got enough rooms. They'd . . . they'd do it up.'

During the time she was speaking she was rubbing her right hand up and down her thigh as if to ease away a pain, and she watched his expression change, his face brighten as he said, 'A proper house; I mean, detached . . . they would?'

'It isn't detached; it's connected by a doorway. But yes.' She closed her eyes for a moment and nodded. 'Yes, in a way it's detached. And it could be made really nice.'

He half turned towards the window again, saying, 'Well, I'd have to get a job and . . . and they are not so easy now. Dad's on the buildings and he's been off a month. He used to be able to walk from one job to another, but not any more. So . . . so that'll be an obstacle, the job.'

Her hand stopped its rubbing and joined the other one tightly at her waist, and her voice sounded very much as her

48

mother's did at times when she had to submit to something that her father wanted doing. 'They'll see to that too,' she said. 'Great-gran said there could be a place found for you in the garage.'

His expression took on a lightness.

'Selling cars?'

'No!'

She now clapped her hand over her mouth because the 'no' had been so loud. Then almost in a whisper she explained, 'Dad's over the showrooms, he's manager there. You'd . . . you'd best keep your distance from him. Anyway, you'd be put down in the grease shop to start with, under Mr Brooker . . . no, Mr Stanhope; Mr Brooker is assistant to the general manager, Mr Cartwright.'

His face had resumed its usual expression. 'Grease shop; what's that?'

'That's what they call the repair shop.'

'A greaser? Me . . . mam won't like that.'

She had a great urge to swear like Great-gran did at times and cry at him, 'Damn your mam!' But what she said and grimly now was, 'What would your mam have to do with it? If . . . if we get married you'll have to take on responsibility and . . . and you should think yourself lucky that they are considering giving you a job. Yes, you should.' She was flapping her hand at him now. 'Anyway, who do you think you are, Andrew Jones? You played the big "I am" a few months ago; you acted as if you were a man.' She paused here and they stared at each other in bitterness; and then she added, 'And you lied. You said you lived up the top of Brampton Hill and your father worked in the Town Hall.'

'Oh well.' He made a short sound of embarrassment. 'Half of it was true: Dad was working on the roof of the Town Hall. And anyway, from what I could see of your house from the gate it wasn't like this, was it?' His voice dropped to a hiss and he swept his arm about the room, adding, 'Would you brag about this?'

Her gaze was hard on him, her eyes widening slightly, and in this moment she felt sorry for him; she could see what he meant and why he had pretended to live on Brampton Hill. And because he went to the Grammar School she had never questioned this. And now an odd thought struck her: she had never seen him wear his school cap, which was why, she supposed, he seemed to be so much older than he was. School uniforms and caps revealed your age group.

They continued to look at each other, and the silence now became so deep that it allowed the shrieking and pounding feet of children in the street to enter into it.

He took two steps towards her; then, still looking directly at her, he said quietly, 'I'll marry you; we couldn't be much worse off than we are now, could we?'

She didn't question this, at least her side of it; but after wetting her lips a number of times she muttered, 'All right then.'

He took another step towards her, and now he was within half an arm's length of her. 'We . . . we got on all right together at first, didn't we?' he said; but she didn't answer, only continued to look at him.

'Well, we could again, especially if we're on our own and . . . and they leave us alone.'

To whom was he referring: his people or hers? In a way she could see his people being prevented from interfering with them but not hers, not those three women back there. Oh, dear, dear, what was she saying, those three women! And they had all been so good to her, even Grandma Pollock, who was forever on the whine, she had never really said an unkind word to her; and then she had to say, those three women! and in that tone. What was happening to her? Is this what carrying a baby did to your mind? She had been

50

sick this morning. She had been sick other mornings but nobody had seemed to notice, except that once when it had been put down to the leek pudding. And there had been a row over that leek pudding because Grandma Pollock had made the crust with dripping – her father had refused to eat it – so her sickness had been put down to that. What was more, she had a wash-basin in her room, so she had no need to go to the bathroom. There were wash-basins in all the bedrooms; it was that kind of house. This made her glance round the room in which she was standing and again she felt that pang of pity for Andrew. He must have some finer feelings because he disliked this place.

She said softly, 'We'd better tell them then, hadn't we?'

'Yes.'

'Will you be going back to school?'

'Well, it'll all depend on when . . . when you want the arrangements made.'

'They'll . . . . they'll have to be soon.'

'Yes, yes, I understand.' He nodded, as though he were an authority in this matter. 'It'll be all right, it'll be all right.' His hand was on her shoulder now and she felt herself shrinking from it. She wanted to say, 'Don't touch me,' but that would have been silly when only a short while ago all she wanted was to be clasped in his arms, tightly. Would she ever feel like that again? Yes; she'd have to.

'Come on,' she said.

She preceded him out through the door, across the passage and into the kitchen. And there they were as she had left them, for seemingly no-one had moved: Mr and Mrs Jones at one side of the table, her mother at the other, and Andrew's young sister still standing near the fire.

'Well, then, what's the verdict?' As Mr Jones asked the question Lizzie rose to her feet and, picking up her bag and gloves from the table, she looked as if she were about to walk straight out, for she already knew the answer. But she wasn't prepared for the addition to the answer and it halted her and her mouth dropped into a slight gape as her daughter, looking at Mr Jones, said, 'We've agreed to get married, but we want no interference . . . from either side.' And she turned slightly towards Andrew, her glance emphasising her words, and his mouth, too, was slightly agape as she went on, 'We'll go along with whatever arrangements you decide between you, but once it's done . . . well, we want to manage on . . . on our own.'

Lizzie couldn't believe her ears. Her daughter had gone into that room a hang-dog girl, defiant and dead set against marriage, while at the same time knowing that it was inevitable. But out of that room had come this apparently young woman who was making conditions and it was that thought that prompted Lizzie now to say, 'You're in no position, either of you, to give orders, or make conditions.'

'Oh, yes we are, Mam. We could both say no, couldn't we?' She turned and looked at her future husband, and he, as if imbibing courage from the fierceness of her glance, nodded and said, 'Yes, she's right, we could both say no.'

When the burst of laughter hit the room all attention was diverted, not only to Mr Jones, but to his young daughter, for as he leant back in his chair and let out a roar, Minnie's high-pitched laughter sounded hysterical.

'Shut up! Stop it!' Mrs Jones had sprung to her feet; then, turning to Peggy, she cried, 'Who d'you think you are, miss, coming in here giving your orders! He's my son and he'll do what he's told.'

'He hasn't done so up till now.' Lizzie's cool voice penetrated the woman's yelling. 'I should imagine it was apparent to you. Our visit here today should point that out. And my daughter is right, there'll be no interference, not from our side, anyway.' What was she saying? No interference from

52

her side? There would be open war between this boy and her husband; and if the boy knuckled under to him his life would be hell; and if he didn't it would still be hell. But she wanted to be out of this house, away from these people.

The husband and daughter were wiping their eyes, and now it was the man who spoke again. The rumbling laugh still in his voice, he looked at Peggy, saying, 'I know who's going to wear the trousers in this union. Good luck to you, lass.'

It came to Peggy at this moment that this man didn't like his son; this was a divided house, father and daughter, mother and son. She was glad she hadn't a brother. But then, hadn't Charlie always been like a brother to her?

Her mother was now saying to Andrew, 'If you'll come around, we'll talk of arrangements.'

'Yes, we definitely will.' His mother was shouting again. But a bawl from her husband silenced her, and his forearm thrust her back into her chair as he said, 'Enough! woman. Enough! Goodbye, missis. Goodbye, lass.' He was nodding towards them. 'See them out, Andy. See them out.'

The boy went before them now, through the passage and to the front door, and there, looking at Lizzie, he won her over just a mite by saying, 'I'm sorry for the carry-on. I'm . . . I'm sorry for everything.'

She paused on the step and, looking at him, she said, 'Well, the future will prove how sorry you are. However' – she swallowed – 'we'll give you all the help we can. Come along, Peggy.'

Peggy paused for a moment, too, and looked at her future husband and what she said to him now surprised not only her mother and the boy, but also herself, as she said, 'You want to stand on your own feet.'

4

'May I come in, Mrs Conway?'

'Oh, my dear, you've never had to ask to come in before.'
May pulled open the door, adding, 'I've been wondering
when you would make the trip; it's a fortnight since I've
seen any of you.'

'Mam misses you. I know she does; she looks lost at
times.'

'Well, she knows where I am. There's been other times
when we haven't seen eye to eye but she's never stayed
away. Sit down; I've just brewed some coffee. Funny' – she
laughed – 'that's my one extravagance, real coffee. Can't
stand ersatz.' She turned to a side table, switched off the
percolator and poured out two cups, saying, 'I don't really
know how you like it; you've never been here at this time
in the morning before.'

'I don't like it very strong . . . milky.'

'Milky it shall be.'

A minute later, when she placed the cup on the table before
Peggy, she asked quietly, 'How did your father take it?'

Peggy looked down into her cup, then picked up the
spoon and ladled two spoonfuls of sugar into it before

she said, 'I think he would have killed me if Great-Gran hadn't hooked him off.'

'Hooked him off? He attacked you?'

'Yes, and she dragged him off me with the handle of a walking stick. He's never spoken to me since.' The spoon moved slowly now in the cup as she added, 'I'm to be married a fortnight today.'

'A fortnight? Well' – May raised her eyebrows – 'the sooner the better, I suppose. Where's it to be?'

'A registry office. Father apparently won't hear of my going to the church.'

'Have you met his people? Well, I suppose you have by now.'

'Yes; yes, I've met them, but only the once.'

'What were they like?'

Peggy took a sip of her coffee, then returned the cup to her saucer before saying, 'Very ordinary. I could have liked the father, he . . . he seemed a sort of fair man, understanding. But the mother, Andrew's mother, no! He has a sister. She could be a bit of a rebel, I think. She was on her father's side.'

'Well, I don't suppose they'll trouble you. It goes without saying, you'll be living next door.'

'Yes, it goes without saying. They're making it nice, though, the annexe.'

'Oh, in the annexe? Oh, yes; that could be very nice. And you'll be on your own . . . well, pretty much.'

'Mrs Conway.'

'Yes, lass? By the way, wouldn't it be nice if you called me Auntie May.'

Peggy smiled now, saying, 'I've always wanted to, but . . . well, you know.'

'I know, lass, but we're on our own now and you'll soon be a married woman and we'll be neighbours; well, you'll be closer to me than they are in the house. And you know' – the smile faded from her face – 'I want you to believe this, lass, I'll always be here if you need me in any way. You've just got to remember that.'

'Thank you.' There was a catch in Peggy's voice now and it was a moment or so before she added, 'Well . . . Auntie May, I need you now because from what I can gather Dad's not going to come to the wedding. Candidly, I don't want him there, but . . . but there's no other male relative and I know Mam would like to ask you and Mr Conway to stand in. Would you?'

'Like a shot, girl, like a shot. The only thing I'll say is . . . oh no, I won't say it.' No, she couldn't say, 'You should be married in a church in a lovely white dress with a train.' No, she couldn't say that to the girl. Instead she said on a laugh, 'I would like to kick your father's backside.' And Peggy's smile, too, was as wide as she agreed, 'You're not the only one.'

'But I have to say this,' May said; 'Frank sees the situation from a man's point of view: only a saint, he says, could live in the same house with three women and one of them being such an old matriarch and letting everybody know it, because your great-gran does, doesn't she?'

'Yes. But she's good.'

'Oh yes, she's good, lass, looking at her from your point of view, but not from your father's. Men are all queer cattle, you know.'

'Yes; men are queer cattle.' She could well believe that. She hadn't seen Charlie since the night he brought her home, and she said so now: 'I haven't seen Charlie for some time.' And May answered, 'Well, you wouldn't; you're not at school now.'

'Is he out?'

'Yes; he's gone for another lesson. He's having two a week. He's thoroughly taken with this new man, and the old fella with him. And he is an old fella, too, well into his seventies; but he can play that guitar! You know, I was never for Charlie taking it up. Listening to all that twanging, twanging, twanging, it used to get on my nerves. But oh, when you hear that man, it's beautiful. You forget he's playing a guitar. You know, you listen to so much on the wireless and you see these bands going twing twang, twing twang, all the time. It's a good job the drums play so loudly it covers it up. But when that instrument's played properly by that old man, oh, it's beautiful. He's travelled the world, you know. He'd still be travelling if his legs hadn't given out. His wife can't speak a word of English, she's Austrian or something, but she smiles all the time . . . ' May changed her track now, and with it her tone. Taking up her teaspoon, she tapped it against the saucer before she said, 'Charlie's upset, Peggy; you know, you being brought up together, and . . . and he's very fond of you.' She looked across the table at the top of the head that had gradually drooped forward as she had talked and she thought to herself, Very fond of her? Crazy would have been a better word. She'd never seen or heard her son cry since he was six years old when he had come in with a bleeding nose, but the other night while passing his door she had heard the sobs. She had gone in and she had held him, but she hadn't asked him why he was crying, and he hadn't said why he was crying. Not one word passed between them, but she had cried too whilst she had tucked him up in bed, as she used to do when he was small. Afterwards she had gone into her own room and there she had continued to cry. And Frank had come up and found her in a state and, as he held her, he had said something very strange, 'He'll get what he wants in the end. He's made that way. He's like me, he can wait . . . remember?'

Yes, she remembered: leaving school at sixteen to look after her mother, who had taken to her bed with arthritis and who, over the next five years, had come to enjoy being an invalid; then her father, worn out with so many things, having a heart attack; and all the while Frank on the side, never saying, 'When is it going to end? What's going to happen to us?' just saying, 'Don't worry; things will pan out.' Even when she told him to go, what had been his answer: 'Where will I go without you?' And she had dared not go to bed with him just in case she got into the same situation as this lass sitting opposite to her. And this brought her back to the lass: 'Come on,' she said brightly, 'don't look so down in the mouth. Don't upset yourself. As my Frank always says, in twenty-three and a half nobody street there's a blind man and a deaf woman and both their sets of parents are alcoholics. Just think.'

Twenty-three and a . . . Oh – Peggy began to laugh now – Mrs Conway . . . Auntie May was always quoting her Frank. Twenty-three and a half nobody street. Yes, she supposed she was right; there were other people worse off than her. But then the sympathisers and the advisers weren't experiencing what you were experiencing. In a way, it was easy to offer parables when they weren't experiencing the pain they were pitying.

Oh, what was the matter with her? She was always trying to explain things to herself. Well, didn't she know what was the matter with her? She didn't want to get married. It wasn't that she had come to dislike Andrew; in fact, she felt as sorry for him as she did for herself. It was that she didn't like the idea of living with him day after day, and more so, night after night. But when the baby came she would likely feel different. It would take her mind off things when the baby came. But it was a long time to December.

She rose from the table now, saying, 'I'll have to go. It's close on dinner time and we must all be at the table at the correct time, mustn't we?' There was a touch of bitterness in her voice. 'That'll be one good thing when I have a place of my own, I won't miss the soup if I'm five minutes late.'

'You miss the soup if . . . ?'

'Oh yes. Dad's orders: you're there on time or else.' The bitterness now changed to cynical laughter as she said, 'But it only seems to apply to me because Mam and Gran are always there. Great-gran usually has her tray upstairs. Moreover, I have to eat my crusts. Right back as far as I can remember I've had to eat my crusts. Oh' – she grinned – 'wait till I'm on my own. I'll cut all the crusts off a loaf as soon as it enters the house.'

'Go on with you!' May pushed her over the step, only to halt her by gripping her shoulders and, bending above her, saying, 'Tell your mother to pop in. Tell her I miss her. Say that.'

'I will. I will, Auntie May,' and impetuously now, she leaned up and went to kiss May's cheek and found herself hugged in a tight yet tender embrace. Then she was running through the garden and into the woodland; and there she stopped and, leaning her head against a tree, she began to cry, cry as a child might.

5

'I won't have it!' he said. 'I just won't have it! Do you hear me? I'll go and see her this minute and give her the length of my tongue. It's about time.'

'Len.' The quiet voice Lizzie used in speaking his name conveyed a sadness, and she spoke it again: 'Len,' she said, 'you know what happened before when you gave Gran the length of your tongue, you nearly lost your job. I had to do a lot of talking that time.'

She was looking at him. His face was almost purple and his left eye was twitching again. She felt sorry for him. How often during their married life had she felt sorry for him? But it was like feeling sorry for a stranger, someone who had no real connection with your life. She had lain in bed with this man for seventeen years but he was still a stranger to her, although she knew every facet of him, every reaction he would make to everything she said, and his reaction to everything her grandmother said.

Presently he turned from her and, gripping the edge of the desk, he leant partly over it, and, his head bowed, he said, 'I can't stand it. I can't.' Then suddenly whipping round to her, he cried, 'I won't! I just won't! I won't have that fellow in the shop.'

She kept her voice down as she answered, 'He won't be in the shop. He won't be anywhere near the salerooms. He'll be with Ken Stanhope all the time, and Ken will keep him busy. There's no doubt about that.'

'I will be bound to run across him and I won't be able to keep my hands off him.'

'I wouldn't try anything like that, if I were you; he's a young fellow and I think he'd be able to hold his own. That would be a mistake on your part if you hit him or even attempted to. Ignore him if you will, but I would advise you to keep your temper and your hands to yourself.'

He sat down suddenly in his chair and, taking out a handkerchief, he wiped the sweat from his brow. Then looking at her he said, 'Have you spoken to her about when Cartwright goes?'

'No, I haven't, and I have no intention of doing so. He's got some months to go before he retires and there's Harry Brooker to consider.'

As if he had been prodded with a fork from the chair seat, he was up and confronting her again, crying now, 'I've been there for twenty years! By God! in heaven, if she were to put him in front of me, I'd do something to her. I would that. There's many a time I've felt like swinging for her but if she did that . . . '

'Shut your mouth! Don't you dare say such things. And let me tell you, Len, once and for all, she can do what she likes. The business is hers, this house is hers, and at the end she could leave the lot to the Salvation Army and you or I or anybody else couldn't stop her. But it's you, remember, who'll be more likely to make her do it. Let's face it once and for all, we are here on sufferance, both of us, and Peggy. She had no need to let us stay here, neither at the beginning, nor since. Just as many another couple had, she could have made us take a council house or such. I was in one the other day, the home of your future son-in-law, and you know what I thought? and don't look like that and put your fist out to me, because he will be your son-in-law; and I repeat, you know what I thought? This is the kind of house we could have been in for years, a bit cleaner, yes, but the same kind, because your money would never have provided us with anything else at the beginning, and not even now. So don't you talk of swinging for her else somebody might swing for you. And tell me this: why, if you thought you were worth something better than manager of the showrooms, didn't you go out and get another job? No; you've hung on here hoping that she'd die and that I'd come into everything, or most of it, because it wasn't likely she'd leave the control in Mother's hands. That's been in your mind, hasn't it? Well now, let me tell you, she's far from dying, she'll see my mother out and I shouldn't be a bit surprised if she sees me out too. And let me tell you something finally: if she's going to leave anything to anyone, it's more likely to be to Peggy. And who'll reap the benefit of that? That young fellow you don't intend to tolerate and who you are going to bash if ever you come across him. And when he marries your daughter in just over a week's time you're not going to be here to see it, are you? because you've taken your fortnight's holiday early; you're going off on a tour. You know something, Len Hammond? You make me sick. Well, there I've said it, *you make me sick*, and you have for years. And when you go off on your tour I hope you meet somebody more suitable to you, for I'd be pleased to give you a divorce tomorrow. There's more unlikely things have happened, you know. You're only thirty-seven and when you're spruced up you look attractive, even if you don't sound it. Think on it.' She turned and walked towards the door, but there stopped and, looking back at him, said, 'But make sure she's got money, or her people have, because you're the kind of man who really needs someone to work for you.'

She had quickly closed the door before his voice brought her shoulders hunching as he yelled, 'I just might! I just might, at that.'

When she reached the hall, her mother, who was standing at the foot of the stairs, suddenly displayed an unusual gesture: quickly approaching her daughter, she put an arm around Lizzie's shoulder and guided her towards the sitting-room, saying, 'Come and sit down; and I'll tell you what, we'll have a glass of sherry.'

In the room Victoria pressed Lizzie down on to the couch and stood for a moment looking at her before she said, 'Don't worry; perhaps something'll happen to him. Don't worry.' Then lowering her head down towards Lizzie, she whispered, 'Perhaps he'll get run over while he's on his holiday, at best fall under a bus.'

It was many a long year since Lizzie had heard her mother make a joke, and this macabre one caused an upheaval in the pit of her stomach. It started as a rumbling laugh and when it reached her throat it almost choked her. Her head went back on the couch, her mouth opened wide and she let out a roar of laughter such as she had never before heard herself make. And her mother was now sitting beside her, holding her hand, and she, too, was laughing. But when the tears began to run down her daughter's face she pulled her into her arms, saying, 'There now. There now. Give over. Give over.'

Neither of them was aware that the door had opened until Victoria looked up and saw her mother standing above them. And she said to her, 'Lizzie's upset, Mother.' And Emma Funnell nodded, saying, 'Well, there's nothing like a good cry to clear the system. And the next best thing is a glass of sherry, eh?'

Lizzie pulled herself from her mother's arms, lay back on the couch again and, looking up at her grandmother, her tears turned to laughter once more, and almost on a gurgle she said, 'A glass of sherry, Gran? Yes, a glass of sherry. This must really be an occasion, for Mother, too, suggested it, and we only have sherry on occasions.'

'Well, we will make this an occasion, dear,' said Emma Funnell. 'As we drink our sherry we'll discuss the wedding and whether we're going to have a little reception here or at an hotel. After what you have told me about his people, though, I myself think an hotel would be preferable. Anyway, we'll discuss the matter over the sherry. Go and bring the bottle, Victoria, and the best glasses, too. And there are those new biscuits that came from Fortnum and Mason's. And if Peggy's in her room, bring her down too; she should be in on this.'

Lizzie let her chin droop on to her chest. 'Bring Peggy down too,' Emma had said, 'she should be in on this.' Dear God! Life was really funny when you came to think of it, because it was made up of families, and there was nothing funnier than families, was there? or more tragic, or more sad or more hopeless and desolate. And it was all inside of her.

6

It was the night before her wedding and Peggy was standing in the little sitting-room of her new home. Her mother and gran had worked wonders with it over the past four weeks, and for the last week her Auntie May and Mr Conway — she couldn't even now think of him as Uncle — had been of enormous help. And so the whole place was looking fresh and shining. The rooms were mostly emulsioned a delicate shade of mauve, the doors and woodwork painted a bright yellow-sun colour. For the sitting-room they had brought down furniture from the attics, but her great-gran had fitted the kitchen out with a new electric cooker, a washing machine and dryer, and cupboard fitments, besides a kitchen table and four chairs. She had also bought her a modern bedroom suite. The bedroom carpet and the landing and stair carpets were new. They had found two comparatively good carpets in the attic, one blue for the dining-room and one pink for the sitting-room. There had been no talk of fitting out the second bedroom as a nursery, not as yet. There was a small scullery going off the kitchen and it was here the door connected with the house. There had been no lock or bolt on the connecting door, and when she saw Mr

Conway putting a lock on she didn't know whether he was doing it off his own bat, or her mother had suggested it, and she didn't enquire.

It was from the small dining-room at the far end of the annexe, away from the house, that another door led into the yard and almost on to a path which, in turn, led to the tradesmen's entrance. And this was plainly stated on a wooden board at the lower gate. It was by this way that Andrew had made two recent visits to his future home, and on each he had been ill-at-ease, for both her mother and gran had been present.

But now she was waiting for his coming and she was alone. She walked round the sitting-room. It seemed small, box-like after the one in the house. But there was one consoling thought: it was to be her own . . . well, not quite her own, because he would be with her. And what was more, she would have to cook for him. She wouldn't mind that though, for she liked cooking. Her mother had been showing her how to cook for some time.

She walked into the dining-room. The table could seat six. There was a nice little sideboard. She opened the middle drawer. In it was a cutlery section, and there were six pieces each of what was necessary for a dinner. These had come from the dining-room across the way. She was already thinking of her home as the house across the way.

She went back to the sitting-room and sat on the couch before the electric fire. She felt lonely. She had felt lonely since she had left school. She hadn't seen any of her friends until yesterday, when she met Jane Power and Betty Rowlands in the market place. They had obviously been undecided whether or not to stop and speak to her. When they did, it was Jane who said, 'Hello, Peggy. How are you?' And she had answered, 'Fine.' But when Betty

Rowlands asked, 'How does it feel?' she had stiffened as she replied, 'How does what feel?'

'Well, you know, to have a baby,' said Betty.

Then that new self that had emerged in her replied, 'Why not ask your mother: she had you, didn't she?' and had immediately walked off, leaving them gaping after her. She knew they would be gaping for, as the headmistress had said to her on the day she left, 'It is so uncharacteristic of you, Peggy. I'm really surprised.'

Yes, a lot of people had been surprised, but no more than she was at what had happened to her; and at what was going to happen to her in the future: she was going to live with a boy hardly older than herself. But he would grow into a man and she into a woman and the child would grow. And what then?

A knock on the far door startled her and she jumped to her feet and hurried towards it. When she had pulled it open she paused for a moment before she said, 'Come on in. Oh, you're wet.'

'Yes, it's started to rain.'

'You haven't got a mac on.'

'No, it was dry when I left.'

Andrew paused and looked around the dining kitchen; then he smiled at her and said, 'It looks lovely, doesn't it?'

'It's all right.' Her voice sounded abrupt as she led the way into the sitting-room. Here he again paused: 'It's all finished then,' he said.

'Yes, except we'll have to get food in when we come back.' The last words were muttered; but then brightly she said, 'Sit down,' and pointed to the couch that was set opposite the fire.

He sat down, then slowly looked around him at the room and when he said with obvious admiration and a little awe, 'You've made it lovely,' she answered, 'Oh, I had very little to do with it. You know, you saw them; they were all at it.'

He was sitting on the edge of the couch, his hands clasped between his knees, and his head was lowered as he said, 'They've all been very good, kind.' She did not follow up this remark, but lowered herself down on to the far end of the couch, and she too, sat on the edge and looked towards the fire. After a moment she said, 'I'm sorry I can't offer you a cup of tea or anything yet; there's nothing over here.'

'Oh' – he lifted his head – 'I've had me tea.' Then turning abruptly to face her, and almost on a demand, he said, 'How d'you feel? I mean . . . I mean about tomorrow?'

'How do you expect me to feel? It's all settled, I can't do anything about it.'

'Do you still want to get married?'

'I can ask you the same thing: do you want to get married?'

He looked away from her for a moment before saying, 'I didn't, not at first. That's the truth. But . . . but lately . . . well.'

'Since you've seen this place and because it's better than your home?'

'No! No!' She was startled because he had yelled at her, and she cried at him, 'Please don't yell at me like that.'

He pushed his fingers through his hair now, saying, 'Well, you're suggesting it's just because I want to come and live here and you're wrong. I . . . I feel I've gone back to where it started . . . I mean when I first met you and I wanted you. Yes; yes, I did, I wanted you.' He was again looking towards the fire. 'But I can tell you this, I hate the idea of you being forced into marrying and, in a way, of me being so, too. It's your mother and them on your side, and my dad on my side. He thinks it's only right. Of course, my mam's up in the air. Well,

70

you saw what she was like. She always thought I would get to the university, but I knew I never would. I'm no flier: I only got four O-levels and just scraped into the sixth because of art. It's odd—' He now lifted his head and looked upwards and seemed to ponder for a moment before he added, 'People like her, and Dad too, they think the world is at your feet if you get into a grammar school. I thought so too, at one time, because there weren't many round our way got there. Joe Birkhead did. He's in the next street. Now he is a flier. He's a wizard at maths. He'll go places.'

She put in quietly now, 'So could you, Andrew, if you put your mind to it. I mean, you could study at nights.'

'What? Art?'

He was looking straight at her now, and she answered, 'Yes; or anything else you'd like to take up.'

'Huh!' He gave a shaky laugh, then shook his head, and for a moment he appeared like a grown man to her as he said, 'I'm sure I'll feel like studying at night after Mr Stanhope is finished with me, keeping me on my back lubricating the cars' innards. Greasing their bellies, he calls it.'

When he chuckled at his own words she chuckled too, and their chuckles linked and rose until they were both laughing; and when at last their laughter hiccoughed into silence he drew in a long breath, and presently he said softly, 'It won't be too bad. I'll try to do me best in all ways. It'll be a bigger change for me you know, not so much for you. You've been used to this' – he spread his hand out – 'but my life and Minnie's have been rough and tumble all the way. She sounded a big mouth ... Minnie, but she's all right, really. Ma never took much notice of her, concentrated on me, so she went over to Da.

71

She's all right underneath, though; a bit brash, but she'll grow out of it.'

Of a sudden she felt drawn towards him: he was different; he seemed to have grown up all of a sudden.

When he said, 'I'd better go now, hadn't I? You'll want to do things. It's . . . it's eleven in the morning, isn't it?' she answered simply, 'Yes, eleven.'

He rose to his feet, saying, 'I . . . I wish it was over, don't you? I mean . . . well . . . and we were on our way. Have you ever been to Harrogate before?'

'No, never.'

'It's . . . it's a nice hotel. Da went through and booked it. It's a posh place. He's paying for the week as a kind of wedding present.'

'It was good of him, very good.'

'Da's all right. You could get to like him.'

'Yes, I think I could.'

'I . . . I wish I could say the same for your dad.'

'Do you want to know something, Andrew?' she paused; he waited. 'I wish I could say the same myself.'

'Is that a fact? You said something like that before, but I didn't believe it.'

'Well, you can.'

'He'll lead me a rough time if he can at the works.'

'Well, you'll only have to stand up to him.'

'Oh, I'll do that all right. Oh yes, I will. There's another side to me, you know: I won't be pushed around by nobody. I've got that from me da.'

They were standing near the door now looking at each other. His voice changed, he asked quietly, 'Can I kiss you?'

She made a small motion with her head, and he leaned forward, put his hands on her shoulders and his mouth on hers. His lips felt soft and hot, whereas hers remained tightly closed. After a moment he stood back, smiled at her and said, 'Well, ta-ra until tomorrow.'

'Good night,' she said.

When the door had closed on him she stood with a cheek pressed against it and told herself not to cry, because she was no longer sad; yet she couldn't claim to be happy.

7

They sat at a small table in a corner of the large dining-room, and they were almost silent through awe. The room was brilliantly lit with glass chandeliers, and the glass, cutlery, and the napery on the table seemed to reflect the light and spread it over the diners. Only half the tables were occupied: the men were in dinner suits, very like those of the waiters, except for the one who stood by the open glass doors, and he wore tails. Without exception the women wore evening dress, and they all looked old, some of them fifty or over.

The waiter who had served them, first with soup and then fish, was again at the table, but accompanied now by another, who was holding two plates, on each, half a duck. The main waiter had a bottle in his hand and he proceeded to fill their glasses with sparkling wine. Then, bowing first to one and then the other, he placed the champagne bottle to the side, saying, 'With the compliments of the manager.'

'Oh, thank you.' They spoke together, then looked at each other, and, again together, smiled from one waiter to the other and said, 'Thank you.'

'Enjoy your meal, madam . . . and sir.'

They were again left alone.

Peggy felt that she should raise her glass to his before she drank from it, but as he lifted his glass to his lips he just continued to smile at her; and so she sipped at her first taste of champagne. When the bubbles went up her nose she had to turn her head away to try and stop herself from sneezing, which caused them both to laugh softly, and this, not the drink itself seemed to make them feel more at ease, and he, bending slightly towards her, whispered, 'D'you think we'll get through this?' and indicated the duck.

'I think there's still more to come,' she said when, out of the corner of her eyes, she saw the advancing waiter bearing a tray of vegetable dishes.

'One thing's for sure' – his voice was still a whisper – 'we'll be heavier when we leave than when we came.' . . .

It was half an hour later when, the meal finished, they went into the lounge for coffee. Again they sat in the corner, and no-one spoke to them; some smiled when passing them, others acknowledged them with a slight bowing of the head.

'There's one thing I must say,' Peggy said, sitting back in the plush seat, 'your father's got good taste.'

She was smiling widely at him. She was feeling different, happy. Perhaps it was the wine, she told herself; she'd had three glasses. Wait till she told them back home. Sherry was the only thing they ever drank there, and then it had to be an occasion.

After a while, beginning to feel rather warm, she said brightly, 'Shall we take a walk?'

And he answered just as brightly, 'Why not! We can do what we like. For a whole week we can do what we like.'

Yes, he was right: for a whole week they could do what they liked.

*

She had undressed in the bathroom and was now ready for bed. She did not feel so gay now as she had been two hours earlier when they set out to see the town.

Her nightdress had a square neck and it was sleeveless, but there was a matching coat to go with it, a negligée, the shop assistant had termed it. Her great-gran had chosen it, and paid for it.

She had to draw in a number of long deep breaths before she could leave the bathroom and go into the bedroom. And there he was standing near the dressing-table brushing his hair. He was wearing pyjamas and he looked taller, and when he turned to face her she saw the man again. She went and sat on the side of the bed and it bounced slightly under her light weight.

He came and sat down beside her and, putting his arm around her shoulder, he said, 'It . . . it'll be all right.'

'Andrew.'

Her face was close to his.

'Yes?'

She gulped in her throat, closed her eyes for a moment, then looked at him again and said, 'Don't do anything tonight, will you not, please?'

He drew slightly back from her. 'But . . . well, it's . . . it's usual, and it isn't as if we hadn't . . . '

'I know, I know.' She edged away from him now. 'I know all that. That's why we are both sitting here. Don't rub it in. But, somehow, tonight's been so nice, everybody's been lovely. I didn't think it would be after that . . . well after the registry office, but it has been. So . . . so will you . . . I mean, will you not?'

His lips moved over one another, his head bobbed in small jerks. 'All right,' he said. 'All right. There's . . . there's plenty of time, I suppose, but it's usual. Well' – he hunched up one shoulder – 'so they say. But they say so much, don't they?'

'Yes; yes, they do. You . . . you may hold me.'

'No.' He shook his head; then gave a small laugh as he said, 'No; I wouldn't be able to do that because . . . well.'

'All right.' She moved past him and got into the bed, and he went round to the other side and got into the bed. And after she had stretched out her arm and turned off the bedside light, he did the same at his side. Then her other hand groped towards him and found his hand, and she pressed it for a moment as she said, 'Thanks, Andrew.'

'You're welcome, Mrs Jones,' he said, and at this they both began to laugh, she so much that she had to turn on her side and bury her head in the pillow.

It had turned out all right. It augured well for the future.

On the Saturday morning, just prior to their leaving, the chambermaid looked at her and said, 'I hope everything goes all right for you.'

The kind look and the way in which the girl spoke the words strongly suggested to Peggy that the hotel staff must have guessed that she had to get married. Perhaps his father had said something. Anyway, what did it matter? Things had turned out much better than she had expected, helped undoubtedly by the solicitous attitude of both management and staff.

When the manager himself shook hands with them and said that he hoped they would come again; that, in fact, they would continue to make Harrogate their holiday home for many years to come, she felt that Andrew grew in stature the way he answered the manager: 'We will do that, sir,' he said; 'I can promise you. And you have been so kind to us; we'll not forget it.'

It was strange but she was finding out that Andrew could talk to other people with much more ease than he could talk to her. And he had quite a nice voice.

They arrived home in the afternoon and went straight to the annexe. After the hotel, it seemed terribly small, yet welcoming, and so much so that, having taken off their outdoor clothes, they made straight for the kitchen as though nothing were more natural, and she put the kettle on. Only then did she open the cupboard doors to find that the shelves were well stocked with food, dried and tinned goods, and the fridge with perishables, which sight must have brought them back to face reality, for as she went to mash the tea she suddenly stopped, saying, 'What am I doing? They'll be expecting us to go straight across there and . . . and tell them all about it,' and he, his voice flat now, said, 'Yes, yes, I suppose so. And this is where it all starts.'

'What do you mean?'

'Just what I say: the holiday is over, the living starts from now. You'll be at their beck and call and I'll be at everybody's beck and call in that grease shop. But' – now he stabbed his finger at her – 'it won't always be like this; that hotel's opened my eyes. I'm going to get on, Peggy. I am, I'm going to get on.'

'I'm sure you are, Andrew. Yes, I'm sure you are. But in the meantime' – she smiled at him – 'we had better get on across the yard and let them know we're back. Come on.'

For a moment it was as if she had become a schoolgirl again for she darted towards the communicating door, and he followed her, but more steadily. And when they entered the large kitchen and found it empty he stood looking about him in open admiration.

'They must be in the sitting-room,' she said.

In the hall he paused and looked about him. He had been in the house only once before and he had been too scared to take much notice of anything, only that the place appeared huge to him.

She had opened the far door and when he heard her exclaim, 'We're back!' he hurried to join her and watched her run to where her grandmother was rising from the couch exclaiming, 'Oh! my dear, my dear. How wonderful to see you again!' And after she had been embraced he watched her bend over the other woman on the couch and be enfolded in the upraised arm. This then was the great-gran, the boss. And now her strident voice was directed towards him as she cried, 'Come along in. Don't stand there; there's a draught from that door. Close it behind you.'

He did as he was bidden, then moved up the room and, holding his hand out to Victoria Pollock, he said politely, 'How d'you do?'

Victoria didn't actually answer him, but smiled widely at him and shook his hand. Then he was shaking the old lady's hand and saying, 'How d'you do?' She, however, did answer: 'I do very well, young man,' she said. 'How d'you do?' His wide mouth stretched and he laughed as he said, 'Splendidly, thank you.'

'Oh. Oh, splendidly.' Emma Funnell looked at her great-granddaughter. 'That signifies that you've had a very good week,' she said.

'Yes, Great-gran; and it was most enjoyable. I like Harrogate. We are going back there again. They were so nice at the hotel.'

'Sit down. Sit down, and have a cup of tea; we've just had ours, but there's plenty in the pot.'

Victoria was now bustling around the sofa table that stood at the end of the couch. So they both sat down, Peggy next to her great-grandmother and Andrew in a leather chair to the side of the fireplace. But when Emma Funnell demanded now, 'Well, let's have all your news,' Peggy said, 'Where's Mam?'

'Oh, the last I saw of her she was about to slip across to May's. She didn't expect you until later, not until this evening, really.'

'Oh. Then I'll keep it until she comes back.'

'You'll do no such thing, miss, or missis as you are now.' The old lady turned to Andrew. 'Anyway, young man, how did you find your week? What was the hotel like really?'

'Oh, very upstage.'

'What? What do you mean by upstage?'

He looked uneasy for a moment, then gave a little laugh before he said, 'Well, the usual term is posh . . . it was really high-class.'

'And your father paid for that?'

'Yes.'

'Well, well! Tell me what it was like in this upstage-posh-high-class hotel.'

He glanced at Peggy; then his neck jerked in his collar, and this brought his chin out: it was as if he had come to a decision. Smiling at the woman he had already stamped in his mind as a quaint old bossy boots, he went into a detailed description, not only of the hotel itself but also of the treatment they had received from the staff; of the champagne sent with the manager's compliments to their table the evening of their arrival, and of his bidding them goodbye when they left.

As Peggy listened she again saw the man emerging. She also noticed that her great-gran was not only listening to his description of their week in Harrogate but that she was also weighing him up and favourably, too, she thought. As for her grandmother, she was beaming: she had never seen her look so relaxed, even happy. There could, however, be another reason for both their attitudes: her father was no longer in the house. She had forgotten about him being away; now she realised there was a lightness everywhere, that her grandmother was actually laughing. She had been in her presence now about fifteen minutes and she hadn't heard her complain about one of her ailments. Wouldn't it be wonderful if her father never came back! 'Eeh! dear me. Dear me . . . '

'What's the matter, child? You feeling faint?' Emma Funnell had held her hand up towards Andrew to check his flow and, taking Peggy's hand, she asked her, 'Something wrong?'

'No, no, Great-gran; just for the moment I felt a little queasy, that's all. If you don't mind I'll go and get a breath of air. I'll tell you what, I'll go across to the Conways and tell Mam we're back.' As she rose from the couch Andrew, too, got to his feet, but hastily she said, 'No; you stay and go on telling them all about it. Tell them about the old gentleman who kept taking snuff and his wife sneezing, saying, "A-tishoo! Pardon!" '

'Yes . . . Oh yes,' and he smiled as he nodded at her.

And when Emma Funnell said imperiously, 'Sit down then, sit down. And don't worry; she'll be all right. She'll have a number of these turns before she finishes. You'll have to get used to them. But come on, tell us about the man who took snuff.'

Peggy stood outside the drawing-room door for a moment. The guilt feeling brought on by her shocking thoughts was still with her, but more so was she feeling amazement at how Andrew could talk and, more strangely still, how both her gran and her great-gran had accepted him, especially her great-gran. That was surprising.

She walked the well-worn way across the yard, through the garden, down through the strip of woodland, through the gate and into the Conways' back garden, there to see Charlie outside the shed pumping up a tyre of his bicycle.

She stopped a moment, then walked towards him. He had seen her as soon as she came through the gate; nevertheless, he only slowly straightened his back, yet it was he who spoke first. 'So you're back,' he said.

'Yes, I'm back. Had a puncture?'

'Something like that. What kind of a time did you have?'

'Oh' — her face stretched a little but she didn't smile — 'it was very pleasant. The hotel was fine, everybody was very nice.'

'Well then, everything in the garden's lovely.'

'What's the matter with you?'

'What d'you mean, what's the matter with me?'

'Well, the way you're acting. And you never came . . . to the wedding last Saturday. Your mother said you had a cold, but you hadn't, had you?'

'No; I hadn't.' He was holding the extended bicycle pump and he now thrust it closed as he said grimly, 'Why had you to go and marry him?' And before she could reply he went on, 'Oh, I know. My mam told me, respectability and an illegitimate child, bastard, and all that, and the stigma on you, nobody would want you after that.'

She didn't actually move back from him but she pressed her shoulders and head away from this different individual, this different Charlie, who had been easy-going, kindly, very often inarticulate. Moreover she was amazed his mother could talk to him about such things. But then her Auntie May was very open, different. She watched him now turn about and, bending, place the bicycle pump in its frame on the back of the bicycle. And she recognised the old Charlie when he turned back to her and said quietly, 'I would have married you, you know that, like a shot; you only had to wait.'

'Oh Charlie; we've been like brother and sister.'

'Well, we're not brother and sister, are we?' There was that aggressive note back in his voice. 'And you know damn

83

well we haven't been like brother and sister. Yes, you do!'

He was swearing! She'd never before heard him use a swear word. Other boys, yes. Andrew, yes: he had used bloody when he was talking about his headmaster and what he had said to him when he left school; he had called him a bloody narrow-minded prig.

'Anyway, you're now Missis Jones. It's a very common name, you could be Missis anybody.'

'Peggy!'

At the sound of her mother's voice she turned quickly, and, as if escaping from Charlie, she ran towards her and fell into her arms. And Lizzie said, 'I never expected you back so soon. How are you?'

'Fine, Mam. Fine.'

Lizzie held her daughter at arm's length now, saying, 'You look it. You look better than you did a week ago. Where . . . where is he?'

'Talking to Gran and Great-gran.'

'You've left him alone with them?'

'Oh yes.' She grinned at her mother. 'He was getting on like a house on fire, giving them a vivid description of the place we've been staying in for the past week.'

'That's good.' Lizzie's face had broken into a smile, which disappeared as she added, 'What's the matter with Charlie? He's ridden off without a word.'

Peggy did not immediately answer but linked her arm in her mother's and began to walk her down the path towards the gate; then she said, 'He was a bit short with me.' She did not say 'angry' or 'rude' or why he was short; but when her mother said, 'Well, he would be, wouldn't he?' she answered, 'But we were like brother and sister.'

'Don't be silly! you weren't. I'm sure he's had ideas about you in that way since he first started to think of girls.'

The bloom of the day faded. If she had waited and she had married Charlie, would she have been happy? The answer she gave herself frightened her; and when she shivered, Lizzie said, 'You're cold. Of course, you'll be finding it a bit different here from Harrogate. Come on; let me meet the married Mr Jones.'

As they entered the house Peggy pulled her mother to a halt and asked her quietly, 'When does Father come back?'

'I don't know, dear. I haven't had any word from him, and I don't know where he is. So he can't blame me for not telling him that Mr Cartwright took ill last Thursday and is in hospital and that there could soon be a shake-up all round at the Works.'

8

Leonard Hammond returned home the following Friday
night. He had stayed away for the full fortnight. Everyone
in the house knew he had returned when the front door
banged and the study door banged, then the bedroom
door banged.

Emma Funnell was in the sitting-room; she had just
returned from a visit to a friend and afternoon tea. She
had heard the three doors bang and with each she had settled
herself further back into her chair; but she hadn't stopped
reading the paper, only paused for a moment with each bang
and looked in the direction of the drawing-room door.

Lizzie was in the kitchen with her mother, and she said
quietly, 'You'd better lay his place.'

Victoria Pollock's reply to this was to sit down in a chair,
put her hand to the top of her chest and say, 'Oh, dear, dear,
I felt it coming on all day. It's the hernia. It must have been
that cheese I had at lunch. I shouldn't have cheese, Lizzie.
Look; give me one of my pills, the indigestion ones.'

Lizzie went to the delph-rack and from a row of small
bottles took one with blue pills in it. She extracted a pill,
filled a cup half full with milk, then took it to her mother.

And she didn't say a word. There had been no talk of hiatus hernia, stomach trouble, migraine, or phlebitis, for the past two weeks. It was true she had phlebitis, but the migraine, hiatus hernia and stomach trouble seemed to be born separately or altogether on different bouts of friction.

As she was going out of the kitchen her mother said, 'Where are you going, Lizzie?'

'Just to see if he's enjoyed himself.'

'That'll be the day. Oh yes, that'll be the day.'

As she went up the stairs Lizzie repeated to herself, Yes, that'll be the day. But one never knows.

She did know, however, as soon as she opened the bedroom door. He was changing his shirt and as his head came through the neck of it he looked for a moment like a jack-in-the-box, except that there was no pleasant grin on his face.

'Had a nice time?'

'Yes; yes, I've had a nice time.'

She watched him now tugging at his collar, trying to button it. 'I'll have to have new shirts,' he said; 'they're shrinking in the wash, boiled to bits.'

'It couldn't be that you're putting on weight?'

'I've never put on weight.' He looked at her over his shoulder now as he bent down towards the dressing-table mirror.

She waited for him to say something more, but he didn't. And so she walked to the wardrobe and took down a coat, and as she got into it she said, 'A lot of things have happened since you've been away,' and immediately she sensed rather than saw him swing round, saying urgently, 'She didn't marry him?'

'Oh' – she started to put on her coat – 'yes, of course she married him; and things are going very well in that quarter, I should say. No; I'm referring to the works.'

'What about the works?' His hands became still on the band of his trousers.

'Just that Mr Cartwright took ill. He's in hospital and . . . and from what I gather and from what Mrs Cartwright says . . . well, I don't suppose he'll be returning. He's got Parkinson's disease.'

'What! Why didn't you . . . ?'

'Yes, yes; why didn't I tell you? I should have sent a message to the B.B.C., shouldn't I, and had it broadcast? "Will Leonard Hammond, somewhere in England, come straight home, because Mr Brooker is now in charge of the works, the whole works".'

'Stop your bloody sarcasm, woman! This is serious. When did it happen?'

'Well, you left on the Friday night and he was taken into hospital on the Sunday. But you needn't worry; everything's running very smoothly. I went along with Gran on the Monday, not only to put Henry Brooker in charge but also to introduce your new son-in-law to the shop.'

Why was she doing this? She could see it was pure torture. But hadn't she been tortured for years? When had he said one kind word to her? When had he not taken her like a bitch in season? In fact, she had considered for a long time that rape couldn't have been any worse: never a word of love, never a word of kindness, never the question of how she felt. It was three years now since she had put a stop to it; yet she was only thirty-five, and there was a want in her that she could only fulfil with dreams. But there was a face in her dreams, and she saw the real face every time she went to the works.

She watched him now grab his watch from the dressing-table and look at it, and she said, 'They close at five; you wouldn't be able to make it. But you needn't worry, your showroom's still there.'

'Damn and blast the showrooms! woman. You know what this means, and if that old faggot doesn't give it to me, by God! there's going to be a blow-up like you've never seen or heard before.'

'You are thinking about staging it here or in our own house, the one you've been going to buy for years?' Her voice changing now, she said, 'I'll give you a word of warning, Len; you had better go quietly with Gran, very quietly, because if she wants Henry Brooker to manage, she'll have him. And let me tell you this: she can also have a new manager for the showrooms.' She pulled open the door, then paused and, turning and looking to where he was standing as if about to pick up something and throw it, she informed him, 'I'm changing my room. I'm sleeping across the landing. I'll move the rest of my clothes when the new wardrobe I've ordered comes. It was no use asking you to make a move, was it? because going into a smaller room, you'd be lowering your standards, wouldn't you?'

'*You know something?*'

She waited.

'One of these days I'll do for you, and her, because you know what you are? Trumped up nowts, the lot of you.'

'Yes, perhaps we are, Len, perhaps you're right. And you made the biggest mistake of your life when you married me, because I was one of them. But you didn't really marry me, did you? It was this house, it was the works, and it was the fact, oh yes, it was the fact that you couldn't see Gran lasting for very long and you could see yourself running the lot. But what you didn't know about yourself was, you hadn't the brains or the character, or—' and now she bawled, 'even the common sense to run anything. You are an ignorant man and every time you open your mouth you spew it out. You know the saying, "You can't teach your granny to suck eggs", but you thought you could. Oh, you were sure of it,

90

and see where it's landed you. But go, let her have it, and good luck to you.'

And now it was she who banged the door.

Having run quickly down the stairs, she let herself out of the side door, went straight to the garage, and in her own car drove to the works.

The Funnell Works was a large concern of its kind. The forecourt took up as much space as the glass-fronted showrooms, the offices, and the workshops together. The Funnell workshops had a reputation in the town and in the surrounding countryside, and this had been built up on a good job done for a fair price.

The last of the staff were coming out of the gates as she drove in, and she pulled up when she noticed her new son-in-law at the tail-end of them. He was pushing his bike. He was dressed in greasy overalls and she noted he looked tired. She drew the car to a stop and, leaning out of the window, said, 'Another day over.'

'Oh, hello, Mrs Hammond.'

'How's it going?'

'Oh, I think you'd better ask Mr Stanhope about that. I never knew a car had so many bits and pieces.' He laughed. 'I could have told you all the names of them, and that's about as far as my knowledge went; but I'm learning the greasy way.'

'How are you getting on with the other men?'

He straightened his back a little, then said, 'I think all right, at least with most of them. Some were a bit suspicious. I don't know why, seeing I spend my days lying on my back most of the time. Some won't tell you anything and some tell you too much and it's not all correct, but I suppose it's all in the game.'

She looked him up and down, then said, 'I think you must be the only one who goes home in dirty overalls.'

'Oh, there's another set inside, but they're worse than these.'

'You'd better get a third set then, hadn't you? And keep them for travelling. Better still, change out of them when you're finished.'

He bent down to her again and said quietly, 'Starters are not supposed to get above themselves, Mrs Hammond.'

She laughed and said, 'Oh, I see.' Then she asked him, 'Has Mr Brooker gone?'

'No; I think he's still in his office. He was talking to the nightwatchman when I passed.'

She started the car. 'Be seeing you then,' she said. 'I hope she's got a good meal ready for you.'

'She has had so far. Goodbye.'

He seemed to be fitting in in all ways. She didn't know if she had taken to him or not, but one thing was sure, Gran had; and her mother, too, quite liked him. And yet she wondered if there was a sharp side to him and he was playing the same game as Len did when he first came into the house, but in a different way ... get in early with the old girl and you're set. He had been in the house only on the night they had come back from Harrogate and then again on the Monday, when he had started work in the shop. Yet her grandmother had spoken of him a number of times since.

The nightwatchman was coming out of the office with his dog as she was about to enter, and he raised his cap to her. She nodded in acknowledgement and bent down and patted the dog, saying, 'Hello there, Boxer.' Then she went into the office where Henry Brooker was standing behind the desk. She gave him no greeting but said, 'I saw young Jones going out. He seemed to have more oil on him than there is in the tanks. How's he faring?'

'Very well, I should say, by Stanhope's account. He's quick at picking things up ... Doesn't have to be told over and

92

over again like some starters . . . Is there anything wrong?'

'He . . . he came home a short while ago.'

'And you told him about Mr Cartwright?'

'Yes; yes, I did.'

Henry Brooker moved round the desk and stood facing her before he said, 'And he feels sure he's going to walk in here and take over, Monday?'

'No; he's not sure. Yet at the same time he considers it his right, and if Gran doesn't give it to him I don't know what the outcome will be. He doesn't seem quite . . . well, quite sane at times; feels she has kept him down all these years. And she has, you know' – she nodded her head now – 'she has, because of the kind of man he is.'

'I can understand his attitude. I think I'd feel the same way in his place.'

'You would never be in his place, Henry . . . ' The name slipped out, and in doing so it seemed immediately to have crystallised the situation that had developed, in spite of themselves, over the last two years.

Or was it before that, from the first day he had come to be interviewed at the house? His wife had died only three months previously, in childbirth. He had looked sad and lost. She had given him tea in the drawing-room, and she had liked his voice and his quiet manner. And she had learned since about his sense of humour and his sense of fairness.

'It . . . it just slipped out.'

He took a step nearer to her. 'Your name slipped out, a long time ago, Lizzie. We . . . we've been so polite to each other, haven't we, while knowing all the time? At least I did. What about you?'

'Oh yes, yes.'

When her eyelids began to blink and the moisture to ooze from them he turned swiftly and went towards the window and, as he did every night before leaving the office, he let

93

down the Venetian blind; then, just as naturally, he walked back to her, put his arms around her and said softly, 'If he were a different kind of man and I had known you were happy, I should have squashed it at the beginning. I could have done so; I could have moved on. But I didn't, and I know why I stayed. Many a time I've asked myself what I was hoping for, and then quite slowly it came, the look in your eyes, and I felt it might be the same with you.'

After he kissed her a long, warm, lingering kiss, she leant against him, murmuring, 'Oh, my dear. Oh, Henry, what's going to come of it?'

'Would you divorce him?'

'Oh yes, tomorrow. But I'd have to have grounds, you know.'

'Well, we could give him grounds.'

'Oh, that's the other side of it; I'm sure he would never divorce me. If it was only out of spite he would hang on, especially if he had to leave that house.'

'But there are other ways. If you were separated for a certain time divorce would come naturally; and I'll wait. I'm used to waiting; as long as I know you're there at the end. There's one thing, though; I don't think I could stand being an assistant to him if your grandmother decided to bring him in here. Leaving wouldn't worry me. I must tell you' – he now tweaked her nose – 'I had an offer about a month ago from Rankins.'

'Rankins?' She pressed herself from him. 'The firm that wanted to buy us out?'

'The very one. They offered me the post of manager and I turned it down. But I understand they are not very satisfied with their new man. So, if Len gets the job here I can easily go in a different direction to work. It'll only be a five minutes' longer car ride from my cottage. And Rankins is a bigger firm than this, you know, and expanding, so don't think I'll be so

94

very disappointed if your grandmother decides to move him up. In fact, I think it would be all to the good; he might be more likely to let you go then.'

'Not him! Oh no, he can see the whole business coming into my hands when anything happens to Gran; we'd have to bear the brunt of any divorce.'

'Well, my dear, like Barkis, here's somebody ready and willing.'

They laughed; then as if it had always been so, they clung together again; and when at last she muttered, 'I must get back,' he said, 'We've got to make some arrangement about meeting. You won't know my place on the outskirts.'

'No, I don't.'

'Well, it's some way out beyond Brampton Hill and the new estate. It's a good seven miles from here. It's called Holeman's Rise, a very odd name for a cottage. I usually see to the garden on a Sunday and do a bit of cleaning up. I . . . I've never had anyone in since Jane went and it's not as spruce as it should be, but still it's no pigsty; so, do you think you could make your way there some evening or Sunday?'

'I'll . . . I'll try. Oh, yes, I'll try.'

They embraced again, and she muttered, 'Oh, I can't believe this,' and he said, 'Nor I; but it's true, it's happening.'

In seeing her to her car they walked apart, all very circumspect. 'Good night, Mrs Hammond,' he said as he closed the door on her and smiled, while she in her turn said, 'Good night, Mr Brooker.' Then she drove away.

She was a girl again. She was in love. She had been in love for a long time; it had been like an underground spring, but now it had burst through. Life looked bright; there could be happiness ahead. Yes, there could; though there would undoubtedly be trouble, and she was going back to it.

She knew she was right in it as she opened the front door, because there in the hall stood her mother and Peggy. And

Peggy, rushing towards her, said, 'He's in the drawing-room with Great-gran. Listen to him. He's been bawling at her.' As soon as her mother reached her she said. 'I daren't go in, Lizzie. I know I should, but I daren't. I'm dead scared of that man when he's in a temper, and it brings on my migraine. I've had it all day . . . '

'Be quiet! Mother.' She pulled off her coat and placed it on a chair and went quickly towards the drawing-room door. And as she opened it she saw her husband, his arm outstretched, his finger stabbing towards her grandmother as he cried, 'You can't do this, old woman. You won't! By God! I won't let you do this to me. I've worked there all these years, and . . . '

'Len!' Lizzie's voice halted his tirade, and he swung round towards her and yelled at her, 'You knew this! You're another one.'

'Shut up!' Mrs Funnell's voice was louder than either of theirs and her face was screwed up in protest. But it brought the silence it demanded. And now, with an effort she spoke normally again, saying, 'She knew nothing about my decision. And I didn't make it today or yesterday, but years ago. Do you hear me, Leonard Hammond? Years ago, when I took your measure as an incompetent, big-headed bully, aiming to be what he wasn't and could never be, a gentleman in any shape or form. You came into this house under false pretences. And let me tell you, you've been here on sufferance ever since. If it hadn't been for her—' it was she now who stabbed a finger forward towards Lizzie before going on, 'you would have been out on your neck years ago. Yes, Henry Brooker is going to be manager, and if you're wise you'll keep on the right side of him, because I saw him from the beginning as a stronger character than Cartwright and much more capable to run that place. And finally, yes, finally, let me tell you, Leonard Hammond, just you dare to come in here and bawl at me once more, just once more, or if I hear you bawling at my granddaughter, you will have no job and no home, not in this house, anyway. But when you leave it you leave alone. You have thrown your daughter out of your life and, if she's wise, your wife will throw you out. Now I say to you, get out.'

Hammond didn't move. Lizzie saw that he couldn't; he had turned pale and his rage seemed to have paralysed him. His fists were clenched and his arms held out slightly from his sides, and she became fearful as she saw the look on his face that was directed towards her grandmother. The threat that he had made earlier could well take place at any moment. She walked quickly past him and stood by her grandmother's side. And now his infuriated gaze was on her.

When at last he turned from them it wasn't as a beaten man. His head up, his shoulders back, he marched from the room; he even closed the door behind him, an action which in itself added to her fear of the moment.

'Lizzie.'

She started and looked down at her grandmother.

'Why haven't you got rid of him before? Why haven't you left him? Oh' – the grey hair wagged from side to side now – 'what am I talking about? It would have meant you walking out, not him. He'll have to be thrown out of here. And he will, he will be shortly, because I can't put up with him any more. My God! girl, how have you stood him all these years?' She did not wait for an answer but, leaning back in her chair she let out a long breath, saying on it, 'Get me a glass of sherry, will you?'

Her mother and Peggy were still standing in the hall, but in the far corner near the kitchen door, as if they had delayed too long their escape; and Peggy called to her mother: 'He's gone out. There . . . there's the car starting.' She looked towards the front door. 'What happened?'

'I'll tell you later,' Lizzie said, then spoke directly to her mother: 'Take the sherry in, Mother, will you? Gran's a bit upset,' and addressing her daughter again, she said, 'Andrew's home. Hadn't you better go and see to the meal?'

'He's having his bath. I was going out to put something in the dustbin and I thought I heard somebody yelling. I . . . I didn't think it was him. I didn't know he was back; the car wasn't on the drive.'

'It's all right.' Lizzie put a hand on Peggy's shoulder. 'Stop shivering. Go on. Go on over home.'

It was odd, but in her mind the annexe was already cut off from the house – she looked upon it as her daughter's home – yet she had only to step through a door and she was in it.

Before doing as Lizzie had bidden her, Peggy said, 'It's about the job, isn't it? He hasn't got it. What d'you think he'll do?'

'I don't know,' her mother answered her; 'I just don't know. But he'll do something.'

He could have a car smash or go into the river. Peggy took a gasping breath: she must stop thinking like this about him; it was dreadful. She turned away quickly, saying, 'Will . . . will you come in later, Mam?' And Lizzie answered brusquely, 'Yes; yes, later.'

Peggy found Andrew standing waiting for her in the kitchen. He looked fresh and smelt clean. He enquired immediately, 'What's the matter? Trouble?'

'Yes. Great-gran's passed over Dad for the management and he's gone nearly berserk.'

'Well, he shouldn't be surprised at that; everybody in the shop seemed to know that Mr Brooker was set for it.'

'Did they?'

'Oh yes.'

For a moment Peggy felt herself on the defensive, and she said, 'Well, how could they? Why was that? Dad's been there for years and Mr Brooker's comparatively new.'

He turned from her. 'Well, you're not the only one that doesn't like your dad. Anyway, what's that lovely smell?' He now pointed to the oven, and she said, 'It's a casserole.'

'I'm hungry.'

She immediately set about getting the dish out of the oven. She heaped his plate full with the stew and placed only a small portion on her own. And she could not help but feel satisfaction as she watched him eat. 'Is it all right?' she asked.

He raised his eyes and said with emphasis, 'Lovely. Lovely. You can cook.'

'Mam did most of it,' she confessed. 'Well, she showed me how to do it with the herbs and things.'

'Is there any left?'

'A little.' She scooped the remainder of the stew on to his plate, saying as she did so, 'You want to leave a bit of room for the apple pie.'

When the meal was finished and he was sitting back in his chair she said, 'Do you want to go to the pictures?'

After letting out a long breath, he replied, 'Yes and no. Quite candidly I feel too full and tired to move. Anyway, I'd bet you a shilling, within five minutes of getting in I'd slip off the seat and lie on my back, because I seem to spend my life now lying on my back.'

She laughed, then said, 'I'm not particular either. Anyway I feel we should be here in case Dad comes back and starts anything.'

'Huh! What could we do? What could I do? Stand up to him, hit him?'

She laughed again. 'Well, you could have a try,' she said.

99

He sighed as he said, 'He's an old man.' Then he added, 'I'd like to finish that drawing of the car.'

'Oh, go ahead.'

So it was that Lizzie, coming over an hour later, saw for the first time his drawing of a car with a model draped across the bonnet. But what intrigued her more was the border, which was made up of smaller drawings of all the pieces that went to make an engine.

Lizzie was now looking over his shoulder. 'I didn't know you could draw like that,' she said. 'And you've shown all the odds and ends. You're a quick learner.'

'Well, it was the only thing I was good at at school. Likely I would have taken it further had I stayed on.'

'Now if that was in colour it would make a nice poster, especially with a caption.'

He looked up at her and said brightly, 'Yes. Yes, it would, wouldn't it?' as if this very idea hadn't come to him two nights ago, about both the poster and the caption.

Turning to Peggy now, she said, 'He's back. He went straight upstairs. He's had nothing to eat that I know of.'

'Well, Mam, you wouldn't expect him to come down into the dining-room, would you?'

'Yes, I would. Knowing him, I would. There have been rows before, but he's always liked his food.'

'What do you think he'll do?'

'As I said before, dear, you know as much about that as I do. Whatever he does it will be to please himself, you can be sure of that; what he terms the right course. Anyway, we can only wait and see.'

9

Lizzie couldn't understand it. Acceptance in no way matched her husband's character; yet on the Monday he went to the Works as if nothing untoward had happened. All day she had waited for a phone call from Henry to say that her husband had smashed up the showrooms. But he had returned shortly after five and eaten his dinner. Years ago she had arranged that they had their dinner sharp at six; he would have had only a light lunch at a nearby café at noon. Afterwards he went to the Boys' Club. He had for years done two evenings a week at the Boys' Club, Mondays and Fridays. She could never understand why, of all the hobbies and pursuits he could have taken up, he should give his spare time to a group of boys, but especially these who were mostly from Bog's End and would be a rowdy crew. He had never been fond of children. She knew he could have done without having even a daughter, and he had certainly seen to it over the years that she herself did not fall pregnant again.

By the end of the week her fears had subsided, for he was still acting normally; at least he was keeping to character. She had quizzed Andrew as to how the staff viewed his attitude, and he had said that at least those in the workshop felt he had obviously decided to make the best of a bad job, and that he must have thought it a bad job when Mr Brooker had picked Joe Stanhope to take his place in the running of the Works. But then, as everybody knew, Joe had been there a long time and been head of the workshop and what he didn't know about cars wasn't worth learning.

Her husband had taken all this without any show of retaliation. There was something wrong somewhere. It was this feeling of wanting to find out more that caused her, on the Friday night, to pay her first visit to Henry's cottage.

It was getting dusk when she left the house, but she knew her way, for she had made it her business in the daylight to find out where it lay. And now, having left her car in the lane, she knocked on the door.

It was some time before it was opened; and there he was in his shirt-sleeves. He was standing with his back to the light of the room and so she couldn't see the expression on his face, but his voice told her of his pleasure when he said, 'Oh, my dear, come in. Come in,' and his two hands drew her immediately into a long room.

'I've just finished washing up,' he said. 'Fries seem easy until you've got to tackle the greasy dishes. Sit down. Sit down. Come to the fire.'

He led her down the room towards a large, stone, open fireplace where a log fire was burning. 'I've just lit it,' he said. 'It's the first time this year, but it was turning cold. I love a log fire.' He kept talking as he pressed her down on to the cushions of a large wicker couch. Then, dropping down on to the edge of it, his hands still holding hers, he said, 'Oh, my dear. I'm ... I'm delighted to see you. But how did you find your way? It's nearly dark.'

She spoke for the first time, saying, 'I ... I did some detective work during the week.'

They were looking at each other in silence; then the realisation of her intention straightaway brought them clinging tightly together, their mouths hungry to express their feelings. When it was over they lay, their cheeks against the cushion, their glances holding tight. And when he said softly, 'I've got to say it out aloud: I love you, Lizzie. I never thought I'd say that to a woman ever again in my life; but I do, I love you.'

She put her hand up and touched his cheek. There was a light stubble on it. She did not say now, 'And I love you, Henry,' but 'How old are you?'

He smiled as he said, 'Forty-two and I'm sticking to that right to the very last day, because I'll be forty-three next month. I'm over the hill.'

Her head still on the cushion, she turned her face away from his and her voice had a dreamy note in it as she said, 'I'm thirty-five and I've never known love. I had a girlish idea of it, but was soon disillusioned. I know now, though, that I love you, and have loved you for the past two years' – she brought her face back to look at him again – 'and I'll go on loving you no matter what happens in the future.'

Quietly now they enfolded each other and presently, her head on his shoulder, she murmured, 'I wanted to see you so badly, but I also wanted to know what's happening at the works. His reaction is not natural. When he came back last Friday night and Gran told him she had given you the post, he could have killed her. Really; really, he could have killed her. I heard him yelling before I entered the house. He had Mother and Peggy terrified. It was an awful scene, and when he stormed out of the house I thought such was his rage that he would commit suicide or something. But no; he came back quietly. And that's been his attitude since. How has he been to you?' She raised her head now and looked

103

at him, and he said, 'Polite. Stiffly polite. I know the whole shop expected high jinks, especially when I showed my face in the showrooms. But they were disappointed. Yes. Yes' – he nodded at her – 'they were really disappointed. They were looking for a showdown because, you know, he's not popular. Never has been. But there, some of the men don't like me either. They don't like my methods. They could get round Mr Cartwright, in a way; but as is also the way, he left most of the dirty work to me: he made the bullets and I had to fire them; so it was natural that everybody didn't love me. And some will love me less from now on, because there are one or two slackers in that company and it's usually the slackers that have light fingers and cause staff unrest in other ways. In the main, they are a good crowd and the majority are with me. But I don't think one of them would have been with Len. In the first place, you see, they think he got the position he's in now only through marrying you. Anyway, let's forget about him, the works, everything else, except us. What are we going to do?'

'I don't know. I've got a strange feeling. It's as if I'm waiting for something to happen, something that he's going to make happen.'

'There we go again. Come on' – he pulled her up from the couch – 'and let me show you my abode. Now this' – he waved his arm from side to side – 'isn't a bad little room, is it?'

'It's lovely, and so big.'

'Well, come and see the rest.'

The door at the far end led into the dining-room. When he switched on the light she saw it was about half as big as their dining-room but well furnished. 'And off here,' he said, opening another door, 'is the kitchen. Both these rooms look on to the back garden and the hills beyond. It's a very pleasant view in the daylight.'

She was surprised by the modern appearance of the kitchen and she said so: 'It's beautifully equipped.'

'I had it done out' — he paused — 'oh, some four years ago.' And she knew he had been about to say, 'just before Jane died.'

'And off here,' he went on, 'is a walk-in pantry.' He switched on another light. 'And next to it a coalhouse and woodshed, all modern conveniences. And a cloakroom. I would have liked that nearer the front door but there was no place to put it. At one time I was going to have a glass verandah all along the back here, like a long sun-room. I'll still do it, I think. But now for upstairs.'

The staircase was made of teak, open and uncarpeted, and the landing was quite large for the size of the house. Four doors led off it. The first he opened led into a good-size bathroom, much more modern, she saw immediately, than the one they had back home, for the walls were covered in pale blue tiles.

The first bedroom he showed her was of ordinary size, one which would take a single bed and a bedroom suite. But when he opened the door to the main bedroom she was surprised, not only at the size of it, but at the furnishings and colours. It was definitely a woman's room. The carpet was a dull green, the curtains pink, the bedspread matching them. The bedroom suite was modern, cream with gilt handles, the dressing-table being large with three mirrors. There were two easy chairs, upholstered in scarlet Dralon, as was the oblong box at the foot of the bed. She took all this in whilst he pulled the curtains on the two windows; then he turned to her and, on a short laugh, said, 'I keep the place tidy but I'm not much hand at polishing, as you likely noticed downstairs. A duster, yes.' He was standing in front of her now and asking quietly, 'Do you like it; I mean, the whole house?'

'I think it's lovely. Your wife had good taste.'

'Yes' – he nodded – 'she had good taste.'

The tone of his voice seemed to speak of his loss and she felt a strong pang of jealousy, only to ask herself, why? His wife was dead and she was here and he needed her as she needed him.

When he asked now, 'Are you in a hurry to get back?' she shook her head, then said softly, 'Not for a while.'

He put his hands on her shoulders and looked into her face, but neither of them spoke; then gently he turned her around and unzipped her dress.

IO

'Can you remember what you felt like, Auntie May, when you were carrying Charlie?'

May lay back in the deck chair, put her hands behind her head and looked up into the cloudless sky. 'It seems so far away I can't remember ever carrying him. I . . . I think he just popped in from somewhere.' She turned a laughing face towards Peggy, who was sitting in another deck chair, and she, matching her tone, laughed and said, 'He must have given you a surprise, then. Had he his guitar with him?'

They laughed together; then May said musingly, 'I think I sang most of the time right up to the end.'

'It's the end I'm afraid of. I asked Mam, but she won't talk about it. She just said, "Oh, when the time comes you'll take it in your stride." I thought that was funny.'

'Well, she's right, it's all natural. And when you once hold your baby you forget about . . . well, everything. And you're looking forward to it, aren't you, the baby coming?'

'Yes; yes, I am.'

'Is Andrew?'

'He doesn't talk about it. I think he's more interested in his poster at the present moment, and it's good.' She

107

nodded at May. 'And he's tickled to death that Great-gran is having it enlarged and printed for the showroom. He gets on with Great-gran. Funny that, isn't it, Auntie May? Dad never could.'

'Does he speak to you now?'

'He never opens his mouth to me; but then, he hardly opens his mouth to anybody now, not even to bawl. Gran says not getting the manager's job has knocked the stuffing out of him. Yet, I don't know; I cannot imagine him taking this business lying down, not after the way he went for Great-gran that night when she broke the news to him.'

'There's one thing I think you can be thankful for, lass, and that is Andrew's in another department, right away from him. Has he spoken to Andrew yet?'

'Oh no, not a word.'

'He's an odd man. Anyway, what about a cup of tea? But why tea in this heat, I don't know. Would you rather have a lemonade?'

'No; tea, please.'

As May pulled herself to her feet, Peggy said, 'Talking of speaking or not speaking, Charlie barely opens his mouth to me these days, either. He's so polite I can hardly recognise him.'

'Oh, he's the same indoors,' May lied quickly; 'hardly get a word out of him. He spends most of his time twanging the strings on that bit of wood. But I must say he's coming on like a house on fire under Mr Reynolds. He still goes to him twice a week, pays for the second lesson out of his pocket money. He's got it bad.'

After May left her, Peggy sat staring ahead. She couldn't really understand why she should be so hurt about Charlie and his changed attitude towards her; they had always been so pally.

The gate's clicking made her turn her head, and she saw her mother entering the garden; and Lizzie called out, 'This is what you do with your afternoons, then, is it? I wondered where you had got to. I've been over twice.'

'Oh, I haven't been here long. I must have been in the wood; it's cool in there.'

Lizzie let herself down on to the wooden seat attached to the elm tree that gave shade to the two deck chairs, thinking, Well, why didn't she stay in the wood. She's never away from this end.

She knew she was becoming jealous of May; but she couldn't help it, for more than ever now she was wishing to be closer to her daughter, even though she realised she seemed to be growing further away from her. Between them now was Andrew as well as May and Frank and Charlie. Why couldn't she have fallen for Charlie? Charlie, of course, would never have got her into trouble as Andrew had. She still wasn't sure of Andrew. He was so pleasant and seemingly so grateful for his new way of life. Even her grandmother treated him now as if he hadn't disgraced her great-grandchild, but had brought some benefit to her in some way. She was certainly taken with him.

'Hello, there. Oh, I'll get another cup. Isn't it a scorcher! Sit where you are,' May added as Lizzie rose to her feet.

'I just popped over to see if you've got any wool in your scrap bag, this shade. I only need about half an ounce; in fact, not that; it's just to do the sewing up. I finished the coat.'

'Good lord! Mam; that's quick; you only started it at the week-end,' Peggy said.

'Well, it isn't all that big, is it? And yet it will be too large for a first coat.'

'And you're sticking to pink,' May said. 'Well, my bet's still on blue. And look you!' she stabbed a finger at Peggy.

'The only way to settle this is to bring forth two. You understand?'

'Oh, Auntie May, be quiet!'

'Well, you never know. My goodness, how do they manage with three, four, and even five? When Charlie came along I thought I would go round the bend just trying to manage two, one of them already six years old.'

Lizzie looked at her daughter and her friend: they were laughing together, they looked close; it was they who could have been mother and daughter. She felt outside of everything and everyone. Yet she shouldn't; she should be feeling on top of the world now that she had Henry. Yet, the more she saw of Henry, the more they loved, the more frightened she became. What if anyone were to see her? What if it leaked out? Just imagine if her grandmother got to know, even her mother. And what about Len? Yes, what about him? She never thought she would feel guilt with regard to him, but she did, because there was one thing she had come to know: she wasn't cut out for liaisons. There had never been any scandal in the family and scandals outside it were carried on by . . . that kind of person, someone to be ignored, even shunned. But Len was a man she had come to despise, a man who had no real love for her; passion, yes, even lust. That was another thing she'd had to fight. She recalled the times when she would look at him across the breakfast table and hear him talking to her mother and Peggy in his big way while she wondered if they had any idea of what had taken place the night before or even that morning . . .

'Look, your tea'll be cold. You look miles away. By the way' – May leant towards her – 'here's a bit of gossip. You know the Robinsons, three houses down? He's in the Town Hall, she's secretary to a boss in the new factory on Pringle Road. Well, she's divorcing him, her husband, but by all accounts it should have been the other way round. He's gone to live with his sister in Gateshead and the house is going up for sale. A board went up yesterday. The things that happen in Bramble Lane. My! My! You don't need to read the *News of the World*.'

Lizzie felt sick. She leant her head back against the bole of the tree and when she heard Peggy say, 'You all right, Mam?' she straightened up and flapped the front of her dress, repeating, 'It's this heat.' Then she rose, saying, 'I'll get the wool later, May.'

'Yes. Yes,' said May flatly.

Peggy, too, had risen and she said, 'I'll have to be getting across; I've still to think up what to make for supper; likely salad again.' She smiled at May, then turned away and walked by her mother's side, retracing the way through the vegetable patch and into their own woodland. And there, taking hold of her mother's arm gently, she stopped her. 'Are you all right, Mam?' she said.

'Yes, I'm all right.'

'Is . . . is something worrying you? I mean more than me?'

Lizzie now smiled and put her hand out and stroked her daughter's cheek as she said, 'Strangely, you're not worrying me at all now.'

'I'm glad of that, Mam. Is it Dad?'

'Again, strangely, no; he's never been so quiet or pliable. Yet, at the same time it isn't like him, is it?'

'No, it isn't. I haven't heard him go on for weeks now.'

'No; you're right. And he seems to have lost all his bumptiousness. I don't know what troubles me more, this side of him or the other. Anyway, dear, don't you worry. How are you feeling yourself, I mean, physically?'

'Fine, Mam. A nice feeling inside.' She put her hand on her stomach. 'Not that I'm not a weeny bit afraid at times.'

111

'Are you happy?'

There was a pause before Peggy, her head drooped, answered such a simple yet searching question in saying, 'I . . . I don't know how one should feel when one is really happy. Great-gran calls it over the moon; you could say I have a sort of contented feeling.'

'You . . . you don't love Andrew?'

'I . . . I don't know, Mam. Yet, when I ask myself questions I get all mixed-up answers, and so I keep telling myself to take it slowly, it'll come. But Mam, I'm not yet seventeen and I don't think I should be taking things slowly. Do you?'

'It's the baby. That's how you feel; I mean, about taking things slowly. You can't do anything else. After it's born you'll think differently.' Lizzie now put an arm through Peggy's and on a much lighter note she said, 'How are you getting on with his mother?'

'Oh, I don't think I'll ever get on with his mother, Mam. I like his dad and I like his sister. Funny, but I really do like her. You know something, though? Andrew's ashamed of her; not of his sister, I mean, of his mother. And that isn't right because she was all for him, wasn't she?'

'Oh yes, she certainly was.'

'She's getting into the habit of popping in during the evening when we don't expect her. And sometimes Andrew's hardly civil to her. I feel for her then, especially when he pulls her up when she says something like she did the other night.' She gave a little laugh now as she went on, 'She looked around the sitting-room and said, "House proud is as house proud does", and he came immediately back at her cuttingly, saying, "It's handsome is as handsome does, Ma". And she laughed, and she said, "There's my clever clouts". Funny, but I feel sorry for her at times when he looks down his nose at her. And she's no fool, you know,

112

Mam, so she must be feeling hurt. But oh, if only she was a bit different.'

As they emerged from the woodland Peggy said, 'Another week-end. I thought the time would drag but it's flying. If the weather keeps like this tomorrow we're going down to Shields. Remember when you used to take me to Shields sands?'

'Yes, I remember. And your father's going off for the week-end too.'

'Dad? Where's he going?'

'Likely the same place he went for his fortnight's holiday. He just said at dinner time, "I'll be away until Sunday night." That was all, and that was the longest conversation we've had in a week.'

Peggy sighed now, saying, 'How different things would be if *he* were different.'

'Yes, indeed, how different things would be. But things are never as you want them. Are you coming in to see Gran?'

'No. As I said, I've got to think about the meal.'

'Give him an ice cream sandwich and an iced lemon drink. I should imagine that's all he'll want after being in the toolshop all day.'

At this they parted, Lizzie going into the house and Peggy into the side door of her home.

'I wish I could stay the night.'

'Oh, so do I, love, so do I. Well, if he's away, who's to miss you? Oh, I know you'll have to say goodnight and all that; but do that, go on back, say goodnight. Leave the car in the lane so they won't hear it start up.'

'Oh no, Henry; it's too risky. Very often in the night when Mother has decided to have one of her illnesses she'll come knocking at my door. She's just like a child. "Lizzie. Lizzie,"

113

she says; "I'm not at all well." No, it's too risky. But oh, how I'd love to.'

'Something's got to be done, you know, love; we can't go on like this, not forever. And it's no use waiting until he dies, because he's the kind of man who'll hang on until he's ninety.'

'Oh, don't say that.'

'Well, I can tell you this much, my dear, I won't hang on until he's ninety.'

'Just let us get the baby business over; I want to see Peggy settled with the child. You know' – she turned from his hold – 'I'm worried about her in a way: sort of on the side, away from all the other worries.' She gave him a half smile now. 'She's not really happy.'

'You didn't expect her to be, did you? Pushed into marriage at that age. From what you say, she didn't want it. In my opinion it would have been better if she'd had the child on her own.'

'Oh, Henry, you know what's said about such children and girls like her. Sometimes I think we're still in the Victorian age. We are supposed to be enlightened but there's still that stigma on both the mother and child. Anyway, darling, it's getting dark; I'll have to go and I'll have to make up a barrage of answers to the barrage of questions when I get in. That's another thing. What's this friend of mine like that I've started visiting? Why is she bedridden? If she's so ill, why isn't she in hospital? This from Gran. So why aren't you in hospital?'

How prophetic are the little things one says. So Lizzie was to think later.

They embraced a number of times before they parted, and the twilight was deepening as Lizzie drove home.

The house seemed different; it always did when he was out of it. But she hadn't been in her room five minutes when the voice came at the door saying, 'You there, Lizzie?'

114

'Yes, Gran, come in.'

'You got back then?'

'Well, if it isn't me it's my ghost you're seeing.'

'Don't be facetious, girl. How's this friend of yours faring?'

. . . 'Oh, all right.'

'Still bedridden?'

'Yes, Gran, still bedridden.'

'Funny, that: you suddenly find a long-lost friend you haven't seen for years and she's bedridden. Funny I've never heard about her before.'

'There have been lots of things you hadn't heard about before.'

'Yes, Lizzie, yes, there have been lots of things I hadn't heard about before. And there's lots of things I'm not hearing about now, isn't there? You got somebody on the side?'

'Gran!'

'Oh well!' The old lady turned towards the door again. 'I seem to smell a rat.'

'You're always smelling rats.' And this statement roused Mrs Funnell to retaliate in a strident voice and say, 'Well, I wouldn't blame you if you had. No, I wouldn't, not in your case. In fact, I'd give it a blessing.'

'Oh, thank you very much, Gran: I'll remember that and go out looking tomorrow.' Lizzie laughed now. But when her grandmother said, 'Where's he gone? Do you know?' she answered flatly, 'You know as much about his destination as I do, Gran. And quite candidly it's of no interest to me.'

'Well, it is to me. That's another one who very likely has something on the side. Seeing as you moved your camp across the landing, I don't suppose he would be blamed for it. But being who he is, I blame him for everything.'

Yes; yes, that had been part of the trouble right from the beginning, she had blamed him for everything. No use saying

115

he had asked for it. She didn't like him, and that was that, so she blamed him for everything. She was made that way, a law unto herself. How much trouble and unhappiness was caused in this world by people who were laws unto themselves.

She looked hard at the old woman standing by the door. Had she ever liked her? Yes, she had liked her, but not loved her. Strangely, as much as a nuisance as her mother was, she loved her mother because she had recognised that her forced illnesses were a shield against the fierce armour of that old lady going out of the door now with her back as straight as a ramrod . . .

Sunday morning dragged. Sunday afternoon dragged. She would have loved to drive over to the cottage and into Henry's comforting embrace; but he would be visiting his sister this afternoon. She lived in Fellburn. Apart from the fact that she was his only sister and he was fond of her, her husband was rather ill and he liked to give her a break by sitting with him, and so he wouldn't be back until seven o'clock.

She had asked her mother and grandmother earlier if they would like to join Peggy and Andrew in the wood where Peggy was spreading a picnic tea; May and Frank and Charlie would be there.

Immediately, her mother had said, 'Oh yes; that would be nice.' But her grandmother had come back at her daughter, saying flatly, 'Don't be silly, Victoria, acting like a girl at your age. You'll sit down to tea in a civilised manner. You're not supposed to be able to rise from the chair with sciatica, so how are you proposing to sit on the grass, eh?'

Lizzie exploded with laughter when her mother unexpectedly turned on her own mother, crying, 'You act like the Monarch of the Glen, Mother, and you're about as old-fashioned.' And at that she had marched out of the sitting-room, leaving Mrs Funnell to turn on Lizzie to vent

116

her annoyance: 'Don't you dare laugh at her,' she cried; 'Monarch of the Glen, indeed!' Then such was the character of Emma Funnell that her body began to shake and she put her hand tightly across her mouth to smother the sound of her own laughter and, looking at Lizzie, she said, 'The worm is certainly turning. She's never had any spunk. That's why I've trodden on her. But, Monarch of the Glen.' She wagged her head and her body began to shake again. Then, aiming to control it, she said, 'I'm a dreadful old woman, aren't I?'

'Yes, you are.'

'You don't mean that, Lizzie?'

'Yes, I do. You're a dominant, bossy, self-opinionated, seventy-four year old female who acts like half her age and expects other people to believe it and obey her every command.'

'You really think I'm like that, Lizzie?'

'Yes, Gran, I do, I do. You've always been like that.'

'My God! And I've always thought, if no-one else in this house cared for me, you've loved me.'

How could you say to an old woman that you didn't love her? The old hurt easily; they have lost a number of their skins. She said, 'Of course I love you. In spite of you being a terrible old woman, I . . . I love you. And now, if you don't mind, I'm going to the picnic and I'm going to sit on the ground and get sciatica.'

As she laughed the door-bell rang.

Lizzie opened the front door to see a strange woman standing there. She was dressed in a blue linen frock, and a cardigan. 'Mrs Hammond?' she said; and Lizzie answered, 'Yes.'

'I'm Henry Brooker's sister, Jane Shilla. He's . . . he's in hospital.'

'*Henry in hospital?* What's the matter?'

'He's had an accident. Well, not quite an accident but . . . '

117

'Come in. Come in.' Lizzie almost dragged the woman over the step, then looked apprehensively round the hall before saying, 'Come this way,' and in her hurrying almost ran towards the study. Once inside she said, 'Tell me . . . '

'There's nothing much I can tell you except that the police came for me about one o'clock this morning. I got the fright of my life. They had found him battered, lying near the phone. He had managed to dial nine-nine-nine. He was attacked.'

'He isn't . . .?'

'No; but he's very ill. He only came round fully a short while ago. You see, I have been going backwards and forwards to the same hospital; my husband's ill, too – he caught a bug and it's affected his insides – so I was actually with Henry when he came round, but as soon as he saw me he gave me your name. I suppose it's because he won't be in to work tomorrow.' There was an enquiring narrowing of the woman's eyes now before she said, 'Do you . . . do you know him, I mean, besides being in the business?'

'Yes; yes, we are friends.'

'Oh.' The woman's chin went up on the word; then she repeated, 'Oh,' louder this time. 'Well, he wanted you to know.'

'I'll go straightaway.'

'You won't be able to get in before seven; at least, I don't think so; although perhaps you might as he's on the danger list.'

'Danger list? Do . . . do you know who did it or why?'

'All I could get from the police is that it was robbery. His wallet had been opened and all his money taken; and they had strewn stuff around the living-room. Yet he must have been attacked outside because the blood was on the steps and the pathway. He must have come round and crawled in to the phone. How long he had lain there nobody knows, because as soon as the police got there they said they found my number in his telephone book and they got in touch right away. I'll . . . I'll have to be getting back now.'

'Thank you for coming. Oh yes, thank you for telling me. I'll . . . I'll go to the works tomorrow morning and arrange things.' She spoke as if that was the main concern, while at the same time her mind was racing and crying out, Oh, Henry. Henry.

Her actions in contradiction to her thoughts seemed very business-like: she let the woman out; she then ran to her grandmother's bedroom, where she knew she was resting and said, 'I've got to go to the hospital. Mr Brooker was attacked last night; he's in a serious condition. I've got to find out what's happened.'

Before Mrs Funnell could question her she was out of the room, flying across the hall, out of the house, and through the grounds into the wood from where she could hear the sound of laughter. And, standing outside the circle, she spoke to no-one in particular when she repeated what she had said to her grandmother. Within seconds everyone was on their feet asking questions and she spread her hands wide and flapped them, saying, 'I can't tell you anything. I'm going to the hospital. I'll see you when I get back.'

'Will I come with you, Lizzie?' It was Frank Conway asking this, and she said, 'No, Frank; thank you very much, but I'll manage. Go on with your tea. Go on now; you can't do anything anyway.'

She turned and ran back to the house; then, ignoring speed limits, within five minutes she was driving through the hospital gates. Three minutes later she was standing outside a long ward, and a nurse was saying, 'He's in emergency, mind; you mustn't stay long.'

Lizzie looked at the bandaged head and face and an arm encased in plaster, the other having a tube attached with blood flowing through it. She bent over the bed, saying softly, 'Henry. Can you hear me? It's Lizzie.'

She had to say her name three times before his eyes opened, and then, his mouth twisted, he whispered, 'Lizzie.'

'Oh, my dear, my dear. Don't try to talk, don't; there'll be plenty of time. Just lie quiet.' As if he could do anything else. But what did one say?

She sat down on the chair by the bedside and stroked the fingers of the hand that lay spread out on the counterpane with the tube attached just above his wrist. After a moment his mouth opened again and he said something. 'When . . . when?'

'Don't talk, my dear. You can tell me when it happened, later. Don't try to talk.'

She herself could hardly speak now for the tears running down her face. She felt she had to let them run or she would choke.

She didn't know how long she had been sitting there when a nurse came in and said, 'I think you should go now. In his present state, visitors will only disturb him. Come back in the morning; he'll likely be much better,' and she drew Lizzie up from the chair and led her out of the ward.

A policeman was standing by the door. 'Are you a relative of Mr Brooker?' he asked her. 'No; but he's a friend and he manages our firm, Funnell Cars,' she said.

'Oh. Aye, yes.' The policeman nodded. 'Nasty business. We thought he was a goner. If he hadn't got to the phone he would have been, because it got very cold during the night, as it often does, you know, after a hot day.' He again nodded at her.

'Was it robbery?'

'Oh, yes, pure and simple. His money was gone; we found his empty wallet near the gate. But what's puzzling is that the fight or whatever happened took place outside. I think he must have disturbed the intruder as he came indoors and was then hit with a blunt instrument. And it must have been a blunt instrument, for his head was in a mess, his arm was broken and his body battered from top to bottom, all for a few quid. It's amazing what these fellas will do, and the risks they run. They would earn as much, likely, by doing an honest week's work. But that isn't their style.'

She nodded in assent, then walked slowly away. If Henry were to die what would there be left in life for her? She wouldn't love again, not like this. She had never loved before like this. There would be Gran, and her mother, and Peggy, and the baby, not forgetting Andrew, and Len. Oh no, not forgetting Len. She wouldn't be able to go on. She'd put up with this life for nearly eighteen years, but she couldn't go on for another eighteen, not another eight months, not even eight weeks, if anything should happen to Henry . . .

They were all waiting for her when she got back and she told them the little she knew. And Frank wondered why it was always the decent blokes that were let in for it; he had known Henry Brooker for years and there wasn't a nicer fella walking.

It was just on ten o'clock that evening when she heard Len come in. She heard his key in the door, then the door bang. She heard him going up the stairs and his bedroom door bang.

He was back again and immediately the atmosphere in the house changed.

It was well after twelve o'clock when she left the sitting-room and went upstairs, but she couldn't sleep. It was three o'clock before she dozed off. It was seven o'clock when she woke, seven o'clock on Monday morning: Monday, when the week's routine started. There'd be a cold breakfast this morning, just cereals and toast, because it was wash-day. Her mother would go round collecting all the dirty linen, making the same comments as she did every week. Though not quite, for recently one had been dropped: Why had Peggy to change her underwear every day? When she was younger it had been once a week, except when they were going somewhere special, and then they all put on a clean vest and knickers. However, the comment that never varied concerned Len: why did he wear a clean shirt every day, sometimes two: Mondays and Fridays, when he was going to the Boys' Club, he always changed his shirt in the evening.

How soon could she go to the hospital? she wondered. The wards were always very busy first thing, but she could phone.

She phoned, to be told Mr Brooker had spent a comfortable night.

What did that mean?

Breakfast over, her mother was in the utility room sorting the washing. She herself was washing up the breakfast things when Victoria came to the door saying, 'What do you make of that?' She was holding out one of Len's shirts. 'You know, Lizzie, I starch all the cuffs and the collars of Len's shirts every week without fail. I've done it for years and when I haven't you have, but look at that: that cuff's stiff and that one's limp; it's been washed. Look! part way up the sleeve it's been washed. Now why should he do that? He's been up to something when he's been away. And he left cuff links in another shirt. That's not like him. But why should he wash one sleeve?'

'Likely because it was dirty.'

'How do you get one sleeve dirty?'

'You ask me; or better still, you ask him, Mother. But what does it matter?'

Nothing mattered, except getting to the hospital and seeing Henry again. Before she went, however, she would have to go to the Works. Last night she had phoned Joe Stanhope and told him what had happened. He had been shocked and said, 'Don't worry, Mrs Hammond, things will carry on as usual. At least I'll do the best I can.'

And she had no doubt they would all do the best they could; except Len, of course, who would be gloating, and waiting now, desperately waiting to see if he would at last be given his due: there was no better worker than Joe Stanhope, but where management was concerned he was virtually inexperienced.

At half past eight she crossed the yard and went to the side door of the annexe. She never used the communicating door inside the house because she felt strongly that they both must feel it was their house and so was private.

Peggy was concerned not only for Mr Brooker, but also for the way her mother was reacting. It was as if Mr Brooker was a relation or something. 'It's a pity Mr Brooker isn't there this morning,' she said, 'because Andrew's taken his poster in. Gran saw it last night and thought it was excellent. She thought up a slogan for it and is going to have it printed and stuck along the bottom. It's alluding to the girl on the bonnet and it says simply, "It's what's under the bonnet that counts". She's going to pay him for it.'

'Where are they going to put it? In the showcase outside?'

'Oh no; I think it's going in the showrooms.'

Now it was Lizzie's turn to say, 'Oh no!' Then, 'Len isn't going to like that, and that's putting it mildly.'

'It's only a poster.'

'But it's his showroom; and you know what he thinks of . . . of Andrew.'

'Well, it's gone now.' Peggy pursed her lips. 'He'll have to make the best of it.'

'It was quite big. How on earth did he manage that on his bike?'

'He didn't take his bike; his father picked him up in the old banger. Oh, it's a wonder that car doesn't set itself on fire. Anyway, they put it on the top. Andrew had packed it in cardboard ready. I . . . I thought his using all those parts to form a frame was very good, didn't you?'

'What? Oh yes, the tools. Oh yes; I thought they were very good, very good.'

Parts forming frames, posters, Len going mad when he knew who had done that poster, Henry lying in hospital battered to bits, her mother worrying why Len had washed one sleeve of his shirt . . . Yes, why had he washed one sleeve of his shirt? Oh, what did it matter? Nothing mattered. She must get to the Works.

Willie Anderson, looking at the six foot by four poster, commented, 'Eeh! that's grand. By! you shouldn't be greasing, you should be painting.'

'I will one day.' Andrew preened himself.

'Quite an artist, aren't you?' This from Ken Pickford, who was standing to the other side of the poster which had been placed for inspection against the boot of a car. 'You should take it up full-time.'

'I'm going to night-classes now to keep my hand in. It was my subject at school.'

'I'd say!' Ken Pickford jerked his head to the side; then, poking his neck out, he said under his breath, 'But how d'you think Hammond will take your efforts, lad, eh? He seemed to hate your guts.'

'He can't do much about it; Mrs Funnell likes it; she paid me extra for it.'

'She didn't!'

'Oh yes, she did. She gave me five quid.'

'Well, well. Anyway, it can't remain here. Look, Willie' – he turned to one of the men – 'you give him a hand to take

124

it into the showroom. And mind, you'd better do the talking to Mr Hammond, 'cos, I understand, he hasn't opened his mouth to you, has he?' He was addressing Andrew, and Andrew said, 'No, he hasn't opened his mouth to me, but I haven't missed anything he's had to say. Anyway, whether he speaks or not doesn't affect me; I know where I stand.' He looked from one to the other knowingly, and the two men exchanged glances and, nodding, said together, 'He knows where he stands.' And Willie Anderson added, 'Lucky lad who knows where he stands at seventeen.'

'I'm eighteen next week.'

'He's eighteen next week.' Again they had spoken together; then laughing, Ken Pickford said, 'Get on with it! Forward into battle, idiots and fools first.'

Both Willie Anderson and Andrew were still laughing as they carried the wooden-framed poster through the workshop, not without drawing some comments, then across the forecourt, past the main entrance that led to a small hall and the offices, to the double glass doors of the showroom.

The showroom was a large one. It could take ten cars comfortably, styled. Leonard Hammond's office was at the far end of it. It, too, was glass-fronted, so he had an open view into the showroom itself, where the cars were so arranged that his view could take in the main doors and any customer entering.

He had been sitting in his office for the last fifteen minutes. He had a ledger in front of him and a pen in his hand, but he hadn't written anything or even turned a page. He had already been along to the main office and seen Joe Stanhope ensconced in the managerial chair and had been told that Mrs Hammond would be along later to see to things. He'd had to curb his desire not to reach out and drag the fellow across the table and fling him to the floor . . . Mrs Hammond would be along later to see to things. Yes, Mrs Hammond would be along later to see to things, and he would see to Mrs Hammond. If it was the last thing he did, he would see to Mrs Hammond. His mind seemed to be red hot. He could practically see inside his head, and it was flaming. His temples were bursting. It was when he lifted his eyes and looked towards the door that he saw the two young men easing something into the showroom. When the nearer one turned his face and recognition came, it was as if he had been startled by a loud report, so quickly did he spring up and lean across his desk and stare through his dividing glass panel, to see Alec Fox, the chief salesman, walk towards the two, and Pat Kenyard, the second assistant, come from behind the car and join them. He watched them talk for a while; then Alec Fox looked towards the office and him before pointing to a wall where there hung two framed photos of cars. He was further incensed when Fox took down the photos and beckoned the two carrying the poster towards him.

Now he was out of the office and striding towards them, the impeding cars increasing his anger as he cried, 'Hold your hand a minute! Hold your hand a minute! What's this?'

'Apparently Mrs Funnell said this has to go up in the showrooms,' Alec Fox said.

'*Begod! it has*. Mrs Funnell said, did she? Now get that out of here before I put my foot through it.'

'Better not do that.'

Slowly he turned his head and looked at Andrew. The boy's face was red, the lips of his wide mouth pushed out. 'I've done that, and Mrs Funnell paid me for it and says it's got to hang in here. So hang in here it will.'

'*Get out! you scum. Get out!*'

For a matter of three seconds no-one moved; then Pat Kenyard said, 'Look, Mr Hammond, let's talk this . . . '

'Shut up! you, you fathead . . . So you won't get out and you won't take that with you. Well, I'll show you what I'll do

126

with it.' Like lightning he swung out an arm towards a stand and grabbed up the metal vase holding artificial flowers and hurled it at the poster, and it went through it as if it were tissue paper. What followed next no-one was later able to explain: whether it was Len Hammond who sprang forward on the boy, or the boy sprang forward on him, with three men aiming to separate them. When they did, Hammond screamed, 'Get him out! Get him out!' with Andrew yelling back at him, 'You'll not push me out, or anybody else. I'll be here when you're gone ... I'll take your place, and higher. D'you hear? Higher. I'm all set and you're finished.'

Another implement was hurled, and the men scattered, trying to make for the door; but when the second metal vase went through the glass pane, they crouched behind the cars and then watched Hammond wreak his vengeance on one of the cars. Picking up a loose jack from against the wall he smashed through the car's windscreen and was on the point of attacking the bonnet when suddenly he fell to the side and leant against the door. It was Willie Anderson who, rising slowly from behind the shelter of a car, said quietly, 'He's ... he's having a seizure.'

Now he and Alec Fox moved cautiously forward over the broken glass, to see the wrecker slumped on the floor beside the car, his arms folded across his chest and groaning aloud.

'Straighten him out.'

They were all standing round him looking down on the blue face, the mouth gasping for breath, and Alec Fox muttered, 'Phone for a doctor ... no, an ambulance, quick!'

Pat Kenyard said, 'It's a stroke all right. My dad died with one similar to that. My God! Look at this place. He went mad.' He turned now and looked at Andrew, adding, 'All through your bloody poster.'

'It wasn't through his bloody poster,' Alec Fox said, nodding at Andrew; 'he's been going mad for a long time. This isn't unexpected. So, don't let it worry you, son.'

Andrew was leaning against the bonnet of a car; he felt sick, he wanted to vomit. All those weeks of work smashed up. He didn't care if Hammond died; it would be a good job if he did.

As though prompted by these thoughts, a feeling of guilt brought about by his having said he'd get his place, and higher, assailed him: he hadn't meant it to come out like this. He wouldn't like it to get back to Mrs Funnell; he had already gathered that she was a woman who liked you to keep your place until she thought fit to change it. But that madman could have done for him if that vase had hit him.

Suddenly all their thoughts were brought together again by the opening of the door. Mrs Hammond stood there. No-one spoke as they watched her eyes move from the wall and the shattered poster to the broken windscreen on the first car, then come to rest on the scattered glass about her feet. When she moved slowly into the showroom it was Alec Fox who said, 'Your . . . your husband's had an attack, Mrs Hammond. We . . . we've sent for an ambulance.'

She walked over to the figure lying curled up on the floor of the showroom, and she put her hand over her mouth before she said, 'What happened?' She said it merely for something to say, for she knew what had happened: there was evidence to the side of her; he couldn't take the poster or the fact that his son-in-law had dared to enter his sanctum.

She was saved from further action or comment by the siren proclaiming the arrival of the ambulance.

They were all pushed back, and the ambulance men were bending over the figure, straightening him, testing his heart. Then gently they lifted him on to a stretcher. And one of them, turning to her, said, 'You a relative, ma'am?'

128

'I'm his wife.'

'You'd better come along then.'

She went along, sitting next to the blue-faced figure on the stretcher, now and again putting her hand out, as did the ambulance man, to stop it from rocking. Then as the ambulance drew to a stop, the man leant over and placed his hand over Leonard's heart. He lifted his eyelids, then slowly turned to Lizzie and said, 'I'm afraid, missis, I'm afraid . . . '

By the time they got him into the theatre it was confirmed that Leonard Hammond had died following a stroke.

Five days later he was cremated at twelve noon. The parson from the church was there because his presence was necessary; the members of the family, the three women and the young married couple, were present; neither of Andrew's parents had come: his mother was at work and his father said openly he wouldn't be a hypocrite, for the man hadn't recognised his son so he could see no reason why he should recognise him, even in death. Only four men represented the Works because Mrs Funnell had pooh-poohed the idea of closing it for an hour or so. Two young men represented the Boys' Club.

Mrs Funnell saw to it that the men from the Works were given a glass of spirits and the choice of some eatables in the dining-room, and by two o'clock the whole business was over, and the house returned to normal. There was no need for a solicitor to be present for there was no will to read. Leonard Hammond had had nothing to leave except, as Lizzie was to discover, the evidence that he had tried to murder Henry.

It was when she had been going through his things in the bedroom on the day after his death that Lizzie found his

131

suitcase in the bottom of the wardrobe. It was locked, and none of the keys she found in the room or those in his clothes, which had been returned from the hospital, would fit. She had taken a screwdriver and wrenched the case open, all the while feeling that she would find something in it. What she found was his dark grey suit, with bloodstains on the sleeves and down the front of the coat and one trouser leg. Evidently he hadn't had time to dispose of the clothes before death had hit him unexpectedly. But the condition of the suit linked up with the washed soft cuff of his shirt that her mother had found so odd.

After the discovery, she had sat on the edge of the bed and questioned why he had done it; that he was willing to murder a man because he had been given a position he thought should be his. He had intended murder, and so it would have been if Henry hadn't had such a strong constitution and managed to get to the phone . . .

It was three days later that Lizzie found out her husband had another reason for wanting to murder Henry.

She had defiantly donned a brown mackintosh instead of her black coat. The weather had changed over the past two days and there was now intermittent rain.

In the hall, she saw her grandmother talking to Andrew. She was saying, 'Well, it's up to you now, Andrew,' and the young fellow replied, 'Yes, Mrs Funnell, I know that, and I won't let you down.'

In spite of the life she had experienced with Len and what he had aimed to do to Henry she felt a spurt of deep anger on his account. If only her grandmother had spoken to him like that from the beginning, how different things might have been. And there entered her mind a faint suspicion of her young son-in-law's motives. Looking at him now, she thought he was too pleasant to be genuine. And what was more, why wasn't he at work with the rest of the men?

132

Andrew smiled at her, nodded, then turned away. And her grandmother said, 'Where are you off to? It's raining.'

'I know that.'

The old woman looked her up and down, saying now, 'You've quickly shed your black.'

'For God's sake! Gran, don't be a hypocrite.'

'Lizzie! Lizzie! Now you be careful.'

'Well, you are, you are. You loathed him. You're glad he's dead. And, oh yes, yes, yes' – her head was bobbing now – 'you're not the only one. But to chide me because I'm not keeping in mourning to portray my loss is . . . well—' She made a scornful motion with her hand, then opened the door, bringing forth the immediate reaction of, 'May I ask where you're off to?' from her grandmother.

'Yes, you may, Gran, I'm off to the hospital. And I may have news for you when I come back. But I don't know what time that'll be, so I'd keep awake.'

'Dear Lord! Dear Lord! What's come over this house?'

Lizzie repeated the words as she got into the car: What's come over this house? Well, there would be more coming over this house, if her gran only knew it, because she would be leaving it, please God, at the first opportunity . . .

Henry was propped up on his pillows. The tubes had been taken away, but his head was still bandaged, as was his arm. But he was more lucid than he had been for days. He held tightly on to her hand as he said, 'Well, you've got it over.'

'Yes, yes, I've got it over. But apart from that, how are you feeling?'

'Better, except when I move. I never knew there were so many bones and muscles in one body.' He smiled wanly. Then the smile disappearing, he added, 'I've got something to tell you.'

'Yes?'

'I know who did this to me.'

'And I know, too.'

'*What! How?*'

'I found his clothing all bloodstained.' She shook her head. 'To think he could have killed you – he meant to – just because you got that place. It's all Gran's fault. At bottom, it's all Gran's fault.'

He squeezed her hand tightly, saying, 'It wasn't . . . it wasn't only because of that.'

She remained silent, staring at him for a moment before she whispered, 'No?'

'No. It was because he had found out about us.'

'But how do you know?'

'Well' – he turned his head slowly on the pillow – 'after you had gone, I remained downstairs doing a little bit of work. My mind wasn't really on it. I was thinking of us. And then there was the heat. I had taken my shirt and trousers off and was sitting in my pants; in fact, I was on my way upstairs when I heard the rattle outside. It was as if something was at the dustbin. I thought it was the fox, and I wanted to see her again. You know, I had a fox that reared her cubs in the hillock not ten yards from the back window and I used to watch her. She used to bring them out around twilight, three of them, and they would play, and she would cuff them. I thought it was she making the noise, that she'd come back. I was so pleased. She had become a sort of distant companion to me, but I hadn't seen her for months. Well, it was dark but it wasn't black, and I guessed I should be able to make her out, so I didn't take a torch, and opened the front door and stepped quietly on to the path. And then it came at me, something . . . well, all I can say now it was like something black. As the blow hit me on the head I swung round and glimpsed his stockinged face, and then after something hit my arm I could feel myself falling. I tried vainly to strike out as I fell, but the last thing I remember was the stockinged

134

face staring at me and then of being lifted from the ground, as if I was being pulled up by the shoulders; then the face talking as if through a long tunnel, yelling, "Lizzie. Your dear Lizzie. You stole my job and now you've taken her. But I'll deal with her." I just faintly recall the word "her" echoing down the tunnel. Then something hit me again and the next thing I remember was waking up in this bed. I can't recall phoning or even how I got into the house. But there's one thing sure, he not only used a blunt instrument on me, he used his feet too. It's a good job he's dead, Lizzie, because I would have certainly had him up for this. He didn't intend only to knock me out. The doctor tells me it was touch and go for the first two days ... Don't cry, dear. Don't cry.'

Lizzie swallowed deeply, then said, 'But ... but how could he have guessed?'

'Likely you changing your pattern; and going out at night. Or perhaps he just came out to see where I lived and saw your car. We'll never know. There's only one thing I know now and that is, I'm glad he's dead, because if this had been brought to light, and it would have, the scandal would have been too much for you. Nor would I have been able to stay at the Works. And if you had married me then ... well, you know what people are, we would have had to move, because round here we would have been hounded. But now—' He drew in a long breath before he ended, 'You won't consider proprieties now, will you, Lizzie? I mean, making us wait?'

'No, no; never! Henry. As soon as you're well enough, I'm ready.'

'They'll get a shock; I mean, your people.'

She nodded. 'It won't be before time,' she said.

Lizzie looked from her grandmother to her mother, then to her daughter. They were all gaping at her. And when, after a long pause, her grandmother said, 'I knew there was something going on,' Lizzie came back at her: 'Well, as always, you were right, Gran.'

'You mean to say you're going to be married almost straightaway?' It was her mother speaking, and she answered her, 'Yes, Mother, as soon as Henry is on his feet. By the look of it, it won't be for some weeks, but it will be as soon as he can possibly make it.'

'Oh, Lizzie, Lizzie. You should show a little respect. I know he wasn't nice to you, he wasn't nice to anybody, but he's dead and gone and it isn't proper.'

'Shut up! Mother. No, it isn't proper, and it wasn't proper for him to attempt murder.'

They were all gaping again.

'It was he who attacked Henry and he meant murder, nothing less. What would have happened to me afterwards we'll never know, because he had found out. Like you, Gran' – she now looked at her grandmother – 'he smelt a rat, as you would say. And let me tell you, he did the best thing he ever did in dying, because otherwise he would have gone to prison, and for a long stretch. Henry was determined to name him and' – she thumbed to the ceiling – 'up there is a case with the evidence, which I would have produced. Oh yes, I would.' Her head was nodding to emphasise her words. 'There's a bloodstained suit up there that he hadn't been able to get rid of. So what about your proprieties now?'

No-one spoke for a moment; then her grandmother again said quietly, almost in a whisper, 'You'll be leaving us, leaving the house?'

'Yes, I'll be leaving the house, Gran. And not before time. I've been a slave to it and you, all of you, from the day he brought me back here, hoping that he'd be greeted with open arms. Even before that, it was the house, wasn't it, Gran? Always the house.'

When no-one spoke, she said, 'I've had a very tiring day, I'm going to bed.' And on this she walked out of the room, leaving her mother crying, her grandmother fuming, and her daughter silent.

Peggy walked slowly across the yard to the annexe. In the kitchen she sat on a high stool and placed her forearms on the table and joined her hands tightly together. Her mind was in a turmoil, amazement, anger, bitterness, all churned into one thought: She's been doing this, carrying on, yet she made me get married for respectability. She didn't at this moment consider the pressure that had been applied by her great-grandmother; no, only her mother's attitude to the disgrace of an illegitimate baby.

With a sudden jerking movement she got off the stool, hurried into the dining-room, from there into the sitting-room, started to go towards the stairs, but then stopped. If she went up there she knew what she would do: throw herself on the bed and cry. She thought of Andrew, and gave vent to her feelings: Why had he to go to his art class tonight! He could have missed for once. He had been art mad ever since doing that poster. And look what that had done. It had killed her father . . . But her father had tried to kill Mr Brooker. Not without cause, though. Oh no, not without cause. Of a sudden she could see her father's side, of his attitude to many things and people, especially to her great-gran! Oh yes, especially to her great-gran. She felt she must talk to somebody or explode.

She stopped running as she approached the woodland, because it was almost dark in there now, cool and fresh with rain still dripping from the trees.

Before she knocked on the kitchen door, she could hear Charlie playing his guitar in his room. After her second knock the playing stopped and she heard a voice yell, 'Mam! there's somebody at the back door.'

137

When May appeared she said, 'Why! it's you, lass. Why didn't you come straight in? I had the wireless on: I'm following a play. Come in. Come in. Come through and into the sitting-room. Frank's at a meeting; he won't be back for another hour or so.' She glanced towards the kitchen clock. 'It's that kind of a meeting: all old boys together; Charlie's upstairs practising.'

As Peggy followed her out of the kitchen she knew that her Auntie May was telling her they'd have the place to themselves for a time if she wanted to talk. And so she had hardly entered the room before she started. She gabbled first, saying, 'I felt guilty when I saw the coffin disappear, 'cos I'd never loved him. Mam said he loved me, but he had a funny way of showing it, Auntie May, hadn't he, when he nearly throttled me? I can't understand her.'

'What can't you understand, lass? What has she done?'

So, gabbling again, she gave May an account of the one-sided conversation that had taken place in the drawing-room a short time ago. But the disclosure brought no immediate response from May, and Peggy went on, 'I needn't have got married, need I, Auntie May? But she kept on about illegitimate children and disgrace, nobody would want me, while all the time she was having an affair.'

May's voice was not condemning, just quiet, as she put in, 'She may not have been having an affair at that time, dear,' while her own mind was practically pin-pointing the time when Lizzie's affair had begun. It was when she had noticed the change in her, a carefree attitude that wasn't in line with her character. 'I don't really think it had begun at that time,' she said.

'Oh, it must have, Auntie May. Anyway, Dad found out and tried to murder Mr Brooker, who I thought was a nice man.'

138

'What did you say? Your father tried to murder him? It was he who attacked Mr Brooker?'

Peggy nodded.

'Oh, my God! Well, all I can say, lass, is, it's a good job your father went the way he did, because if Mr Brooker had charged him he would have been in for trouble. Oh, I can't believe it.'

'You won't tell anybody else, will you, Auntie May? Except . . . except Frank, I mean Mr . . . '

'Don't worry about that: of course I won't; the less said about this the better. And your mother's going to marry him, Henry . . . Henry Brooker?'

'Yes; and she said as soon as possible, as soon as he's able to get up. And she's leaving the house.'

May got to her feet, walked to the fireplace, put her foot out to press a log of wood further back into the open grate: then turning quickly, she wagged her finger towards Peggy, saying, 'You know what the next move'll be? Your great-gran'll want you and Andrew to go and live in that house proper. Don't do it. Now, I'm telling you, girl, don't do it, because that'll mean you would have to take your mother's place and shoulder the lot. I don't blame Lizzie for leaving. No, I don't. But I do blame her if she's leaving knowing that you'd have to take her place over there. They're two old women, both your gran and your great-gran, and they're like leeches. Oh, they're nice old girls in their way. Well, I can say that for your gran but not so much for your great-gran, because she's a dominant old bitch at bottom. But if you and Andrew want any life of your own and peace in which to bring up the child that's coming, stick out and don't go over there. Let them get a housekeeper in. Anyway, they look after themselves now, except for the cooking. They're their own servants. Your great-gran's too mean to employ a couple of girls, and it needs a couple.'

Peggy was on her feet now and saying, 'Oh, surely they wouldn't want that. Anyway, I'm too young to run that place.'

'You're a married woman. You'll soon be a mother. Your mother before you wasn't much older when she had you. But mind, I think you'll have a single-handed fight to wage because Andrew won't mind going and living in the big house, will he?'

No. Her Auntie May was right, Andrew wouldn't mind living in the big house. He was already well in with Great-gran. She had even accused him of sucking up to her, and they'd had a row last week. Great-gran had paid him to do another poster.

May had implied that her great-gran was free with her money only when it pleased her. And apparently Andrew pleased her. Andrew was sly. No, no; she mustn't think that way; he was only trying to keep the peace.

On an impulse she flung herself into May's arms, and for a moment her sobs filled the room until May said, 'Now, now! stop that; it'll upset the child.'

At this moment, however, Peggy couldn't think about the child's welfare, only that it had let her in for this. She was gabbling again, saying, 'I . . . I didn't want to be married. I could have looked after it if Great-gran had only been a bit kind; she could have seen to us both until I got a job. And Mam said nobody would want to marry me. But Charlie would have married me, wouldn't he, Auntie May? Charlie would have married me; and I would have loved to be married to Charlie.'

She found herself suddenly thrust from May's embrace, although May still had her hands on her shoulders and was actually shaking her now and her voice was hissing as she said, 'Never say that! D'you hear, girl? Never say that. You're a married woman now and Charlie's got his own life

140

before him. I want him to marry, too. I want grandchildren. I can't bear to think of him being wasted. He's older than his years. He thinks deep. So don't, I'm telling you, girl, ever say that again. Don't even think it. You're married to Andrew and that's your life. In the annexe or in the house, that's your life.'

'Oh, Auntie May, I'm sorry. I'm sorry.' She had never seen her Auntie May look as angry or upset as she was now. 'I . . . I didn't mean it, I just meant . . .'

'I know what you meant.' May's voice was quieter now. 'I know what you meant all right, and there's nobody would have liked to see it more than me, but it can't be; the pattern's been cut out in a different way. You've got your life and he's got his. Some day he'll be a famous musician. I know he will. He'll be able to travel the world, like Mr Reynolds has done. He's lucky to be taught by a man like that; Mr Reynolds doesn't usually take pupils. He's got a chance, I mean, Charlie has, of a good life. Now go on back home, girl, and think over what I've said, not only about staying put in the annexe but about the other thing an' all. You know what I mean.'

Yes, she knew what Auntie May meant. She turned from her, saying again, 'I'm sorry. I'm sorry.'

'No need to be sorry. Go on now.'

She went out into a deep twilight that wasn't as dark as the feelings inside of her. She felt alone, really alone, as she had never done before. She was in the middle of the wood when she stopped and gasped aloud as the figure moved from the trees and stood before her. And peering at it, she said, 'Oh! Charlie. Oh! you did give me a fright.'

'*I'll never marry*. D'you hear me, Peg? *I'll never marry*. I heard it all. Mam's going to be disappointed. For as long as I can remember I've loved you and have known I always would. All right, you're married, but it makes no difference

141

to how I feel; in fact, it only makes it worse, the feeling. She was right about one thing: I'll be a musician one day, a good one, although probably not as great as she imagines. But with regard to you, I'll always be here, Peg; and . . . and thank you for what you said.'

'Oh! Charlie, I shouldn't have. I . . . '

She didn't mean to fall against him and he didn't mean to hold her; but there they were and their mouths were tight together. Then he pushed her from him, saying, 'I won't do that again. Never fear, I won't. But if you ever need me, I'll be next door. I know Dad waited years for Mam, and I can do the same.'

'No, no, Charlie. No; please, don't say that. Your mother was right, you've got to have a life of your own. You must marry. You'll . . . you'll feel different when you're married.'

'D'*you* feel different?'

She paused before answering, 'In one way, yes; in another, no. Some days I still feel I should be running to school, and others that I'm grown up and' – her head drooped – 'and soon to be a mother. So . . . so Charlie, do as your mother says, Auntie May's right. She nearly always is. I must go now.'

He made no further movement towards her, nor did he speak, and she side-stepped, hesitated for a moment, then went on through the wood, one hand outstretched as if groping her way . . .

Andrew came in at half past nine. He was very bright, and full of talk, until he realised that she was not taking any notice of what he was saying.

'What's up? What's the matter?' he asked her.

'Nothing's the matter.' Then she contradicted herself by saying, 'Yes, there's a lot of things the matter.' And she told him, ending with, 'And one thing is for sure, we are not going to live over there. Do you hear me?'

'But . . . '

'Never mind, "but", Andrew Jones, we are not going over there, and that's final.'

'Talking very firmly, aren't you, all of a sudden?'

'Yes; and that's how it's going to be.'

Three months later Lizzie married Henry Brooker, and Peggy and Andrew moved into the big house. It would be more correct to say that Andrew moved, drawn there by Great-gran, and that Peggy had to follow.

So it should happen in December, 1968, that Peggy gave birth to a daughter in the bedroom which had once been her parents'.

Within a few minutes of her birth the child, to be named Emma, was placed in her father's arms because her mother was too weak to hold her. Thirty hours of intensive labour had taken its toll. But at this moment Andrew Jones was giving his wife's condition very little thought, for he was experiencing a feeling that could only be termed as ecstatic: he was holding something that he had made. He was telling himself that *he* had made this little thing, this live, kicking, beautiful little thing that had a tuft of black hair similar to his own, whose features, he told himself, were his except perhaps for the mouth, which looked like a tiny rosebud. He had owned nothing in his life, and he had never known what love was until this moment, and this was his, his baby, this mite of a girl. He had made it; it belonged to him and always would.

. . . Yes . . . and always would.

PART TWO

Possessions
1973

I

'I think they're lovely, Henry, beautiful. Do you know, I hate to part with them. I would say don't give them away, if they weren't going to Emma. You know, you *are* clever.'

Lizzie picked up a set of strings with handles attached and began to manipulate the beautifully dressed, twelve-inch figure of Cinderella, saying as she did so, 'Walk! Prince Charming.'

Henry picked up another set of handles and in a moment Prince Charming was walking towards Cinderella and bowing from the waist.

When Lizzie tried to make Cinderella curtsey she succeeded only in crossing the puppet's feet, and she started to laugh; then, laying the puppet down, she said, 'But of the three, you know, I think I like Buttons; he's so appealing.' And she added, 'She'll soon have a collection, what with the Seven Dwarfs and Jack the Giant Killer.'

'Oh.' Henry continued to place the puppets in folds of Christmas paper and lay them in their boxes as he said, 'It'll be like last year; the Lord of the Manor will have bought her so much that everybody else's presents will be eclipsed.'

He looked up at Lizzie, saying, 'Did you ever know anyone dote on a child like he does?'

'No, I never have. If Peggy herself had had one tenth of such devotion from her father she would have had a happier time as a child. But then, there's another side to this. I think you can have too much of a good thing. He monopolises her every minute and I have the feeling that Peggy doesn't like it. She doesn't say anything, but you know Peggy. Talk about being thrust into maturity: she's still only a month off twenty-two and there she is with the barracks on her shoulders and my mother still dizzying about, and Gran . . . and Gran kicking eighty, acting skittishly. Honestly, Henry, when I think back to when I first saw Andrew Jones in that mucky room, the thin weed of a lad with nothing about him, I cannot believe he's the same person represented by Mr Andrew Jones, not only head of the showrooms, but . . . Mrs Funnell's right-hand man.'

'Well, you've got to hand it to him. I do myself. He was the first one to get it through to your grandmother that it would be a good thing to use the forecourt on a Sunday for the sale of second-hand cars.'

'Yes; but you had thought about it before, hadn't you? You didn't think she would approve. But it was you who had to fight to get double time for the men who worked on a Sunday.'

'That's beside the point, dear; he got it through.'

'But you started the driving school.'

He laughed. 'Yes, yes, I did,' he said, 'but he topped that with the car-wash.'

'My goodness, yes.' She nodded. 'And what did that cost? It makes me wild when I think, it does really, that Gran's as much taken with him as he is with the child. And there's Peggy: she could be an outsider of no consequence. When you're in the house, it's always Andrew this and Andrew

148

that from Gran. And Andrew's monotone, "What does Mrs Funnell say about it?" Oh! he's got his buttons on all right, that one. I first realised it the day of Len's funeral, when I spilled the beans. That's when his mind started working . . . He'll be after your job next, you'll see.'

'Well, that wouldn't trouble me, my dear. I know I could still step into Rankins. He's a Rotarian, you know, the boss down there. We're not supposed to help each other in a business way, are we?' – he pulled a face at her – 'But I know he would welcome me into his band. So, whatever Mr Jones has up his sleeve, he'll let it slide out one of these days and it won't make the slightest difference to me.'

'You're wonderful. Do you know that?'

'Look out! Look out! the puppets will be dancing on the floor in a moment.' He pushed the box further back on the table, then put his arm about her and gazing into her face, said, 'I worry about nothing, not a thing. I have you and that's all that matters. You brought me happiness that I never thought I would know again in this world, and you've added to it every day.'

She put her fingers to the top of his brow and traced a three inch scar downwards to the back of his ear, thinking as she did so, and not for the first time, that he had nearly paid dearly for his happiness. He still paid with violent headaches, but it could have been so much worse.

Following the first operation, two others had kept him in hospital for two months. It had been four months altogether before he returned to the Works, by which time Andrew Jones had been installed in the showrooms as assistant salesman. What was more, his posters were displayed on every available space on the walls, and on fancy artists' easels here and there between the cars. He was also allowed a car for his own use.

In the house he now wined and dined in a style that not even Grandfather Funnell had ever done, but all paid for

149

by Grandfather Funnell's wife, who seemed to have become rejuvenated by the smart, young, fast-talking Mr Jones.

'Well, come on, woman; are you ready? You carry the puppets and I'll take the case. You sure everything's in there? Don't forget last Christmas when you forgot your mother's and we had to come dashing back for it, and it snowing like blazes. And mind' – he turned to her – 'we're not staying long. We've got our own Christmas tree to see to. And I'm going to get drunk tonight.'

'You're not.'

'We're both going to get drunk tonight.'

'We're not.'

'We're not? All right, we're not. But we'll see. Yes, we'll see.' . . .

Arrived at the house, Lizzie's criticising reaction was still with her. 'My! my!' she said as she opened the door, 'No expense spared. Look at those lights! Every window ablaze. And to think when Peggy was little Gran wouldn't let me switch on the tree lights until Christmas Eve. It meant nothing, she used to say, if they were switched on earlier. And look' – she pointed – 'that's an innovation: fairy lights on these outside trees.'

'Come on, come on, it's Christmas; we'll pull them to bits when we get back.'

Entering the hall, they both blinked against the dazzling lights from the twelve-foot Christmas tree situated to the right of the stairs. Then Lizzie, looking up the stairs to where Peggy was descending with a tray of crockery in her hands, said, 'Who's in bed?'

'Gran.'

'Not again! She does this every Christmas Eve.'

'Give me the tray, lass.' Henry took the heavily laden tray from Peggy's hands and put it on a side-table as Lizzie said, 'Did she have her dinner and tea all at once?'

Peggy looked at her mother, and smiling, answered, 'Well, you should know, Mam; she always had an appetite after a fainting fit. It was the only way she could regain her strength. Remember? How are you?'

Lizzie was taking off her coat and hat now and laying them on a chair as she said, 'I'm fine, fine. The question is, how are you? You look drained.'

'Well, what do you expect, Mam, it's Christmas. Who isn't drained at Christmas?'

'Where is Emma?'

Peggy answered Henry's enquiry by thumbing upwards, saying, 'Having her bath.'

'Will she be going straight to bed?'

Peggy turned to her mother, saying, 'Yes, but not to sleep.'

'Well, in that case we can open the presents and put them round the tree. Before we do that, though, I'll pop up and see her.' She turned towards the stairs, only to have her daughter say sharply, 'No, no!' Then her voice changing, Peggy went on, 'Andrew's up there seeing to her.'

'Well' – Lizzie stopped – 'I don't suppose he'll object to me seeing my grandchild bathed.'

Peggy moved her head in a gesture that brought her mother's and Henry's full attention on her, and they waited for some seconds before Peggy, moving up the hall towards the drawing-room, explained, 'It's . . . it's his particular part of the day; he . . . he likes to see to her himself.'

Lizzie and Henry again looked at each other as they followed her into the room, and sat on the couch. Their minds being on Emma, they waited for Peggy to go on, but after placing a piece of wood on the fire she turned to them with a smile, saying, 'What about a drink?'

'Yes, that's a good idea.' Henry grinned at her. 'I'll have a whisky, neat, and this lady here will have a gin and lime.'

151

Then leaning closer towards Lizzie, he said, 'You're sure you wouldn't like a sherry?' This was a joke between them, and Lizzie retorted, 'No, sir, thank you; as you said, a gin and lime.'

Straight-faced now, Peggy said, 'Sherry is for occasions and this is no occasion, not even special company.'

'Go on with you.'

When the door had closed on her daughter, Lizzie looked at her husband and said, 'What do you make of it?'

'Don't ask me; and this is not the place to discuss it.'

'She was afraid of me going up there, wasn't she? Why? And this isn't the first time.'

'Well, my dear, I don't think you can find anything sinister in the fact that a man wants to see his child bathed at night. And we know he's crazy about her. But then, who wouldn't be? She's beautiful and cute and brighter than most for a five-year-old.'

'He's ruling this house, it appears to me.'

'Well, he has done, dear, since he first came in. He's got the support of the owner, hasn't he?'

'Yes; yes, you've put your finger on it, he's got the support of the owner.'

The door opened again and Peggy entered carrying a tray on which there were three drinks. She handed the whisky to Henry, the gin and lime to her mother, then took the third herself, and her mother said, 'What's that? That looks a dark mixture, what is it?'

'Brandy and port.'

'*Brandy and port?*' Henry got this in before Lizzie got over her gasp. When she did she repeated, 'Brandy and port? When did you take to this?'

'I was told it was a very good pick-me-up, and it is. It takes the heat out of life.'

152

They both stared at the young woman before them, sipping now at a brandy and port. Her maturity seemed to have slipped from her. To Lizzie she looked once more like the young girl who had found herself pregnant and didn't want to marry. But the impression vanished as she repeated to herself: Takes the heat out of life. She was looking, not at a twenty-one-year-old girl, a young and beautiful twenty-one-year-old girl, but a twenty-one-year-old girl that could be taken for thirty, and who was drinking a mixture of brandy and port to ease the strain of her life.

'I got a Christmas Box from Great-gran.'

'What was that? A year's free petrol? or a box of fruits, something that you could all share?'

'Don't be cynical, Mam. My present is alive.'

'Alive? Oh, a dog?'

'No, no. She wouldn't have a dog about the place.'

'A horse?'

'No; don't be silly.'

'Well, come on, put me out of my agony.'

'A daily help, full-time. Thirty pounds a week and her meals.'

'*Never!*'

'Oh yes. I had the go-ahead last week-end and I interviewed the fourth applicant this morning. She's a widow, twenty-nine, likes housework, so she says, can cook, and seems to have a very pleasant disposition.'

'I can't believe it! Wonders will never cease. Is it because you've taken a stand since Mother's been taking to her bed?'

'Well, perhaps.' Peggy took another sip from her glass. It would have been humiliating for her to say to her mother, 'I had nothing to do with it; it was the bright boy who made the suggestion to the grand dame.' And had she told them the reason that was at the back of the suggestion, they would not

153

have believed that either. On second thoughts, yes, perhaps her mother would, if she remembered her previous husband. And had her mother ever said to him: 'Leave me alone, I'm too tired. You have spent most of your day sitting in your office while I, from seven o'clock this morning until ten tonight, have been at the beck and call of two old women; I have seen to the needs of my child, and in between times I have cooked the meals and done whatever I could towards keeping this mausoleum clean.' Yes, very likely she had. But had her husband said, 'Very well, we'll see what some domestic help can do towards inspiring your sex urge.' She doubted it, or else her mother would have had help.

Inspiring her sex urge. He talked like that these days. He had talked like that for a long time now. Did her mother guess there was a battle going on in this house; in fact, various battles? The battle of the bed to start with; then the battle against the combined forces of her husband and her great-grandmother – they were most certainly joined now – and the other battle, an unspoken battle as yet, but one that would soon come into the open. It must. Yes it must.

'Look–' Her mother interrupted her pondering. 'Shall I come over first thing in the morning and give you a hand? I can, you know; I've only got him to see to . . .' and she turned and looked at Henry as though she disapproved of having to do so, while Henry smiled back at her. But Peggy said quickly, 'No, no! Everything's done: turkey stuffed, the pudding has been made this past five weeks. Gran did that, you know, as usual, and she made the cake and I've iced it. Yesterday she made the mince pies, and today I cooked a tongue and a small ham and . . .'

'Good gracious! How many are you having tomorrow?'

'Well, there's seven of us, then Auntie May and Frank and Charlie, so that'll be ten for dinner. Then, in the evening

154

Andrew has invited the showroom staff and their wives. That will be another ten.'

'Oh.' Lizzie raised her eyebrows. 'This is a new departure, isn't it, the staff and their wives being invited here?'

'Well–' Peggy drained her glass before walking to the table and placing it in the tray, and her back to her mother, she said, 'When one is an executive one must act like an executive, mustn't one?' Then looking over her shoulder, she enquired, 'Are you coming up to see Great-gran?' and began to walk towards the door.

Lizzie paused for a moment, then rising, said, 'Yes; yes, of course. You coming, Henry?'

'Must I?'

'No; not if you don't want to.'

'Well, let's say I don't want to.'

This little side-play caused Peggy to stop and wonder, and it also gave Lizzie the opportunity to try to bring a smile to her daughter's face and perhaps ease the tension she saw there. 'You know something?' she said to Peggy. 'He will repeat everything I say, part of it at least, and it can get on your nerves, you know.'

Peggy smiled and, looking towards her stepfather, she said, 'Yes, I can imagine how he gets on your nerves,' at the same time questioning why her mother should be so happy, and she a settled woman forty years old, whereas she was twenty-one and so miserable inside that there were days where she wanted to take to her heels and run. Run away from the two old women. Run from the ambitious young man who was her husband and who was bringing fear into her existence, a horrible fear to which she daren't put a name and which had sprung into life a month ago. She wished she could talk about it to her mother, but that would be fatal. It would be equally fatal

155

to talk about it to her Auntie May. She could to Charlie, though. Yet how could she bring such a subject up to Charlie? Oh, she could talk to Charlie about anything. Oh, Charlie. Charlie.

She said now, 'Have you heard about Charlie?'

'What about Charlie?'

Mother and daughter were walking down the room together. 'He's going to London to give a concert. His agent phoned him last week. He won't be on the stage all the time, he said, his will be just a little spot. He's always playing himself down. Auntie May, though, said there's only a quartet, and after he's done some solo pieces he's playing with them. Mr Reynolds is going with him; if his legs will hold out, that is, Charlie said.'

'My! My! He's certainly going places. Well, May always said he would. And of course he's slept and eaten with that guitar over the past five years. How many hours a day has he been practising since he left school?'

'At least six.'

'Enough to drive anybody mad. But then May thinks the sun shines out of him. She must be stone deaf. For meself, I could never see what's in guitar playing.'

'Well, you've heard him play.' They were going up the stairs now.

'Yes; yes, I do grant you he can play that thing.'

They had reached the landing when the first door in the corridor opened and out stepped a man who seemed to have no connection with the boy Andrew Jones, for here was a handsome, well-built and tall man, and he was naked except for a small towel tucked round his waist. The child in his arms. She too was naked except for a small towel around her shoulders. And it was she who cried, 'Oh, Grandma. Grandma. It's Christmas tomorrow.' Then, 'Mammy, must I go to bed?'

Neither Lizzie nor Peggy spoke, for Andrew, after one glance at them, had hurried along the corridor towards the far end where the nursery was situated.

The mother and daughter walked on towards the third door on the other side of the corridor and which led into Mrs Funnell's room. But they paused a moment outside and Lizzie said quietly, 'Does he always take his bath with her?'

Almost in a hiss now Peggy leant toward her mother and said, 'Yes; yes he does. Is there anything wrong in that? She's a baby.'

After a moment of looking back into her daughter's eyes, Lizzie said quietly, 'She's five years old and children seem to mature quickly these days.' Then, stepping forward, she tapped on the door, saying in a louder voice now, 'It's me. May I come in?' And when the answer came, 'Yes, yes, come in,' she opened the door and they went in, to be greeted with, 'And what were you standing outside whispering about?'

'Well,' said Lizzie, 'it's Christmas and we wondered what to put in your stocking.'

'Don't be funny. It doesn't suit you.'

'How are you?'

'Just as you see me. You're too satisfied with yourself and your life. It won't last. Nothing does.'

'Well, Gran, as long as it lasts I'll try to enjoy it. By, it's hot in here.' She waved her hand before her face.

'We are not as young as we were. We need warmth.'

Lizzie now looked towards the three-bar electric fire. Although it was a large fire, she had never known it have more than one bar on at a time. And the same had applied to the other electric fires in the house. Things had certainly changed. Oh, she wished she was back home. She couldn't think now that this had been her home for so long. She could say she had even hated the house; and now she had come to dislike her grandmother, but more so to dislike

157

Andrew Jones. When she thought of her son-in-law, how he had inveigled himself into this house and into this old woman's good books, she again felt a pity for Len rise in her. All right, he was what he was: he wasn't fundamentally a nice man, yet, had he been greeted in the beginning by this old woman as Andrew Jones had, how different things might have been. It might not have prevented her feelings for him from developing as they had, but it would certainly not have caused a change in the atmosphere in this place, and he might have remained livable with.

'You've put yourself to bed early tonight, haven't you, Gran?'

'Well, at my age I would have thought one could retire when one felt so inclined, without adverse comment. Your tone, you know, not only suggested surprise to find me in bed, but also condemnation that I should be here. Well, I am here, Lizzie, in order to prepare myself for a long day tomorrow, which I think is a wise decision, don't you?'

'I am past thinking about anything, Gran, where you're concerned.' Lizzie turned from the bed, and the action provoked Mrs Funnell to say to Peggy, 'Your mother's in that kind of a mood, isn't she, Peggy? I thought her life was now so happy and gay that she wouldn't be able to find it in herself to be uncivil to anyone, even to her grandmother. Hm! You've been drinking again, Peggy,' and she turned her head away. 'I can smell it from you, and it isn't sherry.'

'No, Great-gran, it isn't sherry, it's brandy and port mixed.'

'Huh! Go along with you.' It was evident that Mrs Funnell could not imagine her great-granddaughter drinking brandy and port mixed.

She addressed Lizzie now, saying, 'Have you been in to your mother?'

'No; not yet.'

'She's getting worse; she'll be gone long before I will. I cannot understand where her weakness comes from. There was no such fiddle-faddle ailments on my side, nor on your grandfather's. But there she is, a rattling pill-box.'

'I'll see you in the morning, Grandma,' Lizzie was making for the door.

'Have you brought the presents?'

'Yes.' Lizzie didn't turn round. 'And I've got yours. I spent three months knitting you a pair of bed-socks. I hope you like them.'

Bed-socks. She wouldn't dare.

Peggy closed the door behind them; but Lizzie held her tongue until they had moved further down the corridor, when she said, 'She gets worse; selfish to the core,' and Peggy reminded her, 'Well, you made your escape, Mam, but you left me with it.'

'Oh no, I didn't; it was up to you. I told you at the time to stick out and then she would have to get a housekeeper in. But then, of course' – she pulled a face now – 'I hadn't taken your husband into account, had I? nor his charm or his wiliness. Anyway, don't let us get back on to that. Now I'm not going into Mother tonight; a medical lesson would just finish me. I'll say good-night to the child, then we'll be off.'

One of the large bedrooms had been turned into a nursery and it seemed to hold every conceivable toy a child could have. Dolls of all shapes and sizes were arranged on shelves, and an outsize doll's house stood in one corner of the room, a miniature swing in the other. There were teddy bears and pandas seemingly fighting for a place in an armchair. There was a miniature rocking chair, and against the end wall a single bed with a miniature canopy over it. And in it now, dressed in a frilled nightie, sat the child, and by her side and combing her thick black

159

wavy hair from her brow was her father, partly dressed in trousers now.

'Grandma, Santa is coming tonight. Do you know what he's bringing me?'

'No, I don't.'

The child bent forward now, glee on her face as she said,

'Bread and cheese
And a bottle of pop,
Two boiled eggs
And a mutton chop,
Plain cold water in a glass.
That's only if you're good, said Father Christmas.'

'My, that's a new one. Where did you hear that?'

'Mammy reads it to me. It's in Bunty Bunny's book. And I can read it.'

Lizzie turned and in a low voice said to Peggy, 'They get their money easy, the ones who write that stuff.'

'You going to read me another story tonight, Mammy?'

'Yes, dear, yes. Now lie down, because, you know, if you don't go to sleep he won't come.'

'I'd like to see him. Couldn't you ask him to stay? He could sleep next door; there's no-one there.'

'But what about all the other children he's got to see to? You know, you're not the only one.'

'But she is the only one, aren't you? Aren't you, pet?' Andrew had his hand on her hair again stroking it back, lifting each strand separately.

The child looked up at him, smiled at him, then settled down into the bed. And as he tucked the clothes under her chin Peggy moved towards the door, and her mother, before following her, called to the child, 'See you in the morning, dear.'

160

'Yes, Gran. See you in the morning, 'cos it'll be Christmas then.'

'Yes, it'll be Christmas then.'

They were on the stairs again before Lizzie spoke, when she said, 'He'll ruin her if you're not careful. You want to put your foot down. He's so possessive; it isn't right. I'm telling you; you want to put your foot down.'

'Mam.' The word was ground out between Peggy's teeth. 'He . . . he loves the child. Can I stop him doing that?'

'There is love and love, girl, and his feelings go beyond it. It's possessiveness, pure and simple, possessiveness. You needn't be here, as far as I can see; you didn't give her birth, you didn't carry her; she's his. I've been wanting to say this for a long time.'

'Well, it's a pity you said it now. I've got my life to live and it's in this house, and I say again, you left me a legacy and I've got to manage the best way I can. So, Mam, keep out of it, will you? Keep out of it.'

'Yes, dear. I'll keep out of it.' Lizzie marched ahead now and, on reaching the drawing-room door, she pushed it open, saying, 'We're going.'

And within three minutes they were out of the house and into the car, and only then did Henry ask, 'What's it all about?'

'I've been told once more to mind my own business. But there's a business going on there that somebody should put a spoke into, before something happens and a life is destroyed.'

'What are you meaning?'

'Emma, the child: she's being utterly controlled by him, in all ways. You know why she didn't want us to go up into the bathroom? Because he has her in the bath with him.'

'Well, she's . . . she's only a child.'

161

'She's five years old! And do you think, if this has been going on all the years it must have, he's going to stop now? I tell you I'm worried.'

'Well, what can you do about it? Nothing. It's their business. As I see it, it's up to Peggy, and knowing her I can't see that she'd let anything happen that wasn't above board.'

'Henry, she can't stop it. That's what's the matter with her. I've noticed the change in her over these last two years.'

'Come on. Come on. We've got to go there tomorrow, so' – he took his hand from the wheel and gave her a quick pat – 'put your neb under your wing until after the holidays and see what transpires then.'

2

Christmas Day turned out to be a success, both at dinner time and in the evening. The credit for the laughter at the dinner table could be said to be shared between Henry and Frank Conway.

In the evening, after the first stiffness wore off and charades were introduced, the party went with a swing. The child was not present: her father had taken what he termed a very tired little princess upstairs, given her her bath and put her to bed.

During the Christmas dinner Andrew had kept a low profile, as it were, but in the evening he had played host under the admiring gaze of Mrs Emma Funnell. And the feeling this generated in both Lizzie and Peggy was much the same: resentment and a dull anger directed, if anything, more against the old woman than the young man.

Boxing Day, like all Boxing Days, was a day of clearing up and trying to get through left-overs.

The day following Boxing Day the new help arrived. Her name was Mrs Rosie Milburn. She was plump and fair, with a pleasant face. And from the beginning Peggy sensed her kindly disposition and felt they would get on well together.

Rosie lived with her bachelor brother at the other end of the town. And after her first day's work, which proved her promise that she liked housework, Peggy plied her with what was left of the Christmas fare.

Her grandmother was now on her feet again; in fact, she had got on her feet on Christmas morning. It was strange, the quick turn Victoria Pollock's illnesses conveniently took. She too had taken to the new helper. As for the mistress of the house, she seemed to be withholding her opinion: new brooms literally always swept clean, she warned.

Andrew's opinion of the new help was that she looked well fed, but he had then further remarked to Peggy that he hoped, now that she had help, he would benefit for, being less employed, she would be less tired. To which and looking him straight in the face, she had answered, 'Don't count on it, ever.' And grimly he had retorted, 'Well, you know what that'll drive me to.' And she had answered, 'The sooner the better. I would have thought you were already known there, anyway.'

On New Year's Eve, and out of the blue, he told her he was going to a party and he didn't know what time he would be back.

They were having a cup of tea in the drawing-room. The cup was half-way to her mouth when she said, 'We won't be seeing the New Year in then?'

'No; well, not here.'

'Does Great-gran know?'

'Yes; she knows, and she doesn't mind; she acknowledges the custom is dying out fast. She'll be in bed, anyway; as will your gran. So what would you have the two of us do sitting here alone and saying, "A Happy New Year, dear, nineteen seventy-four"?'

'We always have May and Frank in.'

'Oh yes, May and Frank. And don't forget Charlie, dear

164

Charlie, the great musician. Look' – he got to his feet – 'I've had enough of May and Frank and Charlie, all I'm going to have. Things are going to be different, and you've only got yourself to blame for that, haven't you?'

'I don't consider I'm to blame for anything that has happened since you came into this house. You've manoeuvred everything very nicely. You've hoodwinked a silly old woman into believing you are what you're not.'

'Oh. Is that it? She would love to hear herself called a silly old woman. Now let me tell you something. Her kindness to me is because I've expanded those Works. Profits went up by ten per cent last month and your stepfather got the credit. But who did the groundwork? Who suggested the alterations, and saw them through? I'm telling you, if anybody should be running that place, it's me.'

Her cup clashed into the saucer. She rose to her feet, and she growled at him, 'That's your aim, is it? Oh yes, I can see it now: right from the beginning, that's been your aim; but let me tell you, Henry is too well ensconced in that job and unless you would like to try and kill him, as my father did, you'll stay put where you are.'

He was gaping at her now, then his eyes narrowed. 'Your father tried to kill him?'

'Yes. Yes; you didn't know that, did you? But he wanted that job so badly he was willing to kill for it. Now why don't you try the same? You're young and strong; your swimming has put muscles on you. Go on, knock him off. But be clever and do it like Dad did; arrange it so it looks like a burglary.'

Quietly now, he said, 'You've kept that close, haven't you?'

'It was best kept close.'

'Does Great-gran know?'

'Yes, she knew, but she wanted things hushed up, so when

Mam said she was marrying Henry she didn't protest over much, because Mam was in such a state then she would have brought the whole thing to light. And there's one thing that Great-gran can't stand and that's adverse publicity in any way. Remember that, Andrew, adverse publicity in any way. And so she wouldn't like to know of your visits to a certain house in Bog's End, would she?'

The colour flooded his pale face and he barked at her, from low in his throat, 'Who drove me there? First, it wasn't good for the baby you were carrying; afterwards, post-natal depression. Another excuse. If I hadn't had my child to take my mind off things, God alone knows what I would have done to you.'

'*Your* child? Yes, you've said it, *your* child. She's *my* child, I bore her. Don't forget that, and don't go too far. There's something I'm going to have out with you, but not tonight, not this night. Perhaps we'll start the New Year with it. Yes, yes; perhaps we'll start the New Year with it. Now you'd better get out to where you are going before I change my mind and dash upstairs into Great-gran's room and tell her where you're going first, before you join your men pals. And I'm quite capable of doing it. Don't forget that.'

She watched his whole body stiffen, his fists clench at each side of his hips, then his big soft-lipped mouth, the feature that marred his otherwise handsome looks, stretch wide as he ground his teeth one set over the other. But her eyes never left his face, and he turned from her and marched from the room.

As if she had just been in actual combat she dropped down on to the couch and sat gasping, drawing in long, shuddering breaths. She wanted to cry. Oh, how she wanted to cry. But in a short while, once he was gone from the house, she'd have to go upstairs and read to her daughter and she knew that already the child was sensitive to her feelings: she would say, 'You sad, Mammy?' or 'You vexed with me, Mammy?' And she would have to smile at the first question and say, 'Oh, no, no, of course not. I've got a bit of a headache, that's all.' To the second, she would enfold her in her arms and say, 'No, darling, I'm not vexed with you. I could never be vexed with you.' And her daughter would put her arms around her neck and hug her. But only, as the last time she had done that and had kissed the child, to be told, 'You have a nice mouth, Mammy; Daddy's mouth is wet.' She shuddered with the feeling that ran through her at the picture the childish words conjured up.

Something would have to be done, and soon. But what? What? Whom could she talk to? There was no-one to whom she could confide, 'I'm afraid of my husband's affection for his daughter . . . my daughter.' To whom could she say that?

She didn't know how long she lay there, but when the door opened she started, then relaxed as she saw it was her grandmother.

Victoria came up the room and seated herself on the couch, and without either greeting or preamble, she said, 'I've had indigestion ever since Christmas Day. I shouldn't eat that kind of food; yet other people can. Why should I be like this?'

But when there was no retort from her granddaughter, she turned her head and looked at the young woman lying with her back against the head of the couch, her eyes closed, the muscles of her jaws showing white through the skin, and, her tone changing, she enquired, 'What is it, dear? What is it?'

'Nothing, Gran, nothing.'

'Oh, you can't hoodwink me. Things aren't right between you and him. He's off again tonight, I see; tonight of all nights. Of course, I wouldn't have stayed up. I never do

167

now; I hear the bells and the hooters from bed. But that's me. I'm no longer young. Still, even when I was young' – she was talking as if to herself now – 'I could see no reason to stay up just because a date was changing, starting all over again, one, two, three, four, five. But then you're different, you're young.'

She was looking at Peggy again. 'And you never seem to have any fun, do you, dear?'

She reached out and took Peggy's hand. 'You know what I think? I think you should never have married Andrew. He's changed this house. Do you know that? Oh, Mother is over the moon with him; but I'm not, Peggy. No; I'm not. Between you and me, I'm not. I don't know, there's just something about him. I won't say it's slyness but it's something. And you don't get on, do you? And then there's Emma. He's obsessed with that child. Do you know that? He's obsessed with her. It isn't right. There's something not right about the way he goes on with her. He's promised now to take her swimming.'

Peggy opened her eyes and turned her head sharply and looked at her grandmother. 'When did you hear that?' she asked.

'Oh, I heard him talking to her. "I'm going to take you swimming in the baths." he was saying. "You'll like that. You'll love that." That's what he said. I'll tell you what. You go over to May's, they always have a bit of a carry-on on New Year's Eve, and I'll keep awake and see to Emma.'

'Thanks, Gran; but you know I never leave her alone at nights, and you're bound to drop off.'

'I'm not bound to drop off.' Victoria's tone altered. 'Look, my dear, I'm not in my dotage yet, and I know I'm a grumbler and a complainer. You could say the only form of comfort I've got are my complaints; I'm forever complaining about my complaints. Oh, I know all about myself. Oh yes, I do, dear. And so, look, I tell you what. Later on you can bring her into my bed and then go over there and see the New Year in. Now you're not to say no. All right, if I fall asleep she'll fall asleep, too. And you know, dear, I've been a mother. I had your mother as a baby, and you know something? She howled for the most part of her first two years. I never knew what it was to have a decent night's rest. Oh, your grandfather took his turn. Give him his due, he was very good. But you see, I was a mother, I've had a baby, I know all about it. Even when you were small and Lizzie had a bad time of it, I saw to you. Oh yes, I did.' Her head was bobbing up and down now, and Peggy, smiling wanly, nodded in return, saying, 'Well, I can't remember what you did in those early years, Gran, but I remember how you used to bounce me on your knees in time with "To ride a cock horse to Banbury Cross".'

'Yes, yes I did. Fancy you remembering that. And do you remember "Wee Willie Winkie" and "There was a crooked man and he walked a crooked mile"? Oh, and so many others. We played games, you and I. That was when your father wasn't in. Oh dear me.' She now lay back on the couch and, staring towards the fire, she said, 'Been a funny house, this, held so many lives and hardly any of them happy, except my mother's.' Her voice took on a high, hard tone now, and again her head was nodding. 'Oh, she was happy all right. And she's been happy ever since, bossing everybody around, playing the queen of the castle. Yes, yes.' She gave a short laugh now. 'We used to play "Queen of the castle" on Shields sands. Do you remember?'

'Yes, Gran, I remember.' And Peggy now patted her grandmother's hand, saying, "If one could only remember the nice things, the pleasant things, and let others go by; but it's always the reverse: the unpleasant things grow like weeds and choke any nice memory you might harbour.'

'I don't like to hear you talk like that, Peggy. You're too young to talk like that. On the twentieth of next month you'll be twenty-two. You haven't really started to live yet, and you're talking like a woman who's experienced life.'

Yes, she was talking like a woman who had experienced life, because she *had* experienced life. Since she was sixteen she had experienced life, and none of it had been good, except that she had given birth to a daughter and also that she had found out what love was, but had experienced the painful futility of it.

'There, that's settled. You slip over now . . . well, as soon as you've seen Emma off to sleep, and tell May that you'll be over later. But wrap up well before you go through that garden because it's enough to freeze you out there. I'm sure we're going to have snow. Later on, put your new blue frock on, the wool one; you look lovely in that.'

Victoria now pulled herself to her feet and, looking down on her granddaughter, she said, 'And not only in that, lass, you're a lovely young woman. There's nobody in the family had your looks. I think Emma might take after you. She's got his hair, but that's all. The main thing is, she'll have your character. You know the saying, "Handsome is as handsome does"; that applies to men, but "Beauty is as beauty does", that applies to women. When all's said and done it's the character that counts.' She turned away now and walked to the fire, and there, looking at it, she stood with her hands joined below her waist like a penitent child and said, 'I spoilt my life and those of others about me, especially my husband's. And I blame myself. But then, when I come to think and ask myself what made me like this, I haven't far to seek the answer. It's sad, you know' – she turned about and looked at Peggy – 'It is sad when a mother outshines a daughter, and aims to do it to the extent of trying to fascinate her son-in-law. So the only

170

way I seemed to be able to keep Arthur was to become dependent on him.'

'Oh, Gran. Gran.' Peggy had her arms around the elderly woman now, and they clung together tightly, and there was a break in Peggy's voice as she said, 'Why didn't you talk about this before? You . . . you could have talked to Mam. Why didn't you?'

'Funny that, dear, I couldn't talk to Lizzie, not to my own daughter. I suppose it was in a way because I knew she didn't really love me. And, too, I always felt slightly inferior to her, if you know what I mean: Lizzie was clever, bright; I never was.'

'Gran, I love you. I do, I do.' And she knew she did, but it was only during this moment that it had happened, in this moment of revelation.

They were both crying now and holding each other tightly, but when they flopped down on to the couch their tears turned to laughter and Victoria, wiping her face, said, 'Do you know something, girl? I think this is the happiest moment of my life.'

'Oh, Gran. Gran. Well, I'll tell you something, if it is, we'll have many more happy moments like it, because I feel I've just found you and I feel sorry for Mother that *she* never *found* you.'

'No, your mother never found me, dear. No. It's strange when people go through life lost to each other. They are living in the same house, eating at the same table, and, in the case of Lizzie, part of my own being. But as you say, she never found me. Oh, my dear Peggy, you know, I don't think I'll need any pills tonight, nor perhaps tomorrow either.'

They again fell against each other, their laughter mingling, and Victoria, her voice firm now, said, 'He's bound to be on his way out, if he hasn't gone already, and so go on up, do your duty and leave the rest to me.'

171

Instinctively, in acceptance, Peggy took her grandmother's face between her hands and gently kissed her; then they went out together.

'May you come over here and see the New Year in? Lass, you may bring your bag and baggage and come over here and live for good.'

'No, she can't! I'm not having another female in this house; we've got enough.' And May leant forward from her chair and stroked the cat and its kitten that were lying on the rug before the blazing coal fire. 'Come over here and live and take the whole house from me? Huh!'

'Well, let her come over here temporary, Mam, while I'm away. She may have my room, and you can arrange it between you what you're going to charge her.'

'Charge her?' Frank Conway turned on his son. 'Charge her! You know, you are a mean scrub. All you can think about is your mistress upstairs. For two pins I'd go up and slap your ukulele in the face.'

There was a burst of laughter now and May fell against Peggy, spluttering, 'Laugh, I nearly died. One of the cheeky monkeys from down the road called after him' – she pointed at Charlie – 'the other day, "Give us a tune on your ukulele, mister." So that's what he's playing now, a ukulele.'

Peggy looked from one to the other. There was so much love and companionship and understanding between these three people that she was hurt by it.

'I won't have to stay long,' she said, 'because, knowing Gran, she'll likely fall asleep.'

Yet even as she spoke she knew that her grandmother would not fall asleep, not tonight she wouldn't. Poor Gran. At this moment she had the urge to fly back to the house, take her into her arms again and say 'I'm going to make it up to you for all the love that I've withheld, and for all the love you've missed in your life.'

May was saying, 'This will be the first time in years that Lucy and Jim and the bairns haven't spent New Year's Eve with us. But she's on her time and not feeling too good. I haven't been long back. Good Lord! I'll be a granny for the fifth time. It won't be all that long before Susan marries and then I'll be a great-grandmother. Oh, I'd hate to be a great-grandmother.'

'You look as old as one now; and anyway, don't be daft, woman, Susan's only seven and in ten years' time you'll be in a wheelchair.'

As Frank was talking his arm had gone round May's shoulder and he was hugging her to him, and of a sudden Peggy felt she must get away from this family scene or she'd burst out crying. She rose to her feet, saying, 'Well, I'll be seeing you, that's if you're all sober enough to see me.'

'Another cheeky monkey, suggesting we've been drinking.' Frank stood up and, taking up an indignant posture, he placed one hand on his hip and pranced towards her, saying, 'No alcohol ever crosses my lips, apart from cooking sherry.'

'Get out of the way, you big goof!' Charlie pushed his father to one side, then said, 'Come on, Peggy; I'll see you across.'

In the hallway, as Charlie helped her into her coat, his mother's voice came to them, shouting, 'Half past eleven the recital starts with the Spanish Fandango.'

Out on the pathway leading to the gate he took her arm, saying, 'She gets dafter as she gets older,' but there was such warmth in his tone that his words could have been translated as, 'Isn't she marvellous!'

She stumbled off the edge of the concrete path, and immediately his flashlight was directed towards the ground and at the same time he pressed her arm more tightly into his side, and like this they walked on until they reached the wood, and there their steps slowed and quietly he asked, 'Where's he gone tonight?'

It was the first time any one of them had asked her reasons for wanting to come across and see the New Year in, and she answered, 'Some men's do, I suppose.'

'Yes, yes, some men's do. He's a big noise now; at least he imagines he is. How are things?'

'Oh, as usual, except—' She stopped and she turned to look at him, but she couldn't make out his face in the darkness of the wood, so it gave her the courage to say, 'I'm worried, Charlie. It's about the child. He practically eats her up. There's never a minute when he's in the house that he'll let her out of his sight.'

It was a moment before he answered, 'Well, in a way that's understandable; she's his daughter.'

'Yes, in a way, Charlie, but . . . but there are other things.'

'What other things?'

'Oh.' She moved restlessly and kicked at the crisp leaves at her feet. 'I . . . I can't explain.' But then, her voice lightening, she said, 'There's one nice thing happened today; I mean, tonight. Just before I came over. Gran and I . . . well, Gran opened up and I know the reason for her succession of illnesses, real and imagined. She's had a loveless life right from the beginning, a life domineered by Great-gran. Maybe it's late, but we've come to know each other, and, you know, I don't feel lonely any more over there.'

'Oh my God! Oh, Peggy, to hear you say that . . . that you're lonely, cuts me to the bone. I lie up there night after night' – she felt rather than saw the motion of his head back towards his home – 'but I'm with you over here. I'm in that house, following your every move until you go to bed. And then I'm pulling you from the bed and him. Oh Peggy. What am I going to do about you? I've tried to get you out of my system. I have. Yes, I have. I even went to the length of taking Kitty McKenna to the pictures last week. But that was a mistake in more ways than one. She sent me a Christmas present; it's a tie, one of those hand-knitted ones.'

The note of laughter in his voice matched the rising gurgle in herself and it came over in her voice as she said, 'Kitty McKenna? Oh, Charlie, you've done it now, because she's been after you for years. Her mother teaches the piano, and, if I'm not mistaken, plays the fiddle. Oh no! the violin. She's very refeened; it would never be a fiddle, would it? Oh, Charlie.' She stopped; and they stood, each silent as if alone. The wind passed over them and rustled the bare branches of the trees and they still stood.

Whose arms went out first they would never know, but suddenly they were holding each other tightly, their mouths hungry for each other. They swayed as if they, too, had come under the pressure of the wind.

When it was over she leant against him, the side of her face pressed against his neck and she was muttering, 'This . . . it shouldn't have happened, Charlie. I told myself it must never happen.'

'It happened a long time ago, my dear, when we were quite small, romping in the wood. The thing now is, what are we going to do about it? Mainly, what are you going to do about it? I'm ready any time. We could go away . . . '

She straightened herself. 'Charlie, Charlie, we . . . we could never go away; there's the child,' she said.

'Of course there's the child. We could take her with us; don't be silly.'

'He'd never let that happen, don't you see? I've told you, he's got this mania for her: not only would he take us to court but . . . but I think he'd kill anybody who dared to stand between her and him. That's . . . that's what I'm frightened of, this unnatural feeling. Well, it is unnatural because he's not like an ordinary father at all. He doesn't act like a father, not that I've got much to go on, remembering mine. But it's as if I'd never borne her, it's as if he himself had given birth to her. She's all his, he has said so. Only tonight we had a row and said things. I stand up to him but underneath I'm frightened; scared to death really.'

'Well, if that's the case, something will have to be done. You can't go on living like this, scared to death. Tell me something. If it wasn't for her would you come away with me?'

'Oh yes, Charlie; yes, like a shot. Oh yes, my dear.' She kissed him again softly, tenderly. Then she said, 'I'm afraid for her; in some strange way, I'm afraid for her. But, Charlie, please don't mention this to your mother or dad, will you?'

'No, no, I won't. But me ma's no fool. She took his measure years ago, as she did your great-gran's.'

'There's another thing, Charlie: you've got your career and it's going to be wonderful; London is only the start. And nothing must spoil that . . . '

'Listen to me, Peggy. I love my music, but I can tell you it takes second place in my life. I think I concentrated on it only because you got married. In fact, I'm sure I did. Likely I would have dropped it and returned to the strumming.'

'Never. Never.'

'Well, that's as may be; but no matter what line my career takes, you'll always come first. Wherever I am, whatever I'm doing, there'll be you always in front of it. Just remember that, will you? I haven't got his looks or his stature. I'm five-foot six and I'll likely run to fat later on because Ma says I'm the image of my grandfather, whom I can't remember ever having seen. But when I think about how I feel for you, it turns me into a Hercules and I feel I can conquer the world.'

'Oh, Charlie.' She gave a small laugh. 'You were always flowery; you got it from reading so much poetry. I still have that little book of selected poems you gave me on my twelfth birthday. Do you still read poetry?'

'Not very often; my ukulele takes up most of my time as you know.'

'Your ukulele?' They laughed together now. 'Charlie.'

'Yes, Peggy?'

'I'm very fond of your mother; in fact, you could say I love her. She seems to have always been there for me to run to. And I know she likes me, but I don't know how far her liking will stretch if she knows I'm the means of you . . . well, not marrying. You mustn't let her know this has happened. And I should say I'll forget it too, but I won't. It's something that will help me to go on. But Charlie, seriously, and I mean this, you've got to make your own life, and it must be a married life because I'll be stuck in that house until Emma is old enough to look after herself. And all I can say is, God help me in the years between, because there's going to be a fight and I don't know if I shall be strong enough or clever enough to last out. But there's one thing sure, Charlie, I'll never leave her, not in his care.'

The wind had an icy tang to it: it swirled about them right down to their feet, disturbing any loose leaves it could find; and for a minute or two its voice was the only sound they heard, until Charlie's broke into it, saying, 'Well, don't worry, at least about me. I know what I'm going to do in the future. Oh, come on, come on. Oh Peggy, don't cry. Please. I can't bear it when you cry. Look, I'll promise you one thing: I'll not marry Kitty McKenna, not even if she sends me another tie.'

'Oh, Charlie. Charlie. But . . . but I will worry if I think you are hanging on waiting, because it's no good. I'll be near forty by the time she's ready for marriage, and that's

177

a lifetime away; and it's your lifetime away, too. And you know something, I'm older than you by two and a half months.'

'Yes, you are; and now let me tell you something: years ago I made up my mind never to marry a woman older than myself. So you see, you have nothing to worry about. Oh Peggy. Peggy.' Again they were enfolded. But quickly now, she said, 'I must go; but I don't regret this, Charlie. Oh no; it'll be something to hang on to.' She didn't add, 'And to know you're still there waiting,' because, knowing Charlie as she did, she knew that that was what he would do, wait, hoping against hope. She had said he must marry only so as not to disappoint his mother; but should he come to her one day and say he was about to marry someone, that would assuredly beat her into the ground. He was all she had to hope for. He didn't know it and he mustn't know it, but nevertheless it was true.

'Happy New Year, darling.' She had called Charlie 'darling'.

His reaction was not some other endearment but a tightening of his holding of her and saying again, 'Oh Peggy. Peggy;' then, 'A Happy New Year when it comes.'

3

Rosie Milburn was a joker; besides which, not only did she keep the house spotless but also she was a good cook. In short, Rosie was a treasure who had brought a lightness to the house. She hummed to herself when she was working and should you pass her when she was on her knees polishing the floor, or slapping dough on the board – she made bread for them all – she would come out with some remark that would either cause you to make a retort in similar vein or have you burst out laughing.

Altogether she was a nice woman, was Rosie Milburn. She got on with Victoria like a house on fire; as for Mrs Funnell, she even chipped that old lady. 'How's your old wooden legs this morning? Mind the splinters!' she would say to her.

Mrs Funnell had got used to this form of greeting, but it wasn't known whether she appreciated it or not. As for the master of the house, she chipped him, too. 'Make way for the Lord Mayor,' she said one day on the front steps, as she moved her bucket aside, and he, bending over her, said, 'Many a true word spoken in jest, Rosie,' to which she had reacted quickly, saying, 'Yes, Mr Jones; but those who sit on horsehair chairs generally get their bums scratched,' bringing from him the reaction of a push on the side of her head and their laughing together.

Yes, Rosie had brought lightness into the house. Peggy was aware that many of her sayings were threadbare, she had heard them many times before, but as the comedian said, it wasn't what was said, it was the way it was told. And it certainly was the way Rosie said it. Apparently, too, Rosie enjoyed herself after working hours. Her widowhood sat lightly on her shoulders, and from what Peggy gathered from her she had a favourite pub.

As for Emma, Emma loved Rosie. 'Rosie's being funny again, Mammy,' she would say. 'She said a funny poem to me about an angel spitting.'

'Angels don't spit.'

'Oh, Rosie's angels do.'

Yes, indeed, Rosie's angels spat. She was a dab hand at couplets, was Rosie.

So all went well, at least in the working part of the house, for more than two years. Then it seemed that all of a sudden Rosie wasn't so merry: her laughter was forced, and she didn't wisecrack as you were passing her, until Peggy felt she must seek the reason. 'Is anything the matter, Rosie? Aren't you well?' she asked her. And Rosie had replied in a sort of mumble, 'I'm all right, Mrs Jones; just a bit worried about my brother. He's not too good lately.'

So that was it; she was worried about her brother.

Then came Monday morning. Her grandmother, as usual, was sorting the washing in the scullery. She herself had just returned from taking Emma to school. That was one thing Andrew couldn't do, because he had to be at the Works by eight o'clock and Emma didn't start school until nine. She had picked up the letters from the wire box behind the front door, dropped off her coat on her way across the hall and gone into the kitchen. And her grandmother called from the scullery, 'Is that you, dear?' And when she answered, 'Yes, it's me,' then added, 'Has Rosie arrived yet?' Victoria came to the kitchen door, saying, 'No, she hasn't. Strange, isn't it? You would think that when she wasn't coming she would have got some word round.'

Peggy sat down at the kitchen table and looked at the mail.

There were three letters and an electricity bill addressed to Mrs Emma Funnell, three circulars and – she picked up the last envelope – a cheap blue paper one and addressed to herself, not as Mrs Margaret Jones, but Mrs Peggy Jones. Who called her Peggy besides those in the household? Charlie. But Charlie was away and this certainly wasn't his writing: last year she had received postcards sent by him while travelling abroad with the quartet, and they were naturally never personal, just stating how the concerts were going.

She slit open the envelope, took out a single sheet of paper, and read,

'Dear Mrs Jones,
    I am sorry but I won't be in any more. My brother is not well and I feel I must stay at home. I am very sorry. Believe me, I am very, very sorry, because I liked working for you.
    I am very sorry.
    Yours,
    Rosie.'

She handed the letter to her grandmother, saying, 'It's her brother. He must be pretty bad if she's got to stay at home.'

'She should have told you. It seems so sudden. Oh my! we're going to miss her, aren't we?'

'Yes, we are, in all ways. Back to square one.' She gave a small, tight smile and her grandmother answered it with,

181

'Yes, in more ways than one, we'll definitely be back to square one. Still, you can try for someone else, although I doubt if you'll get another Rosie.'

'No, you're right there, Gran. Look, I haven't put the car away, I'll slip round and see what I can do. Perhaps I could suggest her getting someone in to look after him and she could come for half time. I really do feel she liked working here as much as we liked having her, and not only for her work; she was such a nice person, so warm and lively.'

'Well, I'd better get that washing on and think about a dinner,' Victoria said; 'but you go along and see what's happening and we'll talk about that when you come back . . . '

Peggy was a little surprised to find that 48, Beaconsfield Avenue was not on the council estate but was one of a terrace of small houses, with front iron-railed, enclosed gardens and all neatly kept. After getting out of the car she bent over and pushed open the gate, then closed it behind her, walked up the short path and rang the doorbell. Within seconds she was confronted by a tall man whom she took to be in his late forties, but who, she guessed, couldn't be quite that if he was Rosie's brother. He coughed twice before saying, 'Yes?' then leaned forward and peered at her as if his sight were bad, then coughed a harsh, chest-tearing cough before asking further, 'Yes, what d'you want?'

'I'm Mrs Jones. I . . . I have come to see Rosie.'

'Oh, you have, have you? You've come to see Rosie, have you? Well, Rosie's not here.'

'I . . . I understood that she was, well er . . . '

'Come in. Come in.' He pulled the door wide; then before she had hardly got over the step he slammed it closed. Preceding her now, he went across a small hall and into a sitting-room. This, too, was small but nicely furnished and comfortable-looking.

He did not ask her to sit down but said to her straightaway, 'What has she told you?'

'Well, she . . . she told me that you weren't well and she had to stay at home.'

'Bloody liar! She's gone off.'

'Gone off?'

'That's what I said, missis, gone off with a bloke. I knew there was something in the wind, has been for weeks. Off she's been at nights; couldn't get in quick enough and couldn't get out quick enough. When her man died I took her in and gave her a home. *He* never did. Come easy, go easy, God send Sunday, that was him. I wasn't like an elder brother to her, I was more like a father. She had a duty to me to stay by me 'cos I stuck by her. Me with me chest like this.' He thumped his chest with his fist now. 'It's me lungs; coal dust on top of bronchial trouble. And me back's gone an' all, a roof fall in the pit. I deserved better treatment than that. What d'you think, missis?'

'I'm very surprised at Rosie. She . . . she always appeared so caring, I mean.' What she meant was she had always appeared so caring to all of them in the house. She could, in a way, imagine what it was like caring for the man before her. She asked tentatively now, 'Has she gone very far?'

'Don't ask me, missis; all I know, wherever she went on those nights, she'd leave here at half-past six and it was lucky if the clock saw her coming in that door at half-past eleven at night.'

'Perhaps she was at the pub. Apparently, she went to a particular pub.'

'Pub? The Boar's Head's never seen her for weeks. By! when I think of it, the sly, sneaking bitch that she is. Left me a note' – he pointed to the table – 'saying it was her life and she was entitled to a little happiness. Well! happiness. You know what I wish her? I hope

183

he's one of those blokes that'll kick her from dog to devil.'

'Don't say that. She . . . she was a nice person.'

'Huh! Well, I'm glad you found her so, missis.'

'Well, I'm sure you did until recently.'

'She was only paying me back for what I did for her, and she should have gone on paying me back.'

'Some people expect too much.'

'Huh! It's well seen whose side you're on. I bid you good day, missis.'

'And I bid you good day, too.'

She turned from him and went out of the room, across the hall and pulled open the front door, which she didn't bother to close behind her, so angry did she feel.

The car didn't glide forward, it jumped. No wonder Rosie had left. That man! But why hadn't she told her? Why hadn't she confided in her? She would have understood.

When she entered the house Mrs Funnell was coming down the stairs. 'What's this I hear?' she said. 'Rosie's left?'

'Yes, she's left, Great-gran.'

'And without giving notice?'

'She was paid weekly; she owed me nothing.'

'That's what you think. She owed us courtesy: she was a servant, she should have given in her notice.'

Mrs Funnell followed Peggy into the kitchen, talking all the way. 'Things are getting worse. People don't know their place. What was her brother like?'

Not only was Mrs Funnell startled, but Victoria was too, and even Peggy herself as she rounded on the old woman, crying at the top of her voice now, 'Like all men of his ilk, with a bloody big moaning mouth, yelling off, I, I, I, all the time, his wants. And he's not the only one. No, he's not the only one. And you know what I'd like to do? Kick their bloody backsides, then rub their noses against a mirror until they could see themselves as they really are. But let's be fair. Oh yes, let's be fair, because they haven't got priority in selfishness, have they, Great-gran? Have they?'

'Peggy! Peggy!' Victoria was holding her now. 'Give over. Give over. Come on; come on out of this.' And Victoria now pulled her granddaughter past the indignant old lady, whose face was expressing shock. And when they reached the drawing-room, she said, 'Sit down there, lass, and calm yourself.'

Peggy sat down. She was still shivering with indignation, but when she looked up at her grandmother, it was to see her shivering too, but with suppressed laughter. And when Victoria put her hand over her mouth and almost fell down on to the couch she said, and with some indignation, 'You find it funny, Gran?'

Victoria gulped in her throat, drew in a long sniffing breath up her nose, then said, 'My mother's face; that was the greatest surprise of her life, I'm sure it was. And you swearing. I've never heard you swear in my life. You know what? You know what?' She was leaning towards Peggy now and, a slow smile spreading over her face, Peggy said, 'What, Gran?'

'What do you bet she doesn't come marching in here and suggest that you have a strong dose of Syrup of Figs?'

It was almost at this moment, too, that the door was thrust open and the indignant lady stood within it and in a loud voice proclaimed in her most officious manner: 'When you have come to yourself enough to apologise, Peggy, I'll see you upstairs in my room. In the meantime, I would suggest you clean your system and your tongue with a large dose of Syrup of Figs.'

As the door banged Peggy and her grandmother threw themselves into each other's arms, one arm only around

185

each other for they had to suppress the laughter that was bursting to escape in loud, hilarious guffaws . . .

Peggy did not go up to apologise to her great-grandmother; she was too busy doing the work that had been Rosie's routine. She did, however, slip next door to May and gave her a rough sketch of what had happened, right up to the Syrup of Figs. And as she was about to hurry away again, she asked, 'Have you heard from Charlie?' May answered, 'Yes; they should be in Milan now, but they'll be there for only two days. They should be home towards the end of the week.'

Charlie would be home towards the end of the week. Charlie would be home towards the end of the week . . .

She had to fit her own routine into the day. She was to pick Emma up from school at half past three . . .

There were three or four cars lined up outside the junior school gates. She knew all the mothers, and particularly had she come to know a Mrs White. She would not say they had become friends, just strong acquaintances. Emma went to Janice's parties and Janice came to Emma's parties. Only last Friday there had been great excitement over Janice's eighth birthday party. And it was about that that Peggy now spoke to Mrs White, saying, 'I bet you had some clearing up after the mob on Friday night.'

'My! Yes.' Mrs White was a woman in her early forties and Janice was the youngest of her four daughters, and she said again, 'My! yes. Especially as I found one of them had been sick in the spare room. And there were some tears, too, when they were all getting ready to go home: someone had got someone else's paper hat; and that was somebody else's whistle; even coats got mixed up between the Pratt twins. Oh, they are funny children, those two, aren't they? That's the last time they'll get an invite, I can tell you.' She was nodding at Peggy. Then more quietly, she said, 'They're all such little liars, the tales they spin about what they have in the house. And Eva, the smaller one, argued with Janice that they had two cars. They nearly came to scratching each other because Janice says they've only got an old banger. But there you are, children all lie. Look at little Emma. Telling them all that when she went swimming with her father she could do the crawl and so many other strokes. Well, perhaps one could believe that, but not—' Her voice dropped further now and her head came towards Peggy, saying, 'Not that you never bathed her, never had bathed her, and that she got in the bath with her father every night. My! my! the wrong impressions children give. They could get you into trouble, couldn't they? She likely said that because she's very fond of him, I suppose; and of course, her being the only one, she would want special attention. Children always want to show off and be different.' She now poked her finger into Peggy's arm, saying, 'Well, there's a cure for that, you know. Oh! Here they come like a swarm of ants.' She turned away, leaving Peggy standing stiff and cold, although the sun was shining and it had been in the seventies all day.

Emma came running towards her, saying, 'Mammy, I got a prize for recitation, look!' She held out a piece of black cardboard with a silver star stuck on it, and when her mother made no effort to take it from her or exclaim her delight and approbation, she stared up at her and then said, 'Mammy?'

'Oh yes. Yes, dear. Oh, that was clever of you. Get in.' She opened the car door and when the child was seated she went round and took her place behind the wheel, then drove off.

'What did you recite?' she forced herself to ask.

'The bit about Pooh Bear, and I made a sound like Eeyore and everybody laughed ... Have you got a head-ache, Mammy?'

'No. No, dear; no, I haven't got a headache.' She wasn't going to lie to the child but she was going to talk to her.

187

Once inside the house the child made for the kitchen, but Peggy stopped her, saying, 'You won't find Rosie there. She's gone; she won't be coming back.'

'Rosie's gone? Why? Why, Mammy?'

'She's . . . she's got another situation. Look; come upstairs with me, I want to talk to you.'

But once in the bedroom and sitting on the edge of the bed, her arm around her daughter, what could she say? Do you like being in the bath with your father? Do you like him bathing you? What she did say was, 'In future there's going to be a new rule: you're going to have your bath before your daddy comes home.'

'You'll bath me, Mammy?'

The child's face lit up and Peggy looked down at her, saying, 'You'd like me to bath you?'

'Oh yes, Mammy. Oh yes. You never bath me; but I'm big enough to bath myself now, aren't I?'

'Yes. Yes, you are, dear.'

'I said that to Daddy yesterday.'

'And what did Daddy say?'

'He said I was still a baby. But I'm not, am I, Mammy? I'll soon be eight . . . well, not till December and I know it's only summer, but I'll be eight in December, won't I?'

'Yes, of course you will, and . . . and being eight, you'll be able to have the bathroom to yourself. But till then, I'll bath you. And—' She turned her daughter's face fully to her and cupped her cheek as she said, 'You must tell Daddy that you want me to bath you. You will, won't you?'

'Yes. Well, he . . . he might get angry.'

'He won't get angry with you.'

'But . . . but he might get angry with you, Mammy. And I don't want him to get angry with you.'

'Don't worry about that. Come along then, dear. Have your tea, then you can either go up to the nursery and play

188

or come in the kitchen with me and help me make a pie, whichever you like.'

'Oh, I'd like to help you make a pie, Mammy. Rosie let me make currant men. Why has she gone, Mammy? I liked Rosie.'

'I liked her, too. But people are free to do what they like with their lives.'

What a silly thing to say: people are free to do what they like with their lives. As she watched her daughter run before her down the stairs, she thought, As long as he lives or until she escapes she'll never be free to do what she likes.

'You've put her up to this. Well, don't think you've won, because she'll have another bath. By God! she will. She's my daughter and I'll do what I like with her.'

'By God! you won't. If you want to expose yourself to someone, then do it to one of your fancy women; you'll do it no longer to my daughter, *my daughter*. Do you hear?'

'You've got a filthy mind, that's what's the matter with you. You're frustrated. You're so frustrated you're using your imagination to satisfy yourself. You're making something nasty out of an ordinary natural event.'

'Natural event! How many men do you know who insist on their daughters being in the bath with them? When you're next at your Table meeting, ask around: "Do you bath with your daughter, Tom, Dick, or Harry?" '

'If they're sensible they do and their daughters will know what it's all about and won't throw themselves at the first lad who looks at them. Yes, throw themselves, begging for it like you did. Now get out of my way! I'm going upstairs and I'm stripping her and taking her into the bath with me.'

'Yes, you do that and I'll go and get Great-gran to come and witness her golden boy stark naked in the bath with his daughter sitting on his lap.'

'You dirty minded bitch! Great-gran knows that I bath her.'

'Great-gran knows nothing of the kind; not *how* you bath her. Why is it that when she's about you go into the bathroom dressed, and you come out dressed. But when you know that she's safely tucked up in bed, you come out with a towel around you. And when she's been confined there for days you sometimes haven't bothered with a towel. Of course, you make sure that Gran isn't about, either: the bathroom door used to be locked until I took the key away . . . You do! You lift your hand to me and touch me just once with it and I promise you you won't be able to walk for days, because I'll smash every movable thing in this room over you. Now, let me tell you, and this is final, in future she will be bathed before you come in, and you attempt to take her into that bathroom once again and, boy, you won't know what's hit you.'

'You know something? I'll do for you. I will, I'll do for you one of these days. You try to separate me from her in any way and I'll do murder. She's mine. I've said that from the beginning. I've thumped it into your ears that she's mine and she'll remain mine. Do you hear? Do what you like, but she'll remain mine, because she already knows she's mine.'

If he had turned from her and rushed from the room, banging the door after him, she would not have felt half as afraid as when he backed slowly from her, his arm bent and his forefinger wagging at her. At the door he did not immediately turn and grab the handle but put his hand behind him and slowly opened the door and in doing so had to walk forward a step. Then he paused before slowly going through it and closing the door quietly after him.

Peggy sank into a chair. Her eyes were tightly closed, her mouth wide. He was mad, mad where that child was concerned, and he meant what he said. The feeling of danger that he had left behind him floated round her like a fog, already darkening her life ahead. Then, as if it had become suddenly tangible she sprang from the chair and threw out her arms as if pushing it aside and, her eyes wide now, she said aloud, 'I'll have to do something. I'll tell Great-gran. Yes, I will!'

She had told Great-gran and now she stood looking down on this eighty-two year old woman who was dressed as a woman of forty might have been, in a pale blue cotton dress, square-necked, which showed surprisingly firm flesh for one her age, short-sleeved, which in this case exposed her real age by the sagging flesh of the underarm. The thick grey hair had been tinted a reddish brown, a process to which she had succumbed only for the last two years, having previously been free in expressing her opinion of those stupid women who aimed to camouflage their age by dyeing their hair. Finally, her face, wrinkled around the eyes and mouth, but the skin held firmly in place by good bone formation.

This was her great-grandmother speaking and she couldn't believe her ears. And the fear in her grew. Just a short while ago she had thought that nothing could increase the feeling of dread that Andrew had left behind him in the drawing-room. But she had been wrong, for added to it now was a feeling of utter hopelessness: she was being confronted by a combined force.

'He loves the child, adores her, always has. And she's still little more than a baby. I'm surprised you should think it's anything other than natural that he should want to bath her.'

She found herself bending over the old woman and hissing at her, 'If it's so natural, Great-gran, why did a woman approach me today, the mother of one of the little girls at school, and suggest that my daughter was fantasising

191

about her father being in the bath with her. The woman was definitely shocked, and by the fact that I've never bathed my child. And I can tell you this: I'm amazed at your *new* modern outlook; I've always known you to be as strait-laced as a Victorian corset and sticking to the narrow principles of that time in which you were brought up. Well, I can tell you something; I'm on my own in this house from now on and I shall see to her bathing, and should he attempt to stop me, I've told him what I'll do; I'll brain him with the first thing I get my hands on. You can emphasise that for me, Great-gran, when you are having one of your little palavers with him. And while I'm on, there's another thing I'll say: I regret the day I was made to marry him. You engineered that. If you had said the word, Mam would have gone along with you and I could have had the child and had a life of my own. But what have I had since she was born, even before that? Since Father died and Mam walked out I've had the running of this house on my shoulders. I only got Rosie's help because he put it to you; of course, it would be in a very nice way, that I was too tired to give him his rights.'

'Well, there, let me tell you, you made a big mistake. A wife has duties and to please her husband is one of them. You've a long way to go yet and a lot to learn. You don't keep a man by turning your back on him in bed, nor criticising everything he does, such as the innocent act of bathing his little child.'

'Oh, God in heaven! woman, shut up!' Peggy stepped back from the old woman. 'Shut up! You know nothing about it. Turning my back on my husband, you say; and yes, I did, because I could still smell the whores of Bog's End on him. Is that news to you? His evening jaunts to this meeting or that are all phoney.'

'You're imagining things, girl. It's right what he says: it's impossible to talk to you.'

'Oh, does he? So he says that? Well, he doesn't find it impossible to talk to you, does he? He's given you a new lease of life, hasn't he, with his flattery, his sucking-up.'

'You'd better leave me before I lose my temper with you, girl, and say something I'll be sorry for.'

Peggy did not move, but after a moment of silence she said, 'I can divorce him. I can easily get proof.'

'That would be the stupidest thing you ever did because he'll fight you for your child and he'll win.'

'Because you'd help him win, wouldn't you? Great-gran, you'd help him.'

'I'd do what I think is right. I always have.'

'My God! You poor, hoodwinked old woman.' And on this Peggy turned and almost flew from the room.

In her own room she stood, her hands clenched and pressed tightly against her breast-bone as if to ease the terrible ache and fear whirling there. She couldn't believe it. That old woman across the landing who was judged to be clear thinking; so much so, even at her age, that she visited the factory every Friday and went over the books with Henry. And should she at any time be incapacitated, Henry had to bring the books to her, and she would scrutinise every penny that went out or came in. She had been mean with money all her life, using her daughter and granddaughter as servants, and even herself at times during the last seven or so years as unhired help, except for the time that Rosie was here.

She felt lost, that her youth had gone, been sucked away by that vain and stupid old woman who had become enamoured of the young boy who had turned into a smooth-talking man. Likely it was because she had recognised in him from the first the trait matching her own: the ability to make money, for especially was she enamoured of his Sunday second-hand car-sales and of the fact that he insisted on working on that day and handling this side of the business himself.

When a tap came on the door she didn't answer, but when it came again, she called quietly, 'Come in.'

Victoria came towards her, saying, 'By! you've upset the apple cart today, haven't you?'

'She's told you? She's told you about the bathing?'

'Yes; yes, her version of it. But I agree with you, girl. It's time that was stopped. She's only a child still, but she's a very knowing child, impressionable and sensitive. Yes, it's about time that was stopped. But you're going to have a fight on your hands. Have you any positive proof that he goes to Bog's End?'

'Only that Frank has seen him a number of times coming out of a special house down there. He told May, and she told me to be careful. But I'd been careful for a long time before that, because I'd sensed something. I could get him watched, and that would be evidence for a divorce.'

'I wouldn't do that, girl; he'd fight you for the child. He'd not get her, I know, but he would be granted some access to her.'

And her Gran was voicing her mother's own words: 'The best thing you can do is to hang on, as grim as it will be for you, until she's able to make a choice. And then you'll still be a young woman and Charlie will still be waiting.'

'Oh, Gran, what d'you mean? What d'you know about Charlie and me?'

'Only that he loves you, always has and always will. He's that kind of a man. It hasn't pleased May but she's accepted it. You're lucky in a way that he's there, and lucky, too, that he's got his music and that it's bringing him a name, for it's some sort of compensation in the meantime, helping his waiting.'

'Oh Gran.' She put her arms around the older woman and muttered, 'I felt so alone, entirely on my own, a few

194

minutes ago, but I've got you and I've got Charlie and May and Frank. Four to two.'

'Yes, four to two, lass. Just hang on to that, four to two. So come on downstairs and we'll have a sherry. It's another occasion. Let's look at it as refreshment before the battle.'

4

'Yes, Daddy, I love you. You know I love you.'

'But do you love me more than you love your mother?'

'I love Mammy, Daddy. Of course I love Mammy.'

'But do you love me more? Say you love me more. Go on, say it.'

'Daddy, you're hurting my arms.'

'Oh, pet, pet, I'm sorry.'

'Don't Daddy, don't; you'll mess up my dress.'

'Mess up your dress? Why do you want to go to a party today? You're going to have a big party tomorrow.'

'But Gwen asked me; she's my best friend. And there's a clown coming and her father's getting dressed up as Santa Claus, and . . . Oh Daddy, don't.'

'You used to like me kissing you.'

'No, I didn't. Well, I mean, Daddy, you're a wet kisser.'

The young girl laughed, then after a moment said, 'Don't be vexed, Daddy.'

'I'm not vexed.'

'Yes you are. I know when you're vexed.'

He was kneeling by the side of the bed, his arms about her

waist, his head on a level with hers. 'Say after me, I love you, Daddy, better than anyone else in the world.'

'But . . . but I love Mammy, too. Oh don't, Daddy . . .'

When the door burst open he sat back on his heels and almost toppled over, and the child straightened up from where she had been thrust against the bed.

Peggy had moved quickly towards her and lifted her bodily. Then she thrust a foot against her husband's side, saying, 'You had your answer, didn't you?'

In the corridor, hurrying towards the stairs, Peggy said, 'Now don't cry, don't cry. It'll be all right. You don't want to go to the party crying, do you?' . . .

They were in the car when Emma said quietly, 'You can love two people at the same time, can't you, Mammy?'

Peggy paused before answering, 'Yes; yes, you can love two people at the same time.' Oh yes, that was certainly true: didn't she love this child and didn't she love Charlie? So yes, her daughter could love two people at the same time. Nevertheless, she was already having to pay for it.

When, a few minutes later, she stopped the car and said, 'I'll call for you at seven. Now have a nice time,' Emma said, 'You won't fight with Daddy, will you Mammy, not tonight, or tomorrow?'

Peggy leaned over and drew her daughter into her arms, saying, 'Oh my dear, no, no. I promise you there'll be no upheavals, not today or on your birthday.'

'I love you, Mammy.'

'Yes, I know you do, darling. I know you do.'

'If Daddy would only believe that, everything would be all right.'

'Don't worry now, don't worry, everything will be all right. I promise you. Just remember this: I love you too, very, very much.'

198

When her daughter put her arms around her neck and hugged her tightly it was almost too much, and to prevent the tears from flowing, she said, 'Your dress will be all crushed under your coat.'

'Doesn't matter, Mammy; it'll soon be crushed anyway, when we start playing games.'

After leaving her daughter in the brightly lit and chatter-filled house she did not immediately drive away. 'Don't fight with Daddy tonight or tomorrow.' And she had promised not to. Yet she was having to subdue the urge to dash back there and scream at him. She had asked herself, time and again lately, what was coming over her. She knew her character had altered completely over the last few years. She could admit it but couldn't control the change. More and more she was acting like a bitch; more than once she had to restrain the urge to hit out at him, punch him in his good-looking, smarmy face, especially when she would come upon him in the drawing-room sitting holding her great-gran's hand, stroking it gently as if it were a cat, and that old woman sitting there and, like a cat, lapping it up.

Thankfully, Charlie would be home today. Later on they might have a few minutes together and he would hold her and she would become herself again. And she would say, 'How long are you here for this time?' praying it would be weeks instead of days . . .

Victoria met her in the hall, saying, 'You look frozen. Come in the kitchen; I've just mashed a pot of tea.'

'Where is he?'

'Oh, he went out shortly after you did, within minutes. He took a briefcase with him, as if he were going back to the Works. May's just phoned. They can't come over to dinner tomorrow; they've got unexpected company. She wants you to slip across when you can.'

'But the turkey! We'll never get through that.'

'Oh yes, we will. We'll have hash for days.' Victoria smiled at her, then said, 'What was all that about upstairs?'

'Love.'

'What d'you mean, love?'

'He was at her, trying to make her say that she loved him better than she did me. I was outside the door, listening. I didn't know he was home and I was just on the point of going into her room when I heard him.'

'Dear God!' Victoria shook her head. 'What'll he be at next?'

'The question is, Gran, what has he been at already? That's what worries me every minute. But what can you do? What can you say? There's no proof, and . . . and she's fond of him and she wouldn't do anything to hurt him or get him into trouble. But there's been a change in her of late. She's refused to go to the baths since she had that cold, but I think she was clever enough to make that an excuse. Dear God in heaven!' She put her hand to her brow. 'What a state of affairs.'

'Look, lass, it's Christmas. There's nothing you can do about it at the moment. Go on, get yourself over to May's and meet her company, whoever they are. She sounded very excited.'

'Well, she expects Charlie home today.'

'Yes, she does, but she said "company", and Charlie isn't company, well, not that kind. She would have just said Charlie's home.'

'Will you take her tea up?' Peggy jerked her head in the direction of the ceiling, and Victoria said on a laugh, 'Yes, yes, I'll take her tea up. And if she gives me any of her pernickety, finicky quips I'll throw it over her. I've wanted to do it many a time.'

They laughed together now, but it was a gentle laugh without mirth . . .

Peggy heard the laughter coming from next door before she left the woodland, and it further burst on her as she opened the kitchen door.

May was at the table piling sandwiches on an already full plate, Frank was cutting into a large fruit loaf, and they both turned and hailed her brightly, saying, 'Hello, there!'

'What's all the noise?'

'You may well ask. It sounds like a tap room, doesn't it? It's the band, the quartet.'

Frank laughed. 'You said it; the quartet, four plus Charlie, but it sounds like a football match, doesn't it? Go on in.'

'Oh no! I . . . '

'Don't be silly! Oh, and by the way, I'm sorry we can't make it tomorrow. They're staying over the week-end.'

'All of them?'

'Yes, all of them. There'll be some shakedowns to make up, but they're used to sleeping in cramped quarters.'

'They are not going home for Christmas?'

'Well, one lives in Scotland, one lives in Ireland, one lives in London. Anyway' — her voice dropped — 'it's a breaking-up party.'

'They're breaking up?'

'Oh, my dear, he'll tell you all about it later. Go on in.'

Reluctantly she went out of the kitchen, across the small hall and towards the sitting-room. The door was open and she stood just outside the aperture taking in the five men. Charlie had his back to her. He was sitting on a pouffe to the side of the fire. And when two of the men stopped laughing and looked over his head, he turned and sprang up and hurried towards her, saying, 'Hello, there,' and reached out to take her hand.

'Hello, Charlie.'

201

'I . . . I was coming across but I was held up by this lot.'
He thumbed towards the men behind him, then said, 'Come on in and meet the gang.'

He led her into the room and, looking at the four musicians, he said, 'This is Peggy, my sparring partner ever since we both crawled on the lawn together. And this' – he spread an arm out – 'is the amateur group I've been supporting over the past years.'

There was a great hoot of laughter and chipping and protests. The men were standing now and Charlie, pointing to a small middle-aged man, said, 'This is Joe, violin and much more.' Joe shook her hand and smiled.

'And this is Ron, viola, but he really should have been playing the cornet, he spends more time on it.'

'How d'you do, Peggy?' The tall man with a long face bent in the grand manner as he took her hand.

'And this too is Ron. The cellist. And believe it or not we've got to put him on a high chair to enable him to manage his instrument.'

The short man's answer was lost amid laughter.

'And finally, this is Percy. Percy can play anything from the triangle to the tambourine. He can also whistle.' Percy took her hand, saying, 'Definitely my art is diffused, but I have never stooped so low as to even touch a guitar.'

She was laughing. They were all laughing, and she was amazed at the feeling of camaraderie among these men and particularly at Charlie's obvious standing amongst them, for all four looked to be in their mid-forties.

'Sit down, dear.' Charlie pressed her on to the pouffe near the fire and then he sat down on the floor beside her.

Solely for something to say to cover her embarrassment, she said, 'When did you get back; I mean, from Spain?'

'Oh, we landed at Newcastle airport' – Charlie turned and looked at the men – 'at three o'clock?'

They nodded, saying, 'Yes, three o'clock.'

For the next ten minutes or so she sat listening to these mature men chipping him, and he, her quiet Charlie, giving them back as much as they sent. This was a different Charlie. She had never imagined him being a popular figure. The man called Percy was now leaning forward and saying, 'Those two old girls in the old people's home, remember? They summed up your guitar playing as nobody else has been able to do.'

The memory caused another burst of general laughter; then Percy, addressing himself to Peggy, explained, 'We were giving this concert in this old people's home. Two old girls were sitting very close at the front. One had a hearing aid and she kept fiddling with it. His nibs here was doing his solo piece, the stage to himself and the old people were comparatively quiet, until the one with the hearing aid asked in no small voice, "I can't get me aid to work; what's he playin'?" And her companion answered in an even louder voice, "It's one of them tinny things. And don't bother with it, you wouldn't like it anyway, it's got no tune." '

The room again exploded with laughter.

And still laughing, Charlie said, 'But I did what you lot didn't do: I came back with an Irish jig, and then, "We'll Meet Again" and "Roll Out The Barrel". But you stiff necks, what did you play? Mozart's Quartet in A Flat, and half of them fell asleep. Of course it could have been in B Minor and then they would all have been carried out.'

'Who does he think he is? And fancy him knowing about Mozart's Quartet in A Flat.'

'Not only A, but B Minor.'

Charlie was about to retaliate when the door opened and May now appeared, saying, 'Well, there it is. If you're hungry, come and get it. It'll fill a holey tooth until later.'

As they made their way to the dining-room Peggy went towards the kitchen, calling to the men, 'I'll be seeing you again.'

Amid their replies Charlie said, 'Carry on, will you? I'll be with you in a few minutes,' and he whipped up his coat from among a stack of luggage and instruments lying in the hall, and taking her by the arm he hurried her through the kitchen.

Out of sight and sound of the house, in the wood, he put his arms about her and kissed her hungrily; and she returned his kisses with fervour, muttering, 'Oh Charlie. Charlie.' Then she asked, 'What's afoot? I mean, your mother said something about breaking up.'

'Yes, this is a sort of parting party. I'm going to miss them. They're a fine bunch of fellas, grand, each one of them.'

'But why?'

'Oh, it's a long story. Anyway, to make it brief, they've got a chance of doing a six months' tour in America from coast to coast. Now two of them, Percy and Joe, they are staying in America, I know that, and I think the other two could be persuaded. It will depend on how the tour goes. None of them has any connections here, not really; they're all bachelors; at least, in a way. One's a widower and another's divorced, and only Joe's parents are alive, so they're free-lance in all ways. But I couldn't see me staying away all that time . . . not from you, and then probably being persuaded to follow their line and make America my home. No, I just couldn't do it.'

'Oh, Charlie, I've spoilt that for you, too. And Auntie May'll be so mad at me. She'll try to hide it, I know, as she always does.'

'Oh no, Auntie May won't, Auntie May's delighted at this arrangement. Anyway, it's been in my mind to step out on my own for some time now. I've enough material to give a full recital. And what's more, I can always teach. And there's more people taking it up seriously now, not just strumming chords. I learnt so much from Mr Reynolds. I do miss him when I come back. But he was old and tired; he's had youngsters falling over themselves to be taught by him. Knowing his methods, I feel teaching could be quite a side-line. I won't starve. And, darling, you wouldn't starve, either. Can't you make up your mind?'

'Oh, Charlie, you know my mind's been made up for years. I could walk out this minute, this very minute, if it wasn't for Emma. But he would and could claim her, you know he would. And there's things going on now that frighten me.'

'Worse?'

'In a way, yes.'

'He hasn't . . . ?'

'Not as far as I know. But I just don't know; she's afraid of rows between us, so she's afraid naturally to say anything.'

'And the great Mrs Funnell?'

'Oh, as enamoured as ever.'

'I can't believe it of that old girl, you know, I just can't. She was such a level-headed, dynamic person; and to be taken in by a scut like him.'

'Vanity's a strange thing. I never realised it until lately, but looking back I can see she has always been inordinately vain. Mother said the same. And that's another thing. Mother used to pop in nearly every day. She doesn't any more. I envy her her happiness – she can't help it shining out of her – but I'm also bitter against her for saddling me with this lot, and for changing me from what I was: she made the young girl into a woman before her time and a bitter one at that. Charlie, I've changed. I'm . . . I'm not the person you knew years ago. I say and do things that shock me.'

He laughed now, saying, 'My dear, dear, Peggy, you'll always be the same to me. You know I've loved you from the very beginning and I'll go on loving you. And now that I'm home for good, at least my bookings abroad will be for just a week or so at a time, that's all, well . . . we're coming together. Do you hear? Really coming together. I don't care where or when. Oh yes, I do, as regards when, anyway, because it's got to be soon. And you needn't have any feeling of compunction about him, for he's been at it for years on the side, and you know it. I must get back now, if for no other reason than that the table will soon be cleared and I haven't had a bite since this morning. Oh, love.' He held her close again, and as they were about to part she said, 'Charlie,' and he said, 'Yes?'

'Have you never wanted anyone else; is that true?'

There was neither an immediate protestation nor confirmation from Charlie; then he said, 'No; I have never wanted anyone else; but that's not to say I've never had needs, and they had to be met. But over the past few years, what with one night stands and travel, there was little energy or time left except for eating and bed.'

He kissed her again, then said, 'I'll see you later tonight. I'm coming over with Emma's present.'

'All right, Charlie.' Even to herself her voice sounded flat.

She did not hurry back to the house.

That's not to say I haven't had needs, and they had to be met, she thought.

She, too, had needs that cried out to be met, but there was no way of meeting them. But Charlie was a man. She had to remember that: though why should she? *Yes, why should she?* Who was to weigh the difference in the urge? Her body was racked at times when the torment had almost driven her across the corridor into Andrew's bed. Only shame and pride had prevented that humiliation.

Damn men! Damn Charlie!

Oh no; never say that. She'd have to pull herself together. But if only he hadn't told her. Oh, come off it. What did she want in a man? A plaster saint? She should remember that she went with a man when she was sixteen. Oh well, didn't she know that? Dear God, didn't she?

But Charlie had been different.

PART THREE

1983

I

'Take her to the doctor,' Lizzie said.

'What can I say to the doctor, Mam? That her teacher says she's not paying attention? That twice this term she's had to leave the classroom because she was sick?'

'Yes, you can say just that, especially the latter ... She's not ... ?'

'Oh, my God! Mam, don't suggest such a thing.'

'Well, my dear, just think back; you weren't many months older.'

'Don't rub it in, Mam.'

'I'm not rubbing it in, Peggy. That's the last thing I would do, you know. I'm just stating a fact.'

'Well, it isn't that, it's him. She's worried in some way about him, but I can't get anything out of her. And if I can't make her open up, how do you expect the doctor to do so?'

'Oh, she'll more likely do so with him than to you, knowing that it's hell let loose every time you look at each other. So do as I say: get on to Doctor Rice and make an appointment.'

'She tells me she's going to a disco tonight.'

'Has she been before?'

'Once or twice. But he doesn't know.'

'Well, you should tell him. Put him in the picture. He's bound to know when he comes and finds her gone or going.'

'He rarely comes home early on a Tuesday night. He has some meeting or other he goes straight to. On a Friday, too. So if there's anything she wants to go to on these nights, I tell her to go.'

'What a set-up for a young lass when her father mustn't be told she goes to a dance,' said Lizzie, which brought forth from Peggy the sharp and quizzical retort, 'Remember, Mam, when I was fifteen I wasn't allowed out at all after six o'clock unless you were with me.'

Lizzie turned in somewhat of a huff and made for the door, saying, 'Things were different then. This is nineteen eighty-three. There was a set of decent rules then; now they're changing partners every night.'

'And having babies at fourteen.'

Lizzie turned from the doorway, saying, 'Don't get bitter, Peggy. What's done is done. And it was done for the best, although I must admit it didn't turn out like that. Anyway, you should be thankful that she's got a clean name, and so have you.'

'Oh Mam, for God's sake! shut up, and go home before I lose my temper. "Clean name, and so has she." With a father like Andrew Jones? Let me tell you something, Mam: I'd have been happy to have had a bastard and to have taken my chance in never being married. But I would have been married and happily.'

'Oh, yes, yes, we know you would, dear, and to Charlie Conway. But it didn't happen like that and you've got to make the best of it.'

As her mother stamped away down the drive Peggy stared after her. Make the best of it, she had said. She got what she wanted and left me with the rough end of the stick . . .

An hour later Peggy was sitting by Victoria's bed. She was holding her grandmother's hand as she said, 'I won't be long. I'm just going to drop her off at the hall. It's the only chance she has of getting out on her own.'

'Peggy?'

'Yes, Gran?'

'I'm going to say something to you now and I want you to promise me something, for I'm not long for this side of the curtain.'

'Oh, Gran; you know you've been bad so often during your life . . .'

'Yes, I know that, lass; I've retreated into illness; but you know, and I know what's wrong with me now. I'm not living on morphine for nothing, am I? Now when I go there'll be a nice bit of money coming to you. She knows nothing about it.' She thumbed towards the wall as if her mother were just beyond and not at the far end of the corridor. 'Father left me a bit and she thinks I went through that a long time ago. She knows I've got some, but I'd never give her the satisfaction of telling her how much. I've always left my bank book locked away in that drawer.' She pointed to the bureau. Then putting her hand under the pillow, she said, 'There's the key. Now, a copy of my will's in there, too, and it's also with the solicitor. Please, dear, please, dear, don't cry, don't cry. Just listen. Now I want you to promise, as soon as I go, when you get that money, you'll take it and the child and go off somewhere abroad for a time. In the meantime, put in for a divorce. You've got enough on him. I know you want proof. Well, engage a private detective. He'll find out his comings and goings to his so-called meetings, twice a week at least. Of course, you'll have to tell Charlie, but by the time you're free, Emma will be of age, such an age that he can do nothing to hold her. Now, promise me you'll do what I ask?'

She forced herself to say, 'Yes, Gran. All right, yes,' knowing that she wouldn't be able to do it; there were so many factors against it: the old woman along the corridor depending on her; Charlie, who had given up a good part of his life waiting for her. However, she had to reassure this woman whom she had never understood but had come to love. And so, bending over her and kissing her softly, she voiced her feelings by saying, 'I love you, Gran.'

'And I you, girl. And I you, and always have. Now go on and dry your eyes, because you don't want to put another worry on that child's shoulders.'

Peggy did not immediately go downstairs but went to her own room. And so it was that she didn't hear Andrew come in and enter the sitting-room, there to see his daughter dressed for going out in her wide-skirted jersey dress, her black hair hanging loose about her shoulders, and wearing, of all things, green-lobed earrings.

He stood within the doorway looking at her for a moment. She had risen from the couch and was awaiting his approach, her consternation evident as if she had been caught out in some misbehaviour.

'And where are we going dressed up tonight?'

He was standing close to her now, not a hand's-breadth between them. And when she replied, 'I . . . I'm going to a disco, Daddy,' he stepped slightly back and his whole face seemed to crumble into disbelief as he said, 'You're what! You're not going to any disco. By God! you're not. Since when have you been going to discos, I ask you? Since when?'

'I've been to two before, Daddy. I . . . I like dancing.'

'You like dancing? Yes, I know you like dancing. We've danced, haven't we? Well, if you like dancing I'm always here. I come home practically every night to be with you, so if you want to dance, we'll dance.'

He now thrust his arm out and pulled her tightly towards him and waltzed her round the table, saying, 'One, two, three; one, two, three; one, two, three. That's how I started you, that's how I taught you to dance.' Stopping now, he held her by the shoulders and, bringing his face close to her trembling one, he said, 'How could you!'

When she tried to shrug herself from his hold, he said, 'Don't do that! Don't ever do that. Now tell me: who asked you to go to this disco?'

'Nobody, not really. All the girls from our class go there.'

'It was a boy, wasn't it?'

'Leave go of my shoulders, Daddy. You're hurting me.'

He closed his eyes tightly; then in a much quieter voice, he said, 'Pet, you know I wouldn't hurt you for the world, but you're hurting me. You want to leave me on my own tonight and go to a disco and let some spotty lout put his arms about you?'

'I'm turned fifteen, Daddy' – her voice trembling now – 'I'm not a child any longer. I don't need . . . well, I've got to say it, I don't need petting.'

'You don't need petting? Well, well! You don't need me to love you any more? So you don't love me?'

'You know I love you, Daddy, and I . . . I want you to love me, but . . . but I've got to . . . '

'Yes? What have you got to . . . ?'

'Well, I've got to live. I mean, like . . . like other girls do.'

'Like your mother did, you mean? Throw yourself into the arms of the first lad who looks at you.'

Emma's long-lashed eyelids blinked rapidly, her mouth opened and shut twice before she said, 'Mother never did.'

'Mother did, and at me. She was a slut. That's how you came about, because she chased me. Well, I'm going to see that you don't do the same.'

'Leave go of me, Daddy. Leave go!'

'I won't leave go. You're mine, you understand? From the minute you were born you became mine. She didn't want you. I did, and you will always be mine, do you hear?' I'll kill you before I let any goggle-eyed, snotty-nosed youth put a finger on you.' . . .

'*Let her go!*'

He swung round, still with Emma in his arms, and not until he saw Peggy dash up the room and pick the long, steel poker from its rest on the brass open-work fender did he release her. And then, his voice falsely calm-sounding now, he said, 'You use that, m'lady, and it'll be the finish of you.'

'Mammy! Mammy!' Emma was clinging to Peggy now, her arms around her neck, crying, 'Don't! Don't! Please, put it down.'

'No, I won't put it down, dear. But stand aside. Go on into the hall; we're going out.'

The girl moved from her mother's side, but now looked towards her father, and he, staring at her, said, 'If you go to that place I'll never forgive you. Do you hear? You go there, and I'll never forgive you. And it'll be the finish of me. If she comes between us—' He now pointed towards Peggy without looking at her and repeated, 'If she comes between us I'll finish it. I will.'

'Go on, dear. Get into the car.'

When she knew her daughter was out of the room, and still with the poker in her hand, Peggy took a step towards him, saying, 'Well, that should be enough for you, shouldn't it? enough proof. You've lost your hold over her. She's going to the disco and she's going to mix with young people of her own age. And no matter how fresh the lads might get they'll have a long way to go before they reach your handling, won't they, Andrew?'

216

His face looked blanched. And now he brought out the words between his closed teeth, saying, 'You think you've won, don't you? But I've told her what you were when you were her age: a slut. And I've told her how she came about.'

The poker wavered in her hand. She told herself not to do it, to turn away from him, to get out of the house. When he said, 'That's shaken you, hasn't it? Now go and explain to her what made you ready to take your clothes off in the barn. Go on, explain it.'

She felt the poker quivering in her hand. Turning abruptly, she flung it with a clash into the fireplace; then she went out and got into the car. And there she sat in silence beside her daughter for a full minute; and neither of them spoke until, in a very small voice, Emma said, 'I . . . I couldn't go to the disco, Mammy.'

As quietly, Peggy answered her, 'Yes, you could dear; and yes, you are! And you're going to forget, at least try to forget what's just happened. But . . . but now you've made a stand' – she turned and looked at her daughter – 'keep it up. Do you understand what I mean?'

Emma looked into her mother's face, and then making a small movement with her head before turning away and, gazing through the windscreen, she said, 'I'm . . . I'm afraid, at times, Mammy.'

'What are you afraid of, dear?'

'Of . . . of his—' Her dark head swung now from side to side before she muttered, 'feelings, possessiveness. I knew a long time ago it wasn't right when he wanted to . . . '

The gulp she made in her throat was audible, and Peggy put in quickly, 'Wanted to what?'

'Nothing, nothing. I'll go to the disco. Come on, let's go. Let's go.'

217

Peggy stretched her left arm and put it around her daughter's shoulders, saying, 'It's all right now. It's all right. Don't get agitated. We'll talk about this later. Now you're going to the dance, and there'll be Susan and Carrie there, and you're going to smile as if nothing had happened here tonight. That's one of the things you've got to learn in life; to smile and cover up your feelings.'

The girl raised her head and looked at her mother, saying, 'He said awful things about . . . about you, Mammy.'

'Yes, I know he did. And when we talk later I'll explain what really happened, and it won't be in the way he put it,' and with similar emphasis she turned the key; but then allowed the car to glide forward.

Five minutes later she dropped Emma at the hall, saying, 'I'll pick you up at ten o'clock. Go on now, enjoy yourself.'

Having turned the car, she wondered if she should make for the cottage to talk out with her mother what her next move should be, but thinking that would leave her grandmother alone too long, she decided to make for home again.

Going up the lane, she saw a car stop and Frank Conway quickly get out and turn as though awaiting her.

When she, too, stopped he said, 'I could see it was you. Can you spare a minute to come in? I've got something to tell you. I think it's important.'

Her heart missed a beat. 'About Charlie?' she said apprehensively. 'Has something happened?'

'Oh no; Charlie's all right. We had a letter this morning and one enclosed for you. He'll be back earlier, on Tuesday. No, it isn't about Charlie. Yet, it could help bring his wishes closer, lass. Come on. The car'll be all right there.'

When they entered the kitchen May's voice came from another room, calling, 'I'll be there in a minute, Frank.'

218

And when presently she appeared in the kitchen doorway she said, 'I didn't know you were here, Peggy.'

'Your husband's dragged me in. There's something he wants to tell me.'

'He's going to leave me for you? I knew it. I knew it.'

'Don't talk daft, woman. This is serious. Is there a cup of tea ready?'

'Yes, sir, yes; it's all ready. In fact, the tea's all set in the dining-room as usual and has been for . . . let me see' – she put her head on one side – 'how many years?'

'Go on, get in there, you idiot.' Then he turned towards Peggy, saying, 'Come in here a minute.'

Seated around the end of the dining-table, both Peggy and May looked at Frank and waited. And what he said, was, 'Well now, I'll have to start at the beginning. It was like this. We got a letter, passed on from the Newcastle office this morning concerning a woman who wants to sell her bungalow. It's out Corbridge way. They always pass out-of-the-way jobs on to us. And this was certainly one. I went out there and found two bungalows set in what looked like nowhere. The lady was very talkative, and I gathered that they were on the edge of a big estate. At one time, apparently, the area all around was to be built up with good-class bungalows, et cetera. But something emerged from the deeds of the estate that put a stop to this development. The two bungalows in question, though, had been standing from the year dot. Well, they were built pre-war, and they were still in good condition and they each had half an acre of land. Now this old girl is getting on and she wants to move into town. She's lonely and she plied me with tea and scones and the rest, and gave me information about her neighbours, whom she seems to like quite a bit. He's a commercial traveller and the wife's a cook in a Newcastle hotel. Both seem to have good cars and to be comfortably off. However, she informed

219

me, she doesn't see much of him, Mr Milburn. Well, she said, you know what commercial travellers are, and laughed and winked. Then suddenly she said, "Good lord! Talk of the devil." And she pointed to the window, saying, "There she is now! She must be seeing him off. He doesn't usually get home in the daytime. Well, I suppose with her being at work he doesn't think it much use." '

Frank looked from one to the other, and then, addressing himself solely to Peggy, he said, 'You'd better hang on to something, Peggy. You know who Mrs Milburn is? Rosie . . . Rosie Milburn. And who should Mr Milburn be but your dear Andrew. Honest to God! There they were going down to the car. I'd seen it along the end of the track. It was a BMW. There's quite a few of them knocking about; I hadn't noticed the number plate; well, there was no need.'

Peggy didn't move. She didn't take her eyes off Frank. She heard May saying, 'Never in the world! Never!' But she still made no comment. Strangely, she found herself thinking along lines similar to those her great-grandmother would likely have thought, putting money first: where does he get the money to keep two houses? She knew he was not actually in the red at the bank, but he was pretty near to it at times, although he was now paid a very good salary, much more than Len would ever have been paid if he had still been alive and in the job. Moreover, Mr Andrew Jones was a neat dresser: he spent a lot on his clothes and quite a lot on Emma, but little on herself. It was presents from Gran that kept her attired as she was. The next thought that entered her head was of divorce: the way was clear. All these years he had been carrying on on the side and now here was actual proof of it. He wouldn't be able to lay claim on Emma.

Charlie. Charlie and her, together at last. No more meeting secretly in the wood in the dark, always in the dark.

May's hand was on hers: 'It's all right, it's all right, dear,' she was saying. 'It's a way out. At last you've got a way out.'

Peggy's voice sounded quiet, even gentle as, looking from one to the other, she said, 'I've been an idiot, haven't I? All these years I've been an idiot. When did Rosie leave? Over seven years ago, and I never guessed. I can't remember once seeing them talking together. No, I can't remember once. And Rosie, she was so nice, so jolly, so kind and helpful.'

She straightened her back and a small smile began to spread over her lips as she said, 'I wonder what Mrs Funnell will say to this? What will her reaction be when she knows that her bright boy, while patting and stroking her and kissing her brow and her blue lips, must have been laughing up his sleeve at her, and thinking what a clever boy he is to be able to live in her fine house and have a big say in her business, while at the same time running a mistress on the side.'

She turned to Frank now. 'You know, Frank,' she said, 'I'm going to take a great delight in telling her, much more so than facing up to the big boy himself, because she it is who has paved the way for all this.'

'I understand what you mean, Peggy, but I can't see how she's paved his way to buy that bungalow. Rosie . . . well, she hadn't any money, had she? And even on a cook's wages she wouldn't be able to rise to that.'

'He may have sold some cars on the side.'

Frank looked at his wife. 'I doubt it, May,' he said. 'From what I understand from Henry, he'd have a job to do that; the old girl has her finger on every penny.'

The ring of the telephone brought May up from the table, saying, 'I bet that's Charlie.' But within a minute she came running back, saying, 'It's Mrs Funnell. Something's happened. She's yelling at the top of her voice. She's calling, "Bring Frank! Bring Frank!"'

221

They were all on their feet now and running from the kitchen, the two women following Frank through the garden, through the woodland and so into the house.

Victoria was standing at the top of the stairs hanging on to the banister. And when they reached her, she said, 'He's taken an overdose.'

In the bedroom, Mrs Funnell was also supporting herself, one hand on her chest, the other on the bedrail, and at her feet lay the doubled-up figure of Andrew clad in only vest and pants.

'Good God!' Frank was now kneeling by Andrew's side, straightening his limbs. He put an ear to his chest, then looked up at them, saying, 'He's still breathing, but his heart's going twenty to the dozen. Let's get him on his feet. You'd better call the doctor, Peggy.'

'No, no!' said Mrs Funnell; 'give him salt and water. It'll bring it up. He hasn't been out that long. I . . . I heard him only a short while ago coming out of the bathroom. Get some salt and water, hot.'

Peggy had been standing near the table. The aspirin bottle was empty, as was the silver-papered, singly wrapped, Panadol square that usually held twelve tablets, but in which she knew there had been only three, for she herself had taken two that afternoon. As for the aspirins, there might have been a dozen in the bottle, but that would have been all. She had made it a habit never to leave medicines lying about since the time she found Emma sucking a Panadol, thinking it was a mint, but thankfully then having the sense to spit it out when she found it wasn't.

Yet if this had taken place in her grandmother's room, he would have found plenty of bottles there, a cupboard-full, going back for two or three years. All in aid of her many illnesses, real and imaginary. And such was her feeling that

222

she might have need of them sometime, nothing was ever thrown out.

She didn't actually run from the room to get the hot water and salt; whatever he had taken was a gesture: it had been enough to knock him out, but it certainly wouldn't kill. This was to pay Emma out, to make her feel guilty and never again to disobey him. But even should she explain it to her as his ruse to get his own way with her, there was still the possibility that the ruse might not have come off; in anyone older than him and less strong, it could possibly have achieved its object.

When she returned to the room with the salted hot water, Frank and May between them had lifted Andrew on to the bed, and there he was propped up and breathing very heavily now. And Mrs Funnell was talking at them all the time: 'I'm not surprised. I'm not surprised. The strain he's been under with one thing and another. But I'd like to know what's brought this on, and I'll get to know. Yes, I will. I will.'

'Get me a bowl, Peggy, will you?' Frank turned from the bed and, taking the mug from her hand, now addressed his wife. 'Pull his jaws apart,' he said.

When the hot, salted water went down Andrew's throat, he gulped, and it would have all spurted out had Peggy, and none too gently, not clamped his jaws together again.

'Get him on his feet and walk him up and down. That's the way. It's no good letting him lie there. Get him on his feet.'

'All right, Mrs Funnell. If you'll get out of the way, we'll get him to his feet.' Frank's voice carried the expression that was on his face, and Mrs Funnell came back at him, saying, 'Don't you bawl at me, Frank Conway! You forget where you are.'

'Shut up, woman!'

This staggered Mrs Funnell into silence, and her feelings were registered on her grim face as she watched this husband and wife whom she had never liked, classing them as common, dragging the almost inert figure up and down the bedroom. And they didn't stop until he heaved and brought up a great deal of liquid into the bowl that Peggy was reluctantly holding.

Following this, they laid him on the bed again, and when he started to groan May said, 'He'll live,' and turning and looking at Mrs Funnell, she added, 'Unfortunately,' before marching out of the room.

Peggy followed her on to the landing. 'Can't believe it, can you, that he would go to such lengths?' she said.

'Oh, his type will do anything. He's a maniac. No, not a maniac, just a devious, two-faced bugger, I would call him. Well, anyway, you've got him where you want him. And as for that old girl in there. Oh, wouldn't I like to be a fly on the wall when you tell her the latest! Anyway, give me a shout if you want me. Frank will realise I've gone home.'

Peggy went into her grandmother's room. Victoria was sitting on the edge of the bed, an arm hugging her waist, and she asked simply, 'He's dead?'

'No; far from it. By what I've reckoned, he took enough just to knock him out. He knew what he was doing. This is all for Emma's benefit.'

'It's a pity he didn't get a surprise and find himself dead. A great pity. Mother went on like someone demented when she found him. It was just by coincidence that she did. If he did as you say, he would have calculated what she would do: when he didn't go in to her and hold her hand she would go and tap on his door, because he never entered the house without visiting her, wherever she was. I once said to him, Mother's in the lavatory but she never locks the door.'

'Oh! Gran.' Peggy wanted to laugh, but she knew if she gave way to it it might turn to hysteria. 'Get into bed, dear.'

She tucked up her grandmother; then bending over her, she smiled at her while saying, 'I think this calls for a glass of sherry. It's an occasion.'

'Oh, Peggy! Peggy!' The bedclothes shook. 'Don't make me laugh. But yes, a glass of sherry. This is an occasion.'

Within an hour Andrew Jones was aware that he was back in the land of the living but that a doctor hadn't been called. Looking up at Frank, he said, 'I'm sorry; a stupid thing to do. Has the doctor gone?'

'The doctor hasn't been,' said Frank tersely. 'Mrs Funnell thought it better not to call him because you'd only taken a small dose. Did you understand that when you made the partial attempt?'

'What . . . what d'you mean, partial . . . attempt?'

'Just that. You took only enough, really, to give you a twenty-four-hour, good sleep. Well now, I'm off. Next time, I'd do the job properly. Take whisky with it, that helps.'

Left alone Andrew Jones closed his eyes and turned his head to the side. He felt terrible. He felt ill. And what had it achieved? Well, he would soon know when he saw her. What time was it? Was she home yet? No, she'd still be in that place, being handled by those young louts. The picture in his mind caused his teeth to clench, and he muttered, 'Oh, Emma, Emma. Don't leave me. Don't leave me.' Then, as if he was being answered, a voice in his head yelled, 'And she'll not leave me! I'll see to that; she's mine. I can't help it. I don't want to help it. She's mine. She always has been mine, and she knows it inside herself. But it's her bitch of a mother. If it wasn't for her, Emma would understand how I feel. But I'll win, I'll beat her yet. By God! yes, I'll beat her yet. Oh lord! I feel sick. Oh Emma, Emma. Hurry up. Come home and see what you've done, what I've done for you.'

There was a rustle by the side of the bed and he opened his eyes to see Peggy standing there. She was smiling and what she said almost brought him up from the bed, his fists flailing. But the sickness caused him to drop back. She had said, 'Better luck next time, Andrew,' and had turned about and walked to the door.

Further along the corridor she tapped on her great-grandmother's door and went in without waiting for permission.

'I'd like a word with you, Great-gran.'

'Well, I'm ready to have a word with you, too. By! yes, I am. This business tonight has opened my eyes.'

'Oh, that's good. I'm glad of that.'

'Don't be perky, miss. And remember who you're talking to.'

'Yes, I am remembering; and please remember, too, Great-grandmother, that I am not a miss any more; I am a married woman who has run your house for years and has had to put up with a man of your choosing.'

'What do you mean, a man of my choosing? Now let me tell you' – the finger was wagging – 'Andrew has been brought to the limit of his patience by your attitude and unwifely behaviour and your lack of understanding with regard to his feelings as a father.'

'Oh, Great-gran, I'll either have to laugh at you or yell at you. But because you're an old-fashioned, besotted old woman I'll laugh at you while I tell you that your dear Andrew has not missed my wifely attentions at all. Do you remember Rosie, our daily help? Dear Rosie, cheery Rosie? She left to go off with a fellow, you remember? Disgraceful conduct, wasn't it? Well, do you know who the fellow was, Great-gran? No, you'd never guess in a thousand years. Well'

– she leant slightly forward – 'the fellow that Rosie went off with was your dear Andrew, the loving father. And he set up house for her in a bungalow further along the river, in a nice secluded part. And that's where he goes to his meetings on Tuesdays and Fridays, and sometimes on a Sunday and any other time his need calls him.'

Mrs Funnell's face was twitching, each feature of it seeming to stretch away from its neighbour: the eyebrows were raised, the eyes wide, the nose was stretched downwards, her upper lip covering her top set of teeth was trying to steady them, while her drooped chin was wobbling; even her ears seemed to be twitching. She did not come back immediately and say, 'I don't believe this, you're lying,' but what she said was, in a very small voice, 'That would have to be proved.'

'Oh, Frank will come over when you like and tell you how he found out. He was called to the next bungalow; the woman's trying to sell it; and there he saw the happy couple saying goodbye to each other. Rosie is a little fatter, I understand. And did you know that your dear Andrew is a commercial traveller? Well, like all commercial travellers, you know what they say about them, as they do about sailors: they have a wife in every port.'

'Shut up! Shut up! You're taking a delight in this, aren't you?'

'Yes, Great-gran, a great delight, because it's paved the way for my divorce; at least, my divorcing him.'

'You won't. You wouldn't dare. I won't have that scandal. He'll be brought to his senses. And I still feel that you're to blame for this: if you had been a wife to him he would certainly not have had to seek comfort elsewhere. No, that's the reason, that's the reason why he's done it. I shall talk to him, and things will be straightened out. I'll put a stop to this. But there'll be no talk of divorce, not in this house.'

'You can't do anything about it, Great-gran, not a thing.'
On this she turned about and walked slowly from the room
with the old woman's voice crying after her, 'You'll see.
You'll see. Oh, yes I can.'

All the way down the stairs she repeated to herself, 'She
can't. She can't do a thing about it.' Yet that dominant, 'Yes,
I can. Yes, I can,' penetrated her certainty.

2

Mrs Funnell was right: she could do something about it, and she did. She informed her great-granddaughter that if she filed for a divorce she would take Andrew's side and say that what he had done in taking a mistress and in finally attempting suicide was because she had never acted as a wife to him. Consequently all his real love had been directed towards his daughter. And if it came to court she would make a plea that he be given the care of his daughter until she became of age.

The morning following Andrew's futile suicide attempt, Peggy had gone into his room and, looking down on to his drawn and sickly countenance, she had asked quite quietly, 'Shall I phone Rosie and tell her that you're indisposed and are unlikely to pay your usual Friday night visit?'

She had thought for a moment that he was going to have a heart attack from shock, but, recovering himself, he had said, 'Well, now you know, what are you going to do about it?' to which she had answered simply, 'Divorce,' and walked out.

When Mrs Funnell had visited him, she had upbraided him firmly for his deception and he, in his most plaintive voice, had said, 'I'm a man, and it was either taking a decent woman or resorting to casual encounters. I took a way out that I thought was best.'

When Mrs Funnell later relayed this conversation to her great-granddaughter, she had ended, 'And I understood his reason perfectly. But he has promised to end the association, so that is the end of that.'

It was when Peggy had come back firmly, stating that it wasn't, that it was only the beginning, that Mrs Funnell had told her definitely which side she was on.

But the effect of all this on Emma was more worrying to Peggy than anything else that had transpired. And so it was that, four months later, she was sitting in the surgery with Emma, waiting their turn to see Doctor Rice.

When the nurse indicated that she should go in, she turned to Emma, saying, 'Sit there a minute; I want to have a word with him first.' But once inside the consulting room she stopped and looked towards the desk behind which was sitting a strange man, a young man. And she was opening her mouth to say, 'It's Doctor Rice I want to see,' when he spoke.

Rising to his feet, he pointed to the chair opposite, saying, 'Doctor Rice is indisposed this morning; I'm taking his place.' Then on a smile, he added, 'Very inadequately, it seems, because I've scared half of the patients away.'

His voice was pleasant and indicated that he wasn't from this part of the country; the South, she imagined.

Slowly she walked to the chair and sat down, then said, 'I . . . I don't think you can be of much help to me, Doctor. You see it isn't about myself I want to talk. I've brought my daughter and . . . and Doctor Rice knows her. And she's in a nervous state, and . . . '

'Well, I don't suppose I'll be able to help you as much as Doctor Rice would, but if you would like to tell me what is wrong, I may be able to offer a little advice. Has she stopped eating?'

230

'Oh no, it's not like that, but she's parky, she still doesn't eat like she used to. No; you see, it's . . . it's a very delicate and awkward matter.' She stumbled over her words and turned her head away before she said, 'It's her father. He's . . . he's so possessive of her, always has been, but it's got worse of late, and . . . and of course it's getting on her nerves.'

'I see. Well, this often happens between fathers and daughters.'

'It does?' The words said: I don't believe it. But he nodded at her, saying, 'I can assure you it does. Now would you like me to have a talk with her, or to listen?'

She stared at him, weighing him up. He spoke with assurance; but he looked so young with his fair hair, grey eyes and slim body, he didn't appear like a doctor at all. But she supposed they had to start sometime.

'How old is she?'

'Fifteen and a half; well, a little older, she'll be sixteen in December.'

'Well now, I could see her for a moment. I don't think that would aggravate her condition.'

Could she say: 'No, you're too young; I'll wait until Doctor Rice comes back'? No; that would sound rude. 'Very well,' she said.

He rang a bell now whilst saying to her, 'Would you mind waiting outside?'

'You want to see her alone?'

'Yes, if you don't mind. I often find that parents are inhibiting to young people.'

His words indicated that he wasn't so young as he looked, and she said, 'Very well.'

When presently the young person came in, he was definitely surprised. He rose from the chair and watched the girl come slowly into the room. She was tall with dark hair and large dark eyes in a pale face. Fifteen and a half, her mother had said. He would have put this girl's age at seventeen, perhaps eighteen. And she carried herself straight and with a certain assurance; or was it defiance? 'Do sit down,' he said, then added on a smile, 'I know I'm not Doctor Rice. So many patients have fled from me this morning because I am not Doctor Rice. I am glad you have decided to see me.'

Emma stared at the man. Her mother hadn't warned her that she wouldn't be seeing Doctor Rice. If she had she wouldn't have come in. Yet this stranger had a different manner altogether from the old doctor who, when he hadn't his hearing aid in place, shouted as if it were you who were deaf.

He was smiling widely at her now, saying, 'I had to tell nurse not to say they weren't coming in to see the doctor they expected. But even so, some of them scarpered.'

It was the word 'scarpered'. She wanted to smile, but she wasn't feeling like smiling, she was feeling sick, she was always feeling sick. Deep inside her there was this constant feeling of nausea. And when her father's hands were on her she felt at times she would vomit all over his suit. It was getting worse. Ever since the suicide business she had become afraid of him, really afraid, because he would do it again, he had said he would.

'Which school do you go to?'

'Fenton High.'

'Oh, I understand that's a very good school. What's your favourite subject?'

'I don't really have one. I'm told I'm good at English but I don't get very high marks.'

'Why not?'

'Because I don't work.'

'Oh.' He sat back in his chair. 'Well, that's straight from the shoulder. And I can recognise the reason . . . '

'You can't!' She almost spat the words at him.

And now he sat forward, his forearms on the desk as he said, 'You'd be surprised, but I can.'

His tone had changed. There was no soft persuasiveness in it now.

'You're not the only one who's had experience or who is having experience with a possessive father; it happens to boys, too, you know.'

Her mouth was open. She was gaping at him while telling herself that her mother would have told him the reason why she was here. But he was going on talking.

'It generally happens the other way round: it's the mother who's possessive of the son. But let me tell you, it's much worse when it's the father. So, you see, I do know the reason why. Watching your every move. Timing you. You must do well at this, that, or the other. You must take all the opportunities that he missed. Is it like that with you?'

'No.'

No; of course, he knew it wouldn't be. It was far worse, more insidious, more destructive. And so he ignored her 'no' and ended with, 'So you see, I know why you don't want to work. And I wouldn't have if it hadn't been for my mother ... You have a nice mother; she's very pretty.'

There was a look of surprise on her face as she said, 'You think Mother pretty?'

'Yes, of course. She's a very smart young woman.'

'She's just over thirty.'

He smiled. 'Thirty? Does that seem very old to you?'

'Well, it isn't young.'

His smile disappeared and his next words seemed to be fired at her.

'What form does your father's possessiveness take? Does he fondle you?'

Her mouth was opening and shutting; she had the urge to run from the room; but then, this man was a doctor. He seemed to know all about such situations. And he wasn't Doctor Rice. Doctor Rice wouldn't have chatted with her like he was doing; he would have bawled at her and said, 'I'll see him. You tell him to come to me.' Or he would have said that to her mother. But this doctor's attitude was different; and he was young, too; well, youngish.

Her head was low as she muttered, 'Yes.'

'And you don't like it?'

'No.'

'Have . . . have you told him? Made it plain to him that you don't like it?'

Her head was up now, her voice spitting out the words. 'Yes! Yes! I have. I've . . . I've told him for years, but I didn't want to hurt him because I loved him. But since he tried to com . . . '

She stopped and looked to the side, and when she didn't continue, he said, 'He's tried to commit suicide?'

Still she didn't speak.

'Has he?'

'Yes.'

'When was this?'

'Some months ago.'

'Did Doctor Rice know about it?'

She was looking at him as she said, 'No. No; my great-great-gran kept it hushed up. My great-great-gran wouldn't have the publicity.'

'What if he had died? She would have had publicity then?'

She looked him straight in the face now as she said, 'She doesn't take such things into account; she's a law unto herself.'

He had heard about the Funnell family and the old matriarch when Doctor Rice was giving him a lightning

234

summary of the patients. Vain, pig-headed old fossil, he had called her, if he remembered rightly.

'Why didn't you talk to your mother about this earlier?'

'Oh, she knows. She's been at him for years. But . . . but it only seems to make him worse.'

'And you have resisted all his advances?' It sounded such a stilted way to put it, but he couldn't find a different approach at the moment.

'Yes; yes, I have.'

'Always?'

She considered for a moment, then shook her head, saying, 'Well . . . years ago I . . . well, I didn't understand . . . well it was Daddy and he loved me. Oh yes, it was always that; he loved me.'

'Has he . . . well, I mean . . . ?'

'I know what you mean, doctor, and no; no, he hasn't, but—' She suddenly sprang to her feet and was standing rigid. He, too, rose, saying, 'There! There!' And slowly he took her hand and drew her to the window and there, pointing, said, 'Look at that! Isn't that a lovely garden? You wouldn't think a man like Doctor Rice would love flowers, now would you? Not with his bawling voice and thumping the table. Oh, you wouldn't know anything about his thumping the table. He does it at least three times during meals. I'm staying with them at present, until I get a place of my own. I didn't like this town when I first came to it, and . . . and I must whisper this, I didn't care much for him either, for his deaf-aid makes him believe that everybody else is deaf.' He was smiling widely at her, then added, 'But isn't that garden beautiful? It was that that made me see the other side of him. If a man could love flowers and arrange a garden like that, then he had a nice side to him. I find that, you know, there's always a different side to everybody. And your father must have a good side, but he must also have

235

a bad one. Oh yes.' Now he was facing her squarely. 'And you must stand out against it. I know you are doing that, but you must put it into words. You mustn't be too kind in a case like this. If he wants to fondle you, you snap at his hands and say, "I'm having no more of it!" Say to him, "If you do that again I'll go to the doctor." That generally scares them. I don't know whether or not it will scare your father. By the way, do you go out . . . ? I mean, play games, dance?'

'I don't go to dances, not any more. It was because I went to a disco that he tried to commit suicide. Mammy said it was an attempt to frighten me. Anyway, I don't go to dances, but I play tennis.'

'You do? So do I. There are two very good courts here. The one on Mowbray Road is excellent. One thing I did excel at was tennis. I was no good at rugby and hopeless at cricket. But you know something?' His head was poked towards her. 'You mustn't let on, because I'd be banned from every club and pub in the county, but I really do dislike cricket. I think it's boring; so slow; hours and days to achieve . . . what? Now, on a tennis court, you can hammer away.'

She was smiling at him. She knew she was smiling at him. He was so different from Doctor Rice. He turned now and led her towards the door, but there he stopped and in a quiet voice said, 'Now, do what I tell you. Stand up to him. Don't be afraid of hurting his feelings. His kind of feelings are unnatural. Remember that; so, fight them . . . I don't suppose I'll see you again, because Doctor Rice will be back in a day or two. But I'm sure he would say as I'm saying now: get out, go to the disco and—' He paused and smiled before he ended, 'play a lot of tennis. There's nothing like it for pushing the world aside.'

He opened the door for her and saw her mother standing waiting, as if impatient for her return.

236

Peggy looked from the doctor to her daughter. Emma was actually smiling. It was the first time she had seen her smile in weeks.

Outside she said, 'Well?'

'He was nice. Different from Doctor Rice. But he treated me like a little girl; part of his training, I suppose.'

'What did he say to you?'

'That I should play a lot of tennis.'

'What?'

'Just that: that I should play a lot of tennis.'

And she played a lot of tennis.

3

'Eighteen thousand pounds! I can't believe it. I knew she kept her statements at the bank and went and saw the bank manager now and again, but I thought it was only a few hundred. And never to leave me a penny.'

'Well, I didn't ask for her money. I knew she was going to leave me something, but not all of it, and not that amount. I tell you I knew nothing about it; I mean, how much she had.'

Lizzie walked towards the fireplace and, stretching out her arm, she gripped the mantel, saying, 'All those years looking after her, pandering to her wants, running for prescriptions.'

'Mam!' Peggy's voice was stiff. 'What you seem to forget is that it's on sixteen years since you left this house. And who has seen to the place since?'

'Who saw to her before? I was thirty-five then, girl. I had the both of them, and Len. Oh yes, and Len.'

'Well, I've had the both of them, Mam, and Andrew. Oh yes, and Andrew. And a fight on my hands that you never experienced.'

'I'm sorry.' Lizzie now took a seat to the side of the fireplace, saying, 'I feel so hurt. Can you understand that? She was my mother.'

239

'Well, Mam, you always said you were never close. But I can tell you this: she and I became very close over the years. I learnt a lot about her and saw her side of why she took up illnesses as a comfort.'

'Well, I'm glad for you. It certainly paid off.'

'Oh, for God's sake, Mam!'

Again Lizzie said, 'I'm sorry. Give me a cup of tea.'

Peggy poured out the tea and handed it to her mother; then sitting beside her, she said quietly, 'She left me the money for a purpose. She . . . she wanted to provide me with something to be able to go off with Emma where he couldn't get at her. That was the sole purpose of her leaving it to me.'

'Well, well. But you needn't have waited for that, need you? You've had it in your hands for months now.'

'As you say, I have. I saw my solicitor again last week.'

'And yes, what did he say?'

'He said it was a pity I hadn't come to him before, when the evidence was there that he was living with this woman, because now the bungalow's been sold and she's disappeared. Also, it is likely that although I will get custody of my daughter, he will also be given leave to see her every week, and likely for a longer period than he sees her now. And there's another thing. I had an ultimatum from Great-gran: if I take up proceedings for a divorce, then I go out of here, but dear Andrew stays.'

'*Never! She wouldn't.*'

'Oh yes, she would. Nothing that her bright boy can do is wrong. It's all put down to nature.'

'What's puzzling Henry,' said Lizzie now, 'is where he got the money to buy that bungalow? It was in her name, too, and being so, she's likely claimed the lot. If she was wise she did, anyway. But where did he get the money from? Henry's been going through the old ledgers but cannot find any sign of a fiddle. Cash or cheques there, they are all duplicated.

240

And of course, as I've told you, it would take some fiddle to get past Gran's lynx's eyes. She might be soft in the head about everything else, but never about money. No, it's a mystery. But as Henry says, he's got the money from somewhere and he means to find out where. By the way, where's Emma? I haven't seen her.'

'She's out playing tennis.'

'On a day like this? It's enough to freeze you.'

'Oh, she'd still play. She plays two or three times a week. And I'm glad; it gets her out and she enjoys it. And she's holding her own these days. She's working better at school, too. Her last report was quite good; at least, compared with the previous ones. I think I can date the change in her since she saw that new doctor. I didn't have much faith in him when I first spoke to him, but apparently he told her to stand on her own two feet. And she's done that.'

'How's Andrew been?'

'Oh, just the same. It's his daughter and she'll always be his daughter, and God Almighty Himself won't dare put a spoke in between them, or else. He's attending the parents' meetings at school now. I don't go when he's there; I just couldn't bear it. The smarminess of him. He came one night when he was supposed to be elsewhere, and there he was, smiling and chatting all round. And Mrs Rogers came up to me and said how wonderful it must be to have a husband who takes an interest in his family; her Dan doesn't know he's got a family and cares less. I nearly said, "I'll swap places with you anytime, Mrs Rogers, and gladly."'

'Well' – Lizzie rose – 'I must be off. By the way, do you hear anything from his people these days? It must be a year since she was this way.'

'Yes, it is a year; about this time. And look at the reception he gave her. My dear Mr Andrew Jones has no use for the Joneses of Doncaster. His father hasn't been here for years.

The last time he came, they had a row and the father called him a bloody upstart. He was a little tight at the time, the father, and it upset dear Andrew. As if he himself couldn't take it. He swills it down at times; of course, on the quiet, after Great-gran's safely tucked up in bed. Oh' – Peggy screwed up her face – 'there are times when I want to spit on him. But anyway' – she nodded her head briskly now – 'it can't last forever. Time's running short for him. She'll be sixteen next month. Do you know what, Mam?' She leant towards Lizzie now. 'I do wish she would meet some nice fellow and run off with him. Yes, I do.'

'And land up in the same condition as you did? Be quiet!'

'Yes, but I wouldn't force her to marry him in order to keep my respectability.'

Lizzie paused on the step and looked at her daughter, and there was a sad note in her voice as she said, 'You've changed, girl. Oh, how you've changed.'

'Well, I've been brought up in a good school these last few years, don't you think? But go on, go on. Drive carefully; the road's slippy. It'll soon be dark.'

She watched her mother get into the car, but she remained standing by the open door until Lizzie had turned the car and then disappeared down the drive. And after closing the door, she still stood and repeated to herself, 'Land up in the same way as you did.' Did she really wish her daughter to run off?

Yes, she did, but not just to live with someone, as was the vogue these days; she would wish her to marry some nice boy. No; not a boy, a man, one who would be able to stand up to her father and say, 'It's done, she's mine.'

4

'That will be our last game until the Spring; the courts close this week, both of them. The hard is too slippery, and there's hardly a blade of grass left on this one.'

Richard Langton stood on the path outside the netting that surrounded the tennis court. He did not look at the girl by his side, who was almost as tall as himself; but he went on talking as she tapped her racquet against the netting. 'How long is it since I first saw you in the surgery? Five months?'

'Nearly six,' said Emma quietly. She, too, was looking through the netting on to the court.

'I'm glad I'm not your doctor.'

'Why?'

'Because what I'm about to say would then be very much out of place and I could lose my practice.'

Emma didn't answer, but she put her hand up and pulled her scarf tightly around her throat as if it would stop the throbbing that was coming up from between her ribs and aiming to choke her.

'I'm twenty-six, Emma; you're not even sixteen until next month. I'm ten years older than you. That's the first obstacle. The second is, I have a career before me. I had no intention of

243

marrying early when I came to this town. In fact, I was only going to stay a couple of years and move on, but . . . but I met you and I knew right from the beginning what was going to happen to me; and it's grown over these months during our supposedly accidental meetings here. Now Emma, I know my own mind, but you're so young and you don't.'

'I do. I do.' She had turned to him now and they were staring at each other. The words had rushed out, but they were vibrant with feeling and certainty as she said, 'I, too, knew from the first. I'm not sixteen yet, as you say. But that's in years . . . otherwise I'm eighteen, twenty. I . . . I never seem to have been young, never had the chance. I've been tied to older people, my father . . . riveted to him. My mother was married when she was sixteen.'

He took hold of her hands now and his voice was gentle as he said, 'Yes, but by all accounts she's paid for it since with a man like your father.'

'But you're not like my father. You're . . . you're like no-one I've ever met or would hope to meet.'

'Oh, Emma, my dear, dear Emma. I want to take you in my arms and kiss you and— ' He looked to the side to where two people were approaching; then dropping her hands, he said on a laugh, 'I've only to be seen doing that in public, even holding your hands, and the place would be set on fire. Now, Emma, listen, I'm going to ask you a question. Will you, when you're seventeen, marry me?'

Emma closed her eyes but for the moment she couldn't answer for the throbbing in her throat. Then on a gasp, she said, 'I'd marry you tomorrow.'

'And I you, my dear Emma, and I you. But that's impossible. What kind of a reception would I get if I were to go to your mother now? I wouldn't ask your father, but your mother would, I'm sure, be up in arms. Anyway, let us arrange it like this: we'll keep it quiet until the beginning of the year, and then, if you haven't changed your mind' – he leant his head towards her, a soft smile on his face – 'I will ask your mother if we can become engaged, and just before you're seventeen or just after, we'll be married.'

Emma's eyes were wide and moist. She gazed at him in silence until he said, 'You're very beautiful, you know, and you'll grow more beautiful with the years.'

'I love you. I love you, Richard. Do you know that's the first time I've said your name? You've always called me Emma.'

'Well, don't in future call me Richard. I'm known as Ricky.'

She smiled softly, saying now, 'I like that ... Ricky; it suits you.'

Richard Langton stared at the young girl before him. He had never been able to take in the fact that she was a fifteen-year-old girl. Right from the beginning she had never talked like a fifteen-year-old girl. As she said, she could be twenty. He knew what Doctor Rice would say when he told him: 'You must be mad.' In his delicate fashion he would likely add, 'If you're so much in need of it, live with somebody. There are plenty available. They've been tripping over you ever since you came here.'

Yes, it was true he need not have wanted for female companionship over the past months. But the only one he had found himself wanting to see was this girl. He had tried, oh yes, he had tried to put the feeling in its place when he first recognised it. But it had become like a hunger: his whole being seemed empty when he was out of her presence. How often, in the beginning, had he stood where he was standing now and watched her play? At least half a dozen times. Then one day, just as if he had come upon her accidentally, he had said, 'You play very well. What about taking me on some-time?' And so it had started; and now it had come to a head.

245

'How are we going to manage . . . I mean, to meet?' he said. 'You couldn't risk going to the theatre with me, not for a while anyway. But look, the park doesn't close until six. Now, should you be coming in the west side' – he pointed – 'that's a very quiet end; let's say around half past five on a Tuesday or Thursday. I don't take surgery those nights. Well, we might just happen to bump into each other, mightn't we? Then what about a Saturday? What do you do on a Saturday afternoon?'

'The senior girls play badminton; others play hockey or netball.'

'Well, do you think you could skip a Saturday and I could pick you up somewhere, then we could take a run out into the country, across into Northumberland, beyond Hexham way; it's wild and wonderful up there. I'm off duty every third week. Anyway, we'll arrange it. Yes' – he leant towards her – 'we'll arrange it, my dear. We must. Now you've got to go, and I've got to go . . . Are you happy?'

'I'm . . . I'm afraid to say how I feel in case it disappears. I can't put a name to the feeling I have for you. If you say it's happiness, then it's happiness. I only know I'm afraid when I leave you; when you are out of sight, I feel lost, lonely.'

This wasn't an answer that a fifteen-year-old girl would give, it was a woman's reply. Quickly he glanced up and down the path. There was no-one in sight. In an instant she was in his arms and he had kissed her, one short, hard kiss, and had pushed her from him, saying, 'Go on. If you don't go this minute I'll go straight home with you, and that mustn't happen yet. Go on.'

She backed three steps from him. There was no smile on her face but her eyes were large and glistening. Then acting like a fifteen-year-old girl now, she turned and ran along the path, around the ornamental clock, and kept running until she reached the east gate of the park. Only then did she walk . . .

'You all right? Have you got a cold?'

'No, no, I haven't got a cold, Mam.'

'Your face is red.'

'There's a frost coming up.'

'Where've you been?'

'Well, look at my racquet, Mam; I've been playing tennis.'

Peggy turned away, asking now, 'Who do you play with, usually?'

'Oh, Pamela Bright. Sometimes a foursome. I like singles best.'

It was no lie, for her mother hadn't specifically said today, she had said 'usually'.

'You'd better come and have your tea. Your gran's been; she was disappointed at not seeing you.'

'Well, she doesn't stay long, does she?'

'What are you going to do tonight?'

'I've got homework and then I must practise I suppose. My piano lesson is on Monday, and I've hardly touched it this week.'

'You're right there; it's a waste of money.'

'I can easily give it up.'

'You're not giving it up. Five years you've been at it now; you should be a concert pianist, and you would be if you had practised.'

Emma had mounted the first step of the stairs and she was unwinding her scarf when she turned and looked down on her mother, saying, 'I would have been many things if I had been brought up in peace.'

Peggy was speechless for a moment. And then almost rushing to the foot of the stairs, she hissed, 'Are you blaming me?'

But Emma didn't answer, and Peggy turned away, saying to herself, What's come over her lately? She's changing. She's different. And she answered herself: She would be; she's growing

247

up. But then she's only fifteen . . . well, just on sixteen.

She went into the dining-room, where the tea was set, and she looked over the table as if there she would find something missing. Then, turning from it, she heard her own voice speaking aloud: 'The quicker I get her away from here the better. And no, no, I wouldn't want her to end up the same way as I did.'

It was half past seven and she was practising Mozart's Rondo alla Turca. She was fond of this lively piece but, on this occasion, her mind wasn't on it because her father was in the house. He stayed in most evenings now, spending some time in his study and some time chatting to his benefactress.

Her hands stiffened on the keys as she heard the door open. She had no need to turn her head to see who it was, for she knew his step.

The piano was situated at the far end of the drawing-room. She continued to play until his hands came on her shoulders, and somehow she kept on playing until his hand lifted her loose hair behind the ear and his mouth came down and touched it. At this, her hands crashed down on the keys and she jerked forward, saying, 'Don't do that, Daddy, please.' She was sitting on the edge of the seat, the front of her body pressed against the piano. 'I'm trying to practise this difficult piece.'

'All right, all right, practise. Go on playing.' His voice sounded calm, even playful. 'But play something else.' He now stood against the end of the piano, his forearms resting on the top of it. 'Play the Skater's Waltz. You know I like that.' He now straightened up, took up the pose of holding a partner and went into a waltz, singing, 'One, two, three . . .'

'Don't be silly, Father.'

As if he had been struck by some unseen force into stillness, he stopped, his right arm still embracing an imaginary

248

figure, his left arm extended. Then slowly he turned his head and looked at her over his shoulder, saying, 'What did you say?'

She bowed her head. 'Well, it is silly.'

He was standing close to her now; his breath seemed to be wafting her hair. 'Since when have you thought dancing with me silly? Eh? You love dancing with me.'

'I never have.' Her head had swung round but it was now bowed again. Then she was being dragged up from the music stool and she was being shaken by the shoulders as he demanded, 'What's this? What's the matter with you? You were never like this to me. She's been getting at you, hasn't she?'

'No. No. Nobody's been getting . . . '

'Then why have you changed?'

She struggled in his hold, pressing herself from him; but he maintained his forceful hold on her and, looking into his face, she said, 'I'm growing up. I'm not a little girl any more. I . . . I want to do the things other girls do.'

'You do, do you? You want to do the things other girls do, like making yourself cheap, going to discos, letting those louts paw you? Well, you're not going to. You're growing up, yes, but you're not grown-up and you won't be for some time, and in the meantime you're still my girl. Aye.' His voice changed and dropped to a quivering whisper as he said, 'My baby. Don't you understand?' He now stepped backwards, pulling her away from the piano and into the middle of the room towards the couch, and he had almost to force her to get her stiff body to sit down on it. His arms were about her now and there was an actual whine in his voice as he said, 'Emma . . . Emma, you're not grown-up but you're not a baby, except in my mind, so you must know how I feel about you, always have. You are mine, do you understand? mine. You're all I've got, all I've ever wanted. You'll never

249

know the torture I've gone through because I've loved you so. Oh! Emma. My Emma.'

As she was pressed back on to the couch her mind raced madly in protest, but all she managed to bring out in a kind of croak was, 'No, Daddy, no.' Then, when her legs were lifted on to the couch, the croak turned into a stilted scream as she cried, 'No! Don't! Stop it! I'll . . . ' Her words were cut off when his mouth covered hers, but when she clawed at him, one of his hands caught her wrists and held them and in a voice such as he had never used before, a deep moaning voice, he said, 'It'll be all right. It'll be all right. I love you. You're mine. Try to understand, I made you and I need you. You're mine.'

'Richard. Richard.'

The name seemed to halt him for a moment, but when his hands were again moving over her, the scream she let out crying, 'Mother! Mother!' almost lifted them both from the couch. It certainly brought the door banging open; and she was still screaming when his body was lifted from her and she saw the poker coming down towards his head. Only the fact that he rolled on to his side saved him from being brained. However, the end of the poker ripped the knuckles of the hand he had thrust up to shield himself and blood was spattered on to his face.

As if from nowhere Henry, too, appeared and, crouching in the corner of the couch, Emma now watched him struggling with her mother, and when he wrenched the poker from her hand and flung it across the room, there was the sound of splintering wood, which brought about an inevitable silence, punctuated only by gasps. But only for a moment.

'You filthy beast!' Peggy yelled at her husband. 'You're rotten, unnatural . . . This is the finish!' She was stabbing her finger at him now. 'You'll go, not me!'

Andrew had struggled to his feet. With one hand he was gripping the knuckles of the other and the look he was bestowing on his wife was one of concentrated hatred. He now stumbled round the head of the couch and from there, leaning against it for support, he growled at her, 'If I go she comes with me.'

'I won't! I won't!' Emma had sprung round from her crouching position now; her whole body was trembling, yet at the same time she looked taut. And now she yelled, 'I'll not go with you! Never! Never! I'm . . . I'm going to be married.'

Her statement startled not only him, but also Peggy, and it showed as surprise on Henry's face, and she looked from one to the other, saying, 'Yes, yes, I am. I'm . . . I'm going to be engaged at Christmas and married next year. And that's for all of you. Do you hear? For all of you.'

Andrew was the first to speak: his mouth in a wide sneer, he said, 'That'll be over my dead body.'

'And it could be. Yes, it could be.'

To the surprise of them all, she was on her feet now. Her body was still shaking but there was no tremor in her voice as she cried, 'I'm marrying Richard . . . Doctor Langton. We arranged it just today.' She turned now and looked at her mother, adding, 'He . . . he was coming to see you at Christmas.'

Into yet another silence her father's voice growled out, 'If he lives that long.' Then they watched him pull himself up from the support of the couch and, keeping his eyes on Emma until he had passed her, he strode from the room.

Emma dropped down on to the couch again and Peggy beside her, and the first question Peggy asked was, 'Is this true?' and Emma nodded, saying, 'Yes, yes, it's true, every word.' Then in a louder voice she cried, 'You took me to see

251

him, do you remember? And from that day it was done for both of us.'

'You're not sixteen yet.'

'Huh!' On the word, Emma turned her head away, the exclamation saying it all.

Peggy could find no reply, no words with which to confront her daughter, such as: He's much too old. You don't know your own mind. You're at a romantic stage. I'll have to see him and talk to him.

And as if Emma had heard her thoughts she turned to her and said, 'You can't do anything, Mam, so don't try. If you do I'll just go off . . . and with him.'

'Have you thought what he might do, your father?'

'Yes, I have; but when he confronts Richard he will be told that he could be taken to court; he's been at me for years. I've had to fight him off. Did you know that? fight him off. Why didn't you do something years ago, Mam? Leave him. You knew what he was like. You blamed Gran-gran for being self-ish, but what about you? You didn't want to leave this house, because you would be leaving Uncle Charlie. Isn't that it?'

'Girl! what are you saying?'

'The truth for once, bringing it into the open; the truth. Do you think I'm blind or stupid? Everybody knows, at least in the family.'

Peggy's head drooped, and Henry, looking at Emma, said, 'Well, that's your mother's business, after all. And who's to blame her, having to put up with those two for years?' He jerked his head towards the ceiling, then went on. 'But from where I stand there's going to be a separation in that quarter and soon . . . Peggy' – he put his hand out towards her – 'I've got him where I want him, where we all want him. There's just one more bit of proof and that'll be in the locked drawer of his desk, because I remember you saying he was like your father in that way: he always kept part of his desk locked up.'

He leant towards her. 'Do you think we can get the key?'

She looked at him as though in understanding, but she couldn't answer him for a moment for there were so many things whirling around in her mind: that doctor and her Emma . . . Good lord! and but for his hand going up she would really have brained him this time, and then where would she have been? And they all knew about Charlie. Well, she had guessed they would, so why was it upsetting her? It was the fact that Emma had accused her of not doing anything to prevent her being molested. And she had been . . . yes, she had been: she had been molested, if only on the surface. Tonight, though, it had gone further than the surface. Oh, yes, yes. What was Henry saying? Andrew had been making money on the side for years? She blinked hard, then said, 'What did you say, Henry?'

'I said, it all came about through the bangers in the backyard. I had given him the usual price list, you know, and we had discussed roughly what we should let them go for. And I remembered one for which we had suggested four hundred. It wasn't at all a bad little car; a bit of rust on the bottom, but nothing that couldn't be covered up. It's usual, of course, to ask a little more to start things off. They're more often that not bought by people passing through, the Sunday buyers, and they like to haggle and feel satisfied when we come down. Well, it should happen that I called in at Gibson's to pick up a suit – I was having the trousers altered – and as I was leaving the shop one of the assistants held the door for me and said, "It's going like a bomb. I'm very pleased with it, Mr Brooker." I stopped for a moment and said, "Oh yes? Which one was that?" "A Ford," he said. "Oh, the Ford," I said, nodding at him; then said, "So it was you who bought the Ford?" as if I was talking about a Rolls, because I could see he was very pleased with himself and his buy. And that's what I said: "Well, I hope you felt you got a good buy."

' "Oh yes, I did, Mr Brooker, for four hundred and seventy-five it was a bargain."

'We noddded at each other and I went out thinking, four hundred and seventy-five. The only other Ford we'd sold that day was a nearly new one from the front. Four hundred and seventy-five. I kept repeating that to myself. Well, I went back to the office and looked up the books, and there it was, four hundred pounds. And there was his signature and the price, four hundred pounds. He had cleared seventy-five pounds at one go. As I said, Peggy, most of that back stuff goes to passers-by, so you never see them again, unless the car turns out to have been stolen, as has happened.

'My God!' He put his hand to his head now.

'When I think of what he's been raking off all these years. Sometimes there's as many as a dozen cars out on the back. No wonder he wanted to work on a Sunday, demanded to work on a Sunday, to please the old girl. Well, I wonder how she will take this? But first I want to get into that drawer, the one in the study he keeps locked. Have you a duplicate key?'

'No.'

'Well, I know a way to get in. Where do you think he's gone now?'

'Oh, likely up to the sanctum to tell her that I nearly brained him and to put his case first, and she'll believe him.'

'Yes, she likely will; she'll believe anything except the fact that he's been doing her for years. Oh, I'm going to be there, and so are you, Peggy, when I present her with the proof . . . Have you got a screwdriver?'

'Yes; two or three of them in the tool box in the boot-room.'

'Let me have them.'

'What are you going to do?'

254

'Well, there's more ways of opening a drawer than from the front, if you get my meaning. And you, Emma, stay in the hall, and if you hear him coming across the landing, stall him.'

'What do you mean, Uncle Henry, stall him?' There was a tremor in her voice.

'Well, let him talk to you.'

'I can't. I can't.'

'All right, all right, don't get agitated. Well, run to the study and give us the tip.' . . .

Five minutes later Henry had taken off the back covering the three side drawers of the desk and had taken out the papers from the only drawer that was still locked. And as he laid them on the table he said, 'Two bank books, look; one in the name of Milburn in a South Shields branch. Two hundred and twenty in that, look. But oh, oh, see here!' He had pulled some documents out of an envelope. 'These are the acknowledgements of Special Deposit, one for a monthly, and two for three-monthly accounts. The bank gives good interest on those. Just look at them, Peggy. My! My! One for three thousand, one for one thousand, five hundred. God in heaven! One for two thousand, three hundred. These are in his own name. And here—' He opened a black-backed book, then muttered, 'Accounts. Oh, I'm going to say it: the clever bugger that he thinks he is, is a bloody fool. Keeping accounts! Look, right back to nineteen seventy; what he's made each week. And what's more, he's done it under my bloody nose.' He straightened up, the book gripped in his hand. 'You know,' he stared at Peggy, 'I could throttle him; on my own account, I could throttle him.' He paused for a moment and looked first to one side then to the other, then bit on his lip before he said, 'But he couldn't have made all that' – he pointed to the Special Deposit accounts – 'just out of his Sunday pickings. Or could he?' He now picked up another book, saying, 'That's one of the shop's receipt books. He's been clever.' He flicked the stubs of the book over, saying, 'He gives them a receipt for what he's charging. All above board. But then he must have another book that he keeps there or somewhere else that he hands to me, and also, apparently, all correct and above board.' Again he was biting on his lip; and now Peggy spoke for the first time: 'Surely somebody else must be in on it; he couldn't have done it all on his own. What about Wilkins, Ted Wilkins?'

'Oh, Ted Wilkins hasn't got the brains he was born with. He shows customers round, does a lot of car-talk that has nothing to do with the money part of it. He can hardly write his own name, but nevertheless he's a good salesman. No, you can count him out. And yet, you know, looking back now to the time I offered the bold boy more Sunday help, he refused; he said, what trade there was he and Ted Wilkins could manage. I remember the words he used: there were hours when they were standing picking their nails, he said. Oh, he's been picking his nails all right, and sharpening them in order to count the notes.' He turned back to the desk, and gathered up the papers and books, saying, 'I'm not going to bother putting that back on, not the night, Peggy, anyway. Come along with me.' Then at the door, before opening it, he said, 'Lass, if I know anything, this is going to be the end of your battle.'

They reached the hall to see Emma standing to the side of the stairs shivering. 'Don't worry; it'll soon be over,' Peggy said to her. 'Come along upstairs and go to your room, and bolt the door. And don't open it, mind, until I tell you.' And she pressed Emma before her, up the stairs and to her room, and waited outside until she heard the key being turned in the lock. Only then did she nod to Henry and precede him along to the end of the corridor. And as they walked Henry whispered, 'Lizzie should be here; I had intended that she should, but things have moved too fast.'

They paused outside Mrs Funnell's door and exchanged glances as the low murmur of voices came to them. Then, without knocking, Henry pushed open the door and, clutching back, brought Peggy forward, and so they entered the room together, there to see the old lady propped up in bed, and seated by her side, a handkerchief wound round his knuckles, was Andrew.

Before either Peggy or Henry had time to speak, Mrs Funnell, looking at Peggy, cried, 'I was just about to ring for you. Have you gone clean mad? Do you want to cause a murder in the house now?'

Peggy walked to the foot of the bed and, nodding at her great-grandmother, said, 'Yes; yes, there could be a murder in the house, but I wouldn't be the one to commit it; I've already missed, so it's your turn now.'

The old lady screwed up her face and her blue lips pouted as she drew in her chin and said, 'What's the matter with you, girl?'

'Nothing, Great-gran; there's nothing the matter with me.'

'Nothing the matter with you, girl, when you nearly brain your husband!'

'Oh, that's nothing to what you'll want to do to him in a minute, Great-gran.'

She now watched Andrew rise to his feet. His slack mouth was wide, but his teeth were close together: he looked like a man about to spit a great distance. Turning to Henry, she said, 'Break the news gently to Great-gran, Henry.'

The old woman narrowed her eyes, pressed herself back on to her pillows and, looking from one to the other, she said, 'What *is* this?' and her gaze came to rest on Andrew. But he was staring at Henry, and something in Henry's face must have warned him of approaching danger for, suddenly gripping his wrist, he turned away and was about to make for the door when Henry said, 'Just a minute.'

'I'll be back shortly,' Andrew growled; 'my hand's aching.'

'Well, you'll have plenty of time to see to that later when I've finished saying what I have to say to you. Just remember, under Mrs Funnell, I'm still your boss, you know. You've forgotten that a number of times lately, haven't you?'

'What you getting at . . . ? And don't push me. Don't you lay a hand on me.'

'I had no intention of laying a hand on you; I'll leave that to the police.'

'*What!*' Mrs Funnell had pulled herself up from the pillows. 'What's this? What are you talking about, Brooker? Police?'

'Yes, Mrs Funnell, I was talking about the police; unless, that is, you would not wish to press the case against him of robbing you for years.'

'What d'you mean, robbing her for years? What you trying to pull?'

'It's no use, Jones. You can put all the faces you like on it but you can't get away from the proof. You've been stupid, you know. You thought you were so clever, didn't you? But when you thieve you should never put it in writing; it goes against you.'

'What is this?' It was a high croak from the bed. 'What are you talking about, Brooker? Spit it out, man. Spit it out.'

For answer Henry moved up the side of the bed and, throwing the cheque book stubs and the notebook on to the bed, he said, 'Your great Sunday business man has made at least fifty pounds a go, sometimes as much as a hundred, on each backyard car he's sold. It's enabled him to buy a house for his mistress and bank thousands under an assumed name. It's all there.'

Mrs Funnell did not look at the evidence lying in her lap, but at the man she had come to love as a son almost from the day he married her great-granddaughter. She'd never had a son; she'd always wanted a son. Her daughter had given off a daughter and *her* daughter had given off a daughter: women . . . women in the house all the time. She did not consider Len Hammond, she had hated him from the beginning, but Andrew Jones was something different. He was young and pleasing and he amused her. He had kept her in touch with all that went on in the Works, underground, that is.

Underground. Her eyes dropped to the evidence on the bed. She picked up one thing after another and scanned it, but her scanning was enough to prove that dear Andrew Jones had been robbing her for years. She turned her head slowly and looked at him. She had known he wasn't a good husband. She had known he had women on the side. She could forgive all that. She could forgive the unnatural feeling he had towards his daughter. But that he would swindle her, that he would do her out of money, her money, this was another thing altogether. She knew she was an old woman and she hadn't all that long to live, and her one regret in facing death was she'd have to leave her money behind. And she had money, a lot of money. She had accumulated it not only directly from the car business, but also from having had fingers in pies that no member of the family knew about. Only her solicitor knew the extent of what she was worth. Even her bank manager hadn't an inkling. And how had she come by all of this money? Through being careful and wise with her investments. She had always seen to her own accounts. When she wasn't able to get up, her solicitor came to her.

She had never believed in God, not since she was thirteen, when she had refused to go to Sunday School; but she had taken to herself a God very early on in life, and its name was 'money'. And during these latter years, when she couldn't get about so much, it had become her main interest in life. Even knowing that she couldn't take it with her, she was

259

determined to have some fun out of life; not that she would actually experience it fully, but she could allow her mind to dwell upon it and be titillated by it: she was going to leave the bulk of what she owned to her second interest in life; in fact, he vied with the first, dear Andrew.

She felt a pain under her ribs as she stared at him. His face was devoid of colour. She wanted to cry at him, 'It isn't true, is it? They've got it in for you because I've made so much of you; they're jealous.' But his countenance at this moment could have hanged him; he couldn't meet her gaze: his eyes were flicking here and there as if looking for a way of escape. And then she screamed, 'You! You've done this to me after all I've . . . ' There was a choking in her throat, and a voice was yelling excuses in her head: well, they're all at it. Everybody's at it. What's a few hundred put on a car? But he had said he only ever thought of her. He . . . he had, in a way, made love to her; her, an old woman: he had not only stroked her hands but massaged her; when she had cramp in her calves he had got rid of it; he had sat her up and manipulated her shoulders; he had made her feel like a young girl, while all the time he was . . . taking her for an old fool. The pain was getting worse. She screamed, 'Get out of my sight! You'll pay for this; I'll have . . . have the police on you.'

'Stop it. Don't agitate yourself. Lie quiet.' Peggy's hand was on the old woman's brow stroking her hair back. She did not turn and look at Henry when she said, 'Ring for the doctor'; the urgency was there, and he hurried out of the room, only to come to a dead stop on the landing when he saw Jones knocking on Emma's door, saying, 'Emma! Emma! Open up. Do you hear me?'

'Yes, she heard you. Now get away from there! And if you're wise, you'll make yourself scarce.'

Jones turned and faced Henry. 'You've always had it in for me, haven't you?' he said. 'Well, you can do nothing.'

'Don't be a fool. And you *are* a fool, you know, and a knave, but not a clever enough one, otherwise you wouldn't have kept the evidence. But you wanted to be reminded each week of where you stood, didn't you? How the sum was mounting; that's been your undoing. Anyway, I'll not expect you into work tomorrow. You understand? And it will all depend on Mrs Funnell where you'll be at this time tomorrow night. You've cooked your goose. And I'm going to tell you another thing: if you don't want to be up on two charges, you leave Emma alone.'

Henry's head jerked backwards when it seemed Jones was about to spring on him; but it was his words that hit him with such force as they were ground out, 'She's my daughter. When I go, she goes.'

'Oh no, she won't.'

'You keep out of this.'

'That's what I'll not do. I'm away to phone the doctor, but before I do that, I'll phone the police. I'll put a stop to your gallop one way or the other; I'll arrange it so you won't be able to lay a hand on her.'

As Henry hurried towards the stairs Jones sent a mouthful of such obscenities after him that his step was checked for a moment; but he stopped himself from turning and going back and banging his fist into the dirty mouth.

Jones now hurried across the landing and into his own room, and there he stood pondering for a second, defiance in his attitude, one which was prompting him to stay and try to talk the old bitch over. His common sense, however, told him that she was past talking over; she would just as likely have him put into jail as not.

His teeth grinding together and like one demented, he began pulling clothes from the wardrobe and from the chest of drawers; then he crammed them into two large cases he had taken from a shelf in the top of the cupboard. The last

261

articles he took were from the dressing-table drawer: gold cuff-links, three watches and two signet rings. Then, putting on an overcoat, he lifted up the two cases and walked towards the door. But there he paused for a moment and looked back around the room, and only then did it really register that, as Brooker had said, he had been a fool: he should never have kept any receipts. But yes, he had found it good from time to time to look on the evidence of his cleverness. Some odd need in him craved for praise, and the only way it could be satisfied was to tot up each week the amounts out of which he had diddled the firm, forgetting that the firm was the old girl. If he had been wise he should have left all the business in the bungalow. But then Rosie wasn't as simple as she appeared to be; she was nosey and liked to get to the bottom of things. He'd always had to keep a watchful eye on her. But oh, what he had lost through this one slip, this one little slip of stupidity: this room, this house, and, aye, by God! the business. Oh yes, she had hinted at that. She had been hinting at it with glee for some time now, telling him that they were all going to get a shock when she was gone, but insinuating in her own way that his shock would be pleasant. Oh, very pleasant.

His reverie over, he put down the cases, opened the door, then lifted up the cases again and went out, and made his going as noiseless as possible. But after putting the cases in the boot of the car he turned and looked back towards the house and to the window of his daughter's room, and it was as if he had yelled aloud, for he could hear the voice in his mind, crying, 'Married? Not if I know anything about it. If that's the last thing I do, I'll stop that. By God! I will.'

5

Mrs Funnell had suffered a slight stroke. Her left arm was affected, and also her mouth was slightly twisted, but she could still talk. And talk she did, alternating from venom to supplication. The venom was directed against her once dear boy, and never a day passed but she demanded to know if the police had yet found him.

Her supplication was aimed mainly at Peggy. Peggy wouldn't leave her, would she? Oh, she knew all about her and Charlie, and she wouldn't mind Charlie coming into the house once the divorce was through. No, she didn't want her granddaughter Lizzie and Henry here. Lizzie was hard: she didn't understand her. And she would leave everything to her if only she would stay with her to the end, and the end, as she could surely see, wasn't very far off.

All this cringing had come about because Peggy had stated that, once the divorce was through, she would then lead her own life, that she had had enough of this house and all that was in it. This she had said to her mother in a low voice whilst in the bedroom, imagining that the old woman was asleep. But although Mrs Funnell lay most of the day with her eyes closed, only she knew that she slept very little and that her mind was as active and as clear as it had always been.

They were well into the New Year now; in fact, it was already the beginning of March, and on this day there was a conclave being held in the drawing-room. Present were Lizzie and Henry, Peggy and Emma, Charlie and May. They all held cups of tea except Peggy, and she sat at the side-table, a hand on the teapot as she listened to her mother, saying, 'They should have put the police on to him straightaway. He should be behind bars.'

'Well, we decided against that, feeling that it could be bad for business. Probably many of those people he had done, or even hadn't done, would come asking for refunds.' Henry turned now and looked at Peggy, saying, 'You really think he's gone abroad?'

Peggy slowly poured another cup of tea out before she said, 'That's only what Rosie Milburn thought. The solicitor said Andrew had persuaded her to sell the bungalow – it was in her name – but then he didn't give her a penny of it.'

'Serves her damn well right!'

Peggy glanced at her mother before going on, 'And there's no possible way of making him refund any of the money. Anyway, he's taken it from the two banks. He certainly wouldn't refund any of it off his own bat, the solicitor said; he would have to be taken to court and our case proved to get any recompense.'

'Do you think he'd go abroad without trying to see Emma?'

Peggy looked across the room at Charlie, and it was some seconds before she said, 'I wouldn't think so; but he had hinted as much to Rosie Milburn, suggesting that they would both go. But then, as she told the solicitor, he just disappeared, taking his cases and everything else belonging to him. She had come back from work to the rented rooms

264

in which they were living and found him gone. He left her nothing. And naturally, she's bitter.'

It was Lizzie again giving a grunt of a laugh and exclaiming, 'Bitter! She's only getting what she asked for. It's a pity she's able to work.'

Peggy looked at her mother as the thought again struck her that some parts of her great-gran would never die as long as her mother was alive.

It was she herself who should be feeling bitter against Rosie Milburn, yet she wasn't; in a way she felt sorry for her: she always remembered how nice she had once been, how helpful. And what was more, hadn't she a lot to thank her for? Hadn't she relieved her of the nightly fight and struggle, which always ended in exhaustion?

All this while Emma had sat with her head slightly bowed, staring towards the cup she held in both hands where it rested on her knees. Had her father gone to Australia? Oh, she hoped so; she'd be free then from this awful dread.

She had not been to school for three days, for not only would her mother have had to take her there, she would also have had to wait in the car for her as though she were a small child being met from school. But really this was of little relief, for she always felt more apprehensive in the lane rather than anywhere else that a car would slow up and her father would jump out and grab her. Her mother couldn't be with her all the time.

She had seen him twice: once at the gate at the end of the drive here, when she had turned and flown back into the house; another time when she and her mother were crossing the market. Her mother had stopped to look at a stall selling all kinds of junk, and she had turned and looked behind her as if she had been pulled around by a force, and there he was standing on the pavement only a stall away. She had gripped her mother's arm and said, 'Don't turn round, but Dad's behind.'

Peggy did turn round, her eyes scanning the pavement, and she said, 'You must have been dreaming; there's no-one there.'

'He was, I tell you. He was.'

That night she had asked herself why she should really be so afraid of him; after all, he was her father. And the answer came whipping back: Don't be silly, asking a stupid question like that of yourself.

There had been no real fear of him until the night when the incident took place on the couch; before that, her feelings had touched on slight revulsion at being held so closely and at being stroked and patted as if she were still a child. But on that night she knew he hadn't seen her as a child, and now she questioned if he had ever seen her that way.

She knew she had refrained from reading about such cases in the paper; and only a few months ago she had switched off a television documentary, refusing to believe that she was in any way involved in such nastiness. But now she was fully aware of what would happen if ever her father got her alone, really alone. If only she was married; he couldn't touch her then. But she had promised her mother to remain engaged a year. Yet more often now, she doubted she could keep that promise.

Why couldn't they be like other families, normal? Why did she have to have such a father? But Ricky said it was common for many men to feel for their daughters as her father did for her, and that it had always been so; it was just that it was being brought more into the open now. The public had been made more aware of it these days. Surprisingly, it was often the mothers who were to blame, for they knew what was going on, yet they didn't report the husband.

Her mother had known about it, and she should have done something sooner, shouldn't she? Taken her away.

But what could she do? There was Gran-gran to be looked after, and she had been on her father's side; and on no account would Gran come back to the house. And so her mother's hands had been tied. In a way, too, so had her heart, because if she had left the house, she would have had to leave Charlie; yet wouldn't Charlie have gone with her mother?

The thought of her mother and Charlie made her feel hot inside; yet that her father had a mistress had never really affected her. Why hadn't it? And why, he having a mistress, should he want her, herself? It was all so mixed up and puzzling. Oh, she wished she was away from here: the house, the town, away with Ricky, just the two of them, no-one else in their world. But that was silly; he was a doctor and there would always be people in his world. At times she felt grown-up, at others she knew she had a lot more growing to do and there would be the urge to get on with it.

She raised her head and looked at them, at her mother sitting looking at the teapot again as if she were interested in it. She was a beautiful woman. She had never thought of her mother as beautiful before; nice looking, bonny; but never beautiful. But she was beautiful, as Ricky had said. Then there was her grandmother; she, too, was good-looking, but old somehow; well, she was over fifty, but she was smart, she dressed well. And then there was Charlie. Charlie was a little younger than her mother; thirty-two, nearly thirty-three. He was a plain-looking man, but his face was kindly. He didn't look like a marvellous musician. Yet what would a marvellous musician look like? She couldn't imagine Charlie playing before all those foreign audiences. Yet she understood that he was well known, and she had heard her Auntie May say that he could have been even more so, if it hadn't been for her mother. She had heard this when she had stood outside the kitchen door that time they were having a row; at least, not a real row, just hot words. Auntie May doted on her Charlie. Funny, how she felt about Auntie May: it was likely because she was the only one who would always speak the truth, came out with it; tactlessness, her gran said it was.

Peggy's voice disturbed her reverie. She was saying to Lizzie, 'You'll have to come and relieve me at times, give me a break. I've got her seven days a week, and nights, too. It isn't fair.'

'She's got enough money to engage a night nurse, and a day one at that. Don't be silly; put your foot down.'

Peggy's reaction was to rise to her feet and to answer her mother indignantly: 'You go upstairs and put your foot down and see the reception you'll get. Anyway, Mam, it wouldn't hurt you to come over one night a week and give me a break.'

'I'm sorry.' Lizzie, too, rose to her feet. Her head was turned away, her eyes closed for a moment, as she said, 'I really am, Peggy, but I can't stand being with her. I never thought I would feel like this about her, but since the solicitor hinted what she intended to do, to leave everything to that bastard, and that's what he was' – she now nodded from one to the other as if daring contradiction – 'I can't bear the sight of her; she's a spiteful old witch.'

'She's your grandmother, lass.'

'Oh, don't you start, Henry. I know she's my grandmother, and I know I'm weighed down by the feelings I have against her. You should understand. Oh, let's get away.'

As Lizzie stalked towards the door, Henry looked appealingly at Peggy, then followed his wife from the room. And when Emma saw the way in which her mother was looking at Charlie, she realised that the trouble concerning her was not the only one to be contended with, for there were other intrigues occupying the minds of her mother and grandmother.

She almost flounced from the room, to hear the ringing of a bell from above. Lizzie had stopped at the front door and was looking back towards the sitting-room, but when Peggy didn't appear she turned to Emma, saying, 'You had better go up. And it's no use looking like that; you've got to take your share.'

The words seemed to convulse Emma, for her whole body jerked as she took two steps forward towards her grandmother, demanding, 'Why? Why should I have to make up for your neglect and Mother's coming desertion? Well, here's something for you to ponder on: I'm standing in for neither of you. I'm getting out as soon as possible, and damn a year's engagement! Do you hear?'

'God in heaven!' Lizzie turned and looked at Henry, her eyes wide, her mouth open. 'I would never have believed it.'

Then from half-way up the stairs the voice cried, 'Well, you can believe it now, Gran, and think on it.'

When she reached her great-great-grandmother's door she did not pause even for a moment to calm herself but pushed it open and quickly approached the foot of the bed, asking, 'Yes?'

Mrs Funnell looked at her, her head to one side; then her mouth twitching, she said, 'What do you mean by "yes"?'

'Just what I said, Gran-gran; what do you want?'

'I would like my tea, girl, that's what I want. And may I ask what's come over you? and at the same time add, how dare you speak to me in this manner!'

For answer Emma said, 'Mother's busy at the moment. She'll bring it up in a short while. Anyway, it isn't four o'clock yet.'

The old lady turned slightly to her right and hitched herself up on the pillows; then peering at Emma, she said, 'Come here.' And when Emma moved up by the side of the bed, she added, 'What's happened down there to upset you?'

'Nothing's happened . . . well, I mean, it doesn't matter what happened down there. But I've made up my mind about something: I'm not waiting for the rest of the year before I get married; I'm going to marry when I like and as soon as possible.'

Mrs Funnell leant back tight against her pillows, and her lips went through the process of agitated munching before she exercised her matriarchal control over this youngest member of her family: 'You'll do what you're told. You'll do as I say.'

'Oh, but I won't, Gran-gran. Great-gran had to do as you said, and Gran's had to do as you said, and Mother's had to do as you said, but I'm a different kettle of fish.'

Mrs Funnell looked up towards the ceiling as if speaking to the Almighty, and she might have been as she said, 'Dear God! am I hearing aright?' Then bringing her gaze down to bear on Emma, she said, 'You go your own way, girl, and you don't get a penny of my money.'

'Blast your money, Gran-gran! Do you hear? Blast your money! I'm sick of listening to what you're going to do with your money. You were going to leave it all to Father, weren't you, to spite Mother and Gran? Then you were going to leave it all to me, provided I was a good girl and did what you said, still to spite Mother and Gran. Well now, I don't want your money; what I want is liberty and a life of my own, and I'm going to have it. Do you hear?' Then, as she backed from the bed and saw the old woman beat her breast with her hand, she said, 'And you needn't put on any of your fainting turns for me, either. You've got Mother run off her feet through them, but as the doctor said, you're

270

like an old horse put out to grass; you'll last for years, nibbling away.'

As quickly as the sense of injustice had urged her down in the hall to make a stand, now it ebbed away as she watched the face on the pillow begin to quiver.

Turning swiftly, she ran from the room and down the stairs and burst into the sitting-room, there to bring her mother quickly from Charlie's arms and to turn on her, saying, 'Girl!'

'Never mind "girl", Mother; I've . . . I've upset Gran-gran. She . . . she might be having an attack, I don't know.'

'What have you been saying?'

'I said what I wanted to say, what I'm saying to you now: I'm not waiting another year to be married, I'm going to be married as soon as possible, and you can do what you like about it. And . . . and I told Gran, too, before she left.'

She watched her mother look at Charlie as if she were wanting him to confirm what she was hearing, before thrusting him aside and running from the room.

Mrs Funnell was lying with her eyes closed. Peggy looked at her for a moment, but said nothing; instead, she went to the side-table and took a pill from a box and poured out a glass of water, then returned to the bed, saying gently, 'Here, take this.'

Mrs Funnell opened her eyes and, her voice assuming that of a weak old lady, she said, 'She went for me, Peggy. She went for me, yelled at me.'

'What did you say to her to make her yell at you?'

The head moved restlessly on the pillow, and after a moment Peggy said, 'Lie quiet now. I'll go and bring your tea up.'

As she made for the door the weak voice came at her, halting her: 'Peggy?'

271

'Yes?' She turned and looked towards the bed, but didn't go back.

'You . . . you wouldn't leave me? You . . . you wouldn't walk out and leave me to the mercy of strangers, nurses, would you?'

A slow smile that could have held cynicism passed over Peggy's face before she answered, 'It all depends on you and how you behave yourself.'

She went downstairs and into the drawing-room and found Charlie sitting holding Emma's hand, and Emma was crying.

Standing in front of her daughter, she said, 'Now tell me, what did you say to her to upset her so, besides telling her you were going to get married? That shouldn't have put her into the state she's in.'

Emma blew her nose, wiped her eyes and, looking up at her mother, she said, 'I told her what she could do with her money.'

'Huh!' Peggy laughed now and, looking at Charlie, she said, 'And that would upset her, because she's been holding her' – she nodded towards her daughter – 'as the carrot to keep me in place. Oh, I'll go and make her tea.' And Charlie rose to follow her, but stayed long enough to pat Emma on the head and say, 'Don't worry, love. You do what you want; she'll be with you.'

It was almost an hour later when Peggy confronted her daughter in the hall, saying, 'Where are you going?'

'I'm going to see Ricky and tell him.'

'Tell him what?'

'That we are going to be married, and as soon as possible.'

'Now look here, Emma!'

'You look here, Mother. You can give your consent or you can withhold it, but it makes no difference. I'm over sixteen and if I don't marry Ricky I'll go and live with him. How about that? It's quite the thing today; in fact, it's more fashionable than getting married.'

'Don't be brash, Emma; it doesn't suit you.'

'Yes, it does suit me, Mother, but it doesn't suit you to think that I'm a young woman, not a young girl. And I'll tell you something else, Mother, while I'm on. I hate this house. I'll be glad when I leave it. There's been no happiness in this house since I can remember; not real happiness. There's always been somebody at somebody else's throat. Well now, Mother, if you will move away from the door; if you don't, I'll only have to go out the back. Don't look like that and say you could slap my face for me.'

Peggy forced herself to take two steps away from the door and away from this girl, this beautiful girl who had become a stranger; not overnight, but within a matter of minutes. Slowly she turned away and as slowly Emma opened the door and went out, saying, 'Charlie said you'd be with me, but he was mistaken, wasn't he?'

She was half-way down the drive when she stopped and put her hand tightly over her mouth: what had come over her? She wasn't sorry for the things she had said to her great-great-grandmother, nor to her grandmother, but why had she spoken like that to her mother? Because she loved her. She had the desire to turn around and run back and put her arms around her and say, 'I'm sorry,' but were she to do so she knew she would be persuaded to let things remain as they were, and that she couldn't do.

Their rendezvous in the park was a seat situated about ten yard from the ladies' convenience, and if Ricky wasn't there at the appointed time she would often wait just inside rather than sit on the bench and be eyed by passers-by.

Tonight he wasn't there, nor could she see anyone on the path beyond the convenience that led to the lake and the land beyond the bench and path was screened by a rhododendron hedge.

She was still in an agitated state, mostly because of her manner towards her mother. She wasn't worried as to what Richard's reaction would be to her proposal of an early marriage; she knew his love for her was of an intensity that set fire to her own. This had shown itself at their parting after the one and only time he had taken her to his flat, when he had laughingly said to her, 'Miss, you're a danger to humanity. And that is the first and last time you'll be invited in there until after the deed is done. You understand me?' And she had answered simply, 'Yes, doctor, I understand you.'

She sat on the bench, her head turned to look towards the main gate. A number of people were entering but only one woman passed her; the rest took a short cut over the lawn that would take them to the bottom gate.

She looked at her watch and made an impatient movement with her head. It had gone fast again; it showed almost a quarter past five and in the distance the chimes of the clock in the market place were just now striking the hour.

When she heard the rustle behind her she didn't turn around; children often made their way up behind the hedge, then would spring out on each other, yelling. But when one hand came on her shoulder and the voice said, 'It's all right. Stay still. Now stay still,' she froze. She literally froze. She couldn't have sprung up if she had tried; it was as if she had become glued to the seat. When the other hand came on her shoulder and turned into a grip, the ice in her body seemed to affect her voice for it came out as a croak, saying, 'Da ... Dad ... Oh, Dad, please, please go away, and leave me alone.'

'I'm ... I'm not going away, baby. I've waited too long. Now listen to me. You're coming with me, do you hear?'

'I'm not! I'm not!' Her voice was a yell now, and when she aimed to spring up, he pulled her back with a thud on to the bench; then he was around it and facing her. His hands gripping her arms now but his voice soft, he said, 'I . . . I can't go on without you. I've . . . I've lost everything, I must have something. But all I want is you. Don't you understand? All I want is you. All I ever wanted was you.'

'Leave me alone.'

'Look; listen to me. You can come quietly or I can make you.' He now left hold of one arm and thrust his hand into his coat pocket and brought out what looked like a narrow tube; then glancing first one way then the other, he said, 'This won't hurt you and you'll come quietly. Now, it's up to you.'

As her foot kicked at his shins and her hand, claw-like, went out to his face, she let out a high scream, and it was so loud that she didn't feel the prick in her arm, and she knew she was still struggling with him, but then, of a sudden, she had the desire to sit down, but his arm was about her. She opened her mouth again and let out a weak cry. Her resistance had all gone.

What time it was when she realised she was being tugged between her father and Richard, she didn't know: it seemed but a second; or was it a week? She knew now that she was leaning against the wall of the toilets, looking down on her father and Richard rolling on the ground. And there were people gathered about. She was next aware of dimly seeing her father lying face down on the path, his hands bent up behind him and Richard with one knee on his back. Richard's face was bleeding and she knew he was shouting up at the people.

'Go to the phone box!' Richard spat the blood out of his mouth, then again cried up at the face hanging above his, 'Go to the phone box outside the gate and phone the

275

police. Do it quickly!' He turned and glanced to where Emma was leaning against the wall. He stared at her for a moment, wondering why she wasn't saying something, why she wasn't moving.

'What happened?' Another face above him was asking the question, and he was about to answer when Jones turned his head to the side and, gasping, spluttered, 'Don't . . . don't bring the police, I'll . . . I'll go.'

'Yes, you'll go, but it will be to jail this time.'

When Jones made an effort to turn on his side Richard growled at him, 'Make another move and I'll break your arm. I mean it!'

'She's . . . she's my daughter.' Jones was now appealing to the faces peering down at him, and a woman almost demanded of Richard, 'Is she? Is she his daughter?'

'Mind your own business.'

Another voice said, 'He's my doctor. That's Doctor Langton, Doctor Rice's partner.'

The man who had gone to the phone came running back, saying, 'Just after I phoned a panda car passed. I waved them down; they're coming.'

When the two policemen stood above him, saying, 'What's this, sir?' Richard answered, 'I'm Doctor Langton. That young lady is my fiancée.' He pointed to the stiff figure still standing against the wall. 'This man' – he jerked the two hands that he was gripping – 'is her father. He is separated from his wife but he has tried to abduct his daughter. I don't know what he's done to her. She seems under the influence of a drug, I think.'

When Jones was on his feet he stood rubbing his arms and spluttering, 'Yes, she's my daughter. I've a right to speak to her.' Then it was as he hunched his coat up on to his shoulders that the glass syringe fell from his pocket to the pavement.

276

Amid silence now, one of the policemen stooped and picked it up, then turned and looked at Emma and, addressing the doctor, he said, 'Yes, you're right: it would appear she has been given something, sir.'

The effect of this sudden confirmation of his fears was Richard's urge to lash out at the face that, like his own, was streaked with blood; but, turning swiftly, he went to Emma, and, putting an arm about her, he drew her forward, saying to the police now, 'I'd better get her to hospital. I don't know what he's given her, but if you don't mind, I'll take that.' He held out his hand for the syringe, but the policeman said, 'I'm sorry, sir, but I must hold this. And I must ask her and you, sir, a few questions.'

'She's not in a fit state, officer. I must take her to hospital.'

'Well, I must have her address, and yours, sir, and I'll see you later.'

'Go to Bramble Lane first; I'll probably be there.'

The officer nodded; then as the two of them urged Jones away with, 'Come on, you!' he turned and shouted at Richard, 'You'll get her over my dead body.'

Having belted Emma in the car and taken his seat behind the wheel, he turned and said to her, 'You're all right. You'll be all right. Do you hear? It will pass.'

She stared at him blankly, then slumped in her seat, which activated him into starting the car and driving as fast as possible to the hospital with the words 'You'll get her over my dead body' ringing in his head.

He would like to think of the man as being mad, but he knew he wasn't; except that is, with an unnatural desire for his daughter.

They were all in the drawing-room again: Lizzie, Henry, May, Frank, Charlie and Peggy, and they were listening to Richard: 'She'll sleep till tomorrow. She'll likely have a very bad headache but she shouldn't have any after-effects. Having said that, though, as long as he's at large she'll be filled with fear and she will need protection. As it is, I cannot give her that until we are married.' He looked around at the faces staring at him, and it was Peggy who now said, 'Well, from what you tell me she hadn't time, or didn't get the chance, to tell you what she meant to do; but she made it plain to me and to my mother that she wasn't going to wait for a year; that she wanted to be married as soon as possible; in fact she seemed determined to be married as soon as possible.'

'She did?' It was painful for him to show his surprise by smiling, for it stretched his face, and he'd had stitches in one cheek and others under his lower lip; but smile he did, and he continued to smile as he said, 'Well, if you are in agreement, that would please me too.'

'We don't seem to have much to say in the matter,' Peggy said with a slight quiver in her voice; then she added, 'Let's hope it will be some protection for her.'

'What do you think he'll get?'

Richard looked at Charlie and shook his head, 'I've no idea. He might have escaped with a caution as being an over-protective father if it hadn't been for the syringe. Even with that, who knows? I can only hope he'll be jailed.'

Peggy reared at this. 'I'll . . . I'll go into the witness box and tell them what he was aiming to do to her,' she said. 'Yes, I will, I will. That'll put him away . . .'

'I wouldn't do that.' Richard attempted to purse his lips. 'That would mean her having to appear to back up your words and you don't want to subject her to that, do you?'

When Peggy shook her head, Lizzie, too, voiced the same feeling: 'No, we don't want that,' she said, then added, 'But there's another thing: he could be brought up for his thieving.

278

He's done my grandmother out of a great deal of money, thousands of pounds.'

'Now, now,' Henry said; 'forget about that part. I've told you, once that's mentioned he'll come back with all kinds of things: V.A.T. and tax and God knows what. So it's best to let sleeping dogs lie.'

'I hate to think of him getting off with it and all that money.'

Peggy lifted her head for a moment. Had her eyes been closed she would have imagined it was her great-gran speaking. Money, money, money. That's all they seemed to think about. Her mother was very like her great-gran. What about herself? Well, money had never meant much to her: she had wanted only enough to live on comfortably, quietly, somewhere with Charlie. And once Emma was married that's what she would do, she would get away from this house and everything connected with it . . . But what about Great-gran?

Yes, what about Great-gran? She was tied here till Great-gran went and that could be years ahead. Where would it end? And now this business tonight, him using a hypodermic needle on Emma. He'd stop at nothing. Yes, let her get married, and as quickly as possible.

She rose to her feet when she heard her mother saying, 'Don't be silly, May! Inform his people. You'd have them here in a swarm. We haven't seen them for years; neither has he. When they hear about this business, let it be from the newspaper report.'

Why did her mother irritate her? She turned to Richard, saying now, 'I think you will be glad to get to bed.'

'I shall, but later on; I'm going back to the hospital first.'

'I'll . . . I'll come with you.'

'No. No; you can do nothing. As I said, she's asleep and she'll sleep until tomorrow. But I would advise you to take your own advice and get to bed. I'll be off now.' And he looked around the company before saying simply, 'Good-night,' then turning away.

Peggy followed him out of the room and to the front door, and there she asked him bluntly, 'Would you move away once you're married?' And he answered as bluntly, 'No. I'm in a partnership here and I'm working to pay it off. I can't just up and go where I please unless I want to lose everything I've worked for so far.'

'Oh.' She nodded, then said, 'I see. It was only a thought. I . . . I imagined she would be safer away from the town.'

'She'll be safe, don't you worry. A taste of prison should stop his capers, and that's what we'll hope for. Good-night.'

'Good-night.'

She didn't know whether she liked him or not, but there was one thing sure: once he married Emma she could say good-bye to her for, in a way, he would possess her as much as her father had done. That she would accept, for that was the penalty of marriage.

But oh, if only she could have married Charlie all those years ago and suffered that same penalty, how different her life would have been.

6

The group outside the courthouse broke up. Lizzie and Henry went towards their car, and Lizzie's voice could be heard protesting none too quietly all the way. Peggy and May, accompanied by Frank and Charlie and Richard, walked across the square to the far corner, and after unlocking the car door, Peggy turned to Richard and said, 'Only three months; I thought he would have got three years.'

'Well, hardly that. I did think, though, he would get twelve months. But he had a good advocate.'

It was May who now said, 'What with the month he's already been in and with good behaviour, he could be out in a few weeks.'

'Yes, he could.'

But Richard reminded them: 'He's on probation for a year and he'll have to be careful or he'll go back again. And if I ever saw fear of prison, I saw it in him back there. Anyway, come Saturday, she'll be under my protection and that'll be the end of it . . . What did you say?'

'I . . . I didn't think I was speaking but I must have been thinking aloud.' Peggy moved her head slowly. 'That solicitor, or whatever he was, saying Emma was the only love he had in his life. Estranged from his wife for years, a man who was full of loving feelings had to find someone to bestow them on, and a mistress wasn't enough. It never was in these cases; blood was thicker than water.' Peggy now dragged open the car door, adding, 'I could have been sick.'

After they were all seated in the car, Richard put his head in the window and looking at Peggy, said, 'Put it behind you; it's finished. You're free and you know that Emma will be safe and happy with me. What you've got to do now is to think of yourself and start a new life.'

'What! With Great-gran? Start a new life, Richard, with Great-gran?'

'She can't last forever. I think she could go just like that.'

When he snapped his fingers she gave a derisive laugh, saying, 'You don't know Great-gran, Richard. She'll last; she'll do it just out of spite. Anyway, I'll see you later. Come round for tea.'

'I'll do that.' He closed the door.

As the car moved away he stood for a moment looking after it, and he drew in a long breath on the thought of how glad he was that he was going to take his Emma away from that house of women. And it was a house of women; it seemed packed with them. It had seemed that every time he had taken Doctor Rice's place and visited that old girl, the granddaughter Lizzie had been present; and, of course, Peggy, often her friend May, and sometimes Emma. The house had always appeared to be full of women, and all at variance with each other. Well, come next Saturday there'd be one less, and he knew that no-one would be happier than Emma. He recalled what she had said to him last night: 'Lately, I've been in a nightmare, dreading something would happen to Mother and I should be the next to look after Gran-gran.'

And yes, she would have had to take over; that old woman was like a leech: first, she had fastened on to her daughter; and then her granddaughter; and now her great-granddaughter; and not forgetting Andrew Jones.

But roll on Saturday, when he would put an end to Emma's nightmare.

7

It was Saturday. It was over. Her daughter was married. There she was going up the stairs to change into her travelling clothes, not from a white wedding gown and veil, as she had often envisaged for her; no, she had been married in a blue silk suit with a grey cape; chic, very chic, but nothing romantic about it. There hadn't seemed to be anything romantic about the wedding at all. It had been very matter-of-fact, not unlike her own at the registry office, even though the ceremony had been performed in the church and the wedding breakfast served in an hotel. Only twenty-five people sat down; Richard's parents being dead, he had but one brother and he a bachelor.

Well, Peggy sighed, if the ceremony and the breakfast hadn't been romantic, they would certainly have a romantic honeymoon in Venice. She looked through the open door towards the drawing-room where Richard was standing talking to Henry and Charlie. Frank was sitting next to her mother on the couch, and they all had glasses in their hands. May was upstairs seeing to Great-gran. She had volunteered to look after her during the time they were all out. She was good was May. She didn't know what she would have done without her over the years, even while she knew she still had a tiny streak of resentment against her for being the stumbling block in Charlie's life, and depriving her of grandchildren.

She would go upstairs and relieve her now, so that she could have a word with Emma.

When she reached the landing, she saw May at the far end of the corridor. She had one hand tightly across her mouth and on seeing her, she stopped and began to beckon frantically towards her. She didn't move from where she was, and when Peggy neared her she grabbed her arm and pulled her back towards the door and into Mrs Funnell's room. Then, closing the door while still holding on to Peggy, she made an effort to speak, and when she did it was a mutter: 'She's dead.'

'Wh . . . at?'

'She was sitting up, going on about . . . about the wedding, and nobody having asked her consent. You know how she does. Then she suddenly lay back and closed her eyes, and I said, 'That's it, have a sleep,' and her hand slid down by her side. She's . . . she's dead, Peggy.'

Peggy slowly walked towards the bed and reluctantly, it seemed, she lifted her great-grandmother's hand and felt for a pulse; but there was no movement. The she lifted her eyelids. She was; she was dead.

'Should I bring Richard up?'

Peggy swung round, seeming to come to life now, saying, 'No. No. Neither of them must know. She's not going to spoil the start of their life. You would think she had done it on purpose. Look, I'll go and tell Emma she's asleep and that it's best not to waken her.'

'But she might want to come in.'

'Well, not if I can help it; but look.' She turned back to the bed and, lifting the limp arms, she put them under the bedclothes and reluctantly she tucked the sheet under the

286

drooping chin. Then turning to May, she said, 'Leave her like that, and . . . and sit there just in case she peeps in, and you can say . . . '

'Oh my God! Peggy, I can't sit here.'

'She's dead, May; she can't hurt you. You've been sitting here all day.'

'Yes, yes of course. It's the shock. Go ahead. Do what you have to do.'

Five minutes later, when the door opened and there stood Emma with Peggy by her side, she rose from the chair and, going towards them, said, 'I wouldn't disturb her, she's . . . she's' – she gulped – 'had a bad night, and she's . . . she's just dropped off. I . . . I . . . I wouldn't waken her.' She pressed them both out on to the landing again, and Emma said, 'Won't she get ratty, Auntie May, if I don't say goodbye?'

'Oh, well, y . . . y . . . you' – she couldn't stop herself from stammering – 'y . . . you know her, she gets ratty about everything. But I'll . . . explain. Oh, you do look lovely. I'll . . . I'll come down and see you off.'

Emma laughed and said, 'I bet you don't get to the bottom of the stairs before her bell rings.'

May and Peggy exchanged a quick glance, and Peggy said, 'Come on with you; Richard is stamping about down there like a wild horse.'

They were only half-way down the stairs when Emma stopped and, looking at her mother, she said, 'Oh, Mother, I'm . . . I'm so happy,' and at this she threw her arms around Peggy, and Peggy, gasping, said, 'Look out! else you'll have us both down the stairs and on our backs.' And there was a break in her voice as she finished, 'Come on with you.'

Richard and the others now came out of the drawing-room and there followed general exclamations of how beautiful the bride looked. But not from Richard; he said nothing, but his eyes told Emma all she wanted to know, and she was now kissed in turn by Henry and Frank, and Charlie, and her grandmother and May, and lastly by Peggy, and all her mother could say to her was, 'Be happy, dear. Be happy.' And Emma, with tears in her eyes, could make no reply, only nod. Then she was seated by Richard's side and they were moving off amid waves and calls of, 'Have a good time. Safe journey.'

When the car disappeared down the drive, Peggy was the first to turn away and hurry into the house, and when they were all once again assembled in the drawing-room, she went to the fireplace and stood with her back to it and clutched a handful of the bodice of her dress and moved it up and down as if trying to pull it from her body.

It was Charlie who spoke first, saying, 'What is it? She'll be all right. She'll be happy. But . . . but what's the matter?'

She looked at him, then at her mother and said, 'She's dead. Great-gran's dead . . . she's dead.' She watched her mother now sink slowly on to the couch and she heard Henry say, 'No, no,' and Frank say, 'But you were with her.' He was addressing his wife, and May nodded as she answered, 'Yes; one minute she . . . she was sitting up, going off the deep end about nobody taking any notice of her; I mean, asking her permission, like, about the wedding, then she lay back and she just went, like that' – she gave a gentle snap with her fingers, and repeated – 'like that,' not knowing that Richard had made a similar gesture of foretelling the old woman's demise.

'You should have called Richard.'

Peggy's head jerked towards her mother and now her voice was almost a shout as she said, 'And spoil their happiness, an' all?'

'Don't shout at me, girl.'

'That's what you forget, Mam, and I don't have to remind you yet again, that I am no girl. And I'll tell you something else: those two are not going to hear about this business until they return. This will be one fortnight in their lives during which this family won't impinge its troubles on them.'

'My God!' Lizzie got to her feet. 'I've seen changes in people over the years, but never as much as in you.'

'We've been through all this before, Mam, about changes and why there's been changes. So we won't go into that. But I shall go now and phone Doctor Rice.'

As Peggy marched out of the room Lizzie shook her head and looked at the men, saying woefully now, 'I just don't know what's come over her lately,' to which May retorted, 'Well, you should, Lizzie; you had years of it yourself.'

It looked as if Lizzie was going to come back at May, too, but thought better of it.

When Peggy returned to the room she said, 'He'll be along within half an hour.'

Both Henry and Frank had been about to say something when they stopped and they, with the rest of the company, stared at Peggy, who was now looking directly at Charlie and, her face bright and smiling, saying, 'I'm free, Charlie. I'm free. Free of this house, free to live my own life for the rest of it. Do you understand that, Charlie? Free! Free!'

As Charlie moved towards Peggy, his hand outstretched, Lizzie sprang up from the couch saying, 'My God! I've heard everything now. Of all the tactless remarks to make, and at this moment. Talk about lack of feeling.'

'Yes, talking about lack of feeling, Mam, let's stop being hypocrites for once. You've wished her dead for years and you can't deny it. Now what you'll be worried about is the will.' And turning abruptly about she again left the room, leaving them all, with the exception of Charlie, open-mouthed; for he had followed Peggy from the room and along the passage and into the study. And there he took her into his arms, and as the sobs shook her body

289

he comforted her, saying, 'There, there. It's all over. As you say, you're free. Oh! Peggy.' He lifted up her wet face and, looking into her streaming eyes, he said, 'You know I've loved you since I was a lad. I don't know at what stage of a lad I began to love you, but I've never stopped loving you since. And if a love can grow deeper with the years, mine has, but I've never loved or admired you more than I did a minute ago when you stood up to your mother and spoke the truth, because the next bone of contention will be the will. But whether the old girl has left you a penny or not, it doesn't matter – she might have left it all to the Salvation Army; I wouldn't put it past her – but there's one thing I'm sure of: we're going to be married. We were in any case, but we're leaving here, this house, and we'll settle some place, even though we may be spending half our lives travelling. I'll take you to places you've never dreamed of. You know' – he held her away from him – 'you've hardly left this town all your life. A few trips to Harrogate, that's the limit of your travelling. Well, all that's going to be altered, and the sooner the better. Roll on the reading of the will and the high jinks to follow.' He pulled her into his arms again and kissed her hard; then he said, 'What do you bet she leaves it equally between the Salvation Army and the Dogs' Home?'

8

The funeral had taken place at ten o'clock. They had returned home at eleven and had a light meal. The solicitor, accompanied by a clerk carrying a heavy portfolio, had arrived at two o'clock and his business was not concluded until four o'clock. Besides them, only Lizzie and Henry and Peggy had been present.

The contents of Mrs Funnell's will had caused surprise, to say the least, and Lizzie almost to faint and Peggy to cry inwardly, 'Oh, no, no. What am I going to do?'

By eight o'clock that evening she knew what she was going to do, and there were assembled in the drawing-room her mother and stepfather, Frank and May, and Charlie.

Her mother had not spoken to her since the solicitor had left the house, when she'd had to be helped upstairs by Henry to lie down and calm down, but she was saying now and vehemently, 'I could contest it.'

'Yes, you could do that, but from what I understand from the solicitor you'd come off badly.'

'It's scandalous, vicious. I looked after her for sixteen years; and not only that, I had to put up with your father, and . . . and she knew what I went through.'

'What you went through with my father, Mother, was nothing compared with what you and Great-gran contrived to make me go through by insisting that I marry Andrew Jones, when I begged you not to let it happen to me. And what I've gone through since didn't affect you. Well now, as a way of payment it seems she has left it all to me, on conditions. But, of course, knowing her, she wouldn't rest in her grave if she thought she hadn't caused complications.'

'Almost a quarter of a million pounds!' – Lizzie's voice was almost at hysteria point again – 'and the Works, besides the bonds and the property that none of us knew anything about. It isn't fair. It isn't fair.' She looked up at Henry, and he, quietly but with a tinge of bitterness in his voice, said, 'No, it isn't fair, dear, it isn't fair. But listen to what Peggy has to say.'

Peggy was staring at her mother; and her face was tight as she brought her words through almost closed lips: 'You think it isn't fair what's happened to you. Well, I think it isn't fair what's happened to me. Great-gran's left me a very rich woman *if*, and it is a big *if*. I always told her that I wanted to get away from this house, but she's fixed me there, for if I leave it within the next ten years I don't get a penny. Charlie was partly right when jokingly he said to me earlier that she could leave it between the Salvation Army and the Dogs' Home. Well, among other charities, she has mentioned the Salvation Army. My first reaction was to let the money go to the Salvation Army and the Dogs' Home, for it wasn't going to tie me here; but then May pointed out something: it says nothing in the will about my taking long holidays away from here, as I remember the wording of the will, only that this was to be my residence.' She looked at May now. 'So I have decided, May, it will still be my residence between times when I'm not travelling.' She now turned to Charlie. 'And as May also pointed out, I can have the place ripped out inside and re-done to my own taste, make it into a modern interior. There's nothing in the will to say I can't do that. This being so, the money, the business, and the rest are mine. I am, as I said, a very rich woman; but I don't want to be a very rich woman, so I've decided to share it. I'm quartering it. Mother, you'll have a quarter of the money and a percentage of the profits from the Works.'

Lizzie's head wagged now and her lips were pressed tightly together before she said, 'A quarter. That's very kind of you; a quarter.'

'It *is* very kind of me, Mother. Think on it; it *is* very kind of me. I'm dividing the money into four.'

'Four? Who are the others? There's only yourself and Emma.'

'Yes, there's myself and Emma and two others.' She now turned and looked at May. 'There is May, and you, Mother.'

'*Oh no!*' May's disbelief was expressed in the wagging of her head. 'No, no! lass, you can't do that.'

'I can do that, May. You have been a friend to every-body in this house for years: you stood by my mother, although she seems to have forgotten that; you certainly stood by me. You also had hopes, great hopes for your son. Well, he has fulfilled them in one way, but not in another. You and I know what I mean, but you never turned against me because of it; you've always been there. And of all the people I'm pleased to share the money with, you are the best because Emma would never have been short of money; Richard would be in a position to see to that.'

'I've heard everything now,' Lizzie said and got to her feet, at which Peggy turned on her, crying, 'All right! If this doesn't satisfy you, there's nothing yet in writing. I'll divide it into three; you might feel better if you have nothing whatever to thank me for.'

'I should have nothing to thank you for, girl, if I was getting my rights.'

'Be quiet! Lizzie. Be quiet.' Henry put his hand on his wife's shoulder, while looking at Peggy and saying quietly, 'Thank you, Peggy. I think you're being very fair, more than fair. And I understand the position you're in.'

'Thank *you*, Henry. It's good to hear you say so.'

As Lizzie shrugged herself from her husband's hold and marched from the room, May, after glancing at Peggy, hurried after her. And in the hall she caught her by the arm, saying, 'I knew nothing about this. I never dreamt. And I know how you feel, Lizzie.'

'Do you, May?'

'Yes, yes, I do.'

The tears now spurted out of Lizzie's eyes as she muttered, ''Tisn't fair. 'Tisn't fair.'

'No, your grandmother was never fair, but Peggy is. She didn't want that money, Lizzie. All she wanted was to get away with Charlie, leave this house and start up a life of her own, that's all she wanted. She's said so again and again. But she's been chained here for years. You know she has. But now there are escape routes for her. So . . . so try to be happy for her.'

'It's all right for you, May' – Lizzie was walking towards the door, Henry by her side now – 'you hadn't to put up with Grandmother.'

'No, perhaps not; but it's all in the past now, so try to make the best of it.'

May remained standing at the door until Lizzie and Henry had got into the car; she then closed it and stood leaning against it for a moment. How people changed. Lizzie would never forgive Peggy; it would always stick in her neck. Yet, really, she should be thinking herself lucky that she'd got anything. Peggy could have kept the lot, but what had she done?

She had divided it up, and even given her a share. Eeh! she couldn't really believe that: no more begging and scraping, making ends meet to keep respectable. She was lucky. Eeh! she was lucky. She hurried back into the breakfast-room now and, going straight to Peggy, she took her hand and she said, 'Peggy, that was something you needn't have done. You owe me nothing, because, like Charlie, I've loved you since you were a bairn. But to think that you've shared that fortune with me, it's like a miracle happening. Thank you, lass. Oh, thank you.' She put her arms around her and held her close, and Peggy said in a small voice and on a broken laugh, 'It's in payment for Charlie.'

9

Apart from the uncontested divorce, two incidents occurred that seemed to close the final chapters on Peggy's way of life and leave the way clear for the new one she was about to start tomorrow, when she would accompany Charlie for the first time abroad. The past weeks had been filled with business meetings with the solicitor and the working out of documents with regard to the division of her money. A fortnight before Charlie and she had been married and had spent a few days of their honeymoon touring the South Coast. Since then, the time had been mostly spent in poring over diagrams for the reconstruction of the house, deciding on colours and wallpapers; also the buying of furniture that was to await their return, mostly beds and carpets. All this, in their absence, was to be supervised by May and Frank because they would be away for at least six weeks, as Charlie had engagements in France, Germany and Spain.

She was going into Newcastle to pick up a suit that she was having altered. She was going in by train, and had left her car in the station car park and was walking towards the station entrance when a woman, coming through the opening, hesitated as she looked at her, then stopped and said, 'Mrs Jones.' Then after a second added, 'You don't recognise me, then? I'm . . . I'm Rosie, Rosie Milburn. I've . . . I've always wanted to meet you and say something.'

Peggy stared at the woman before her; she seemed to have no connection with the Rosie Milburn that had been so helpful in the house. And yet, on closer inspection she realised it was because this woman had hardly any flesh on her bones and Rosie had been plump, all over.

Her voice was stiff as she said, 'What did you want to speak to me about?'

'Well, you know' – the head wagged – 'just to say I'm sorry, but . . . but I couldn't help meself at the time. I knew later I had been a damn fool but . . . but you've got to learn, haven't you? He was a swine but I stuck by him. I'm glad he got his desserts, although it wasn't long enough. He left me high and dry without a penny and I could have claimed the house. I could have: it was in my name. I don't know where I'd have been if I hadn't put a bit by of me own when I was working. But that's not the point; I just . . . well, I always wanted to say I was sorry. But . . . but I did you a good turn, I suppose; well, you know what I mean: took him off your hands at least part of the day . . . you know what I mean,' the head was wagging again.

Peggy felt a rising pity in her for the creature that Rosie Milburn had become, and her voice sounded kindly as she said, 'Are you living in the town again?'

'Aye. I've been back some time. I'm with me brother again. He's bed-ridden, but I'm not goin' to be daft this time. I told him I wouldn't stay unless he put it in writing about the house. When he goes, I'll get the house, and that's something: I won't be left high and dry this time. And by the time he goes I'll have paid for it because he hasn't improved; he's awful to live with; all wants and no thanks. But . . . but that isn't the point, as I said; I . . . I just wanted to say again that I'm sorry. He'll . . . he'll come to a bad end; yes, he will. He was always on about his daughter, you know. He had a mania for her. Well, he's lost her, but he's got two more now.'

Peggy's whole face stretched as she said, 'What do you mean, he's got two more?'

'Oh, he's taken up with a divorced woman yon end of Gosforth, I understand. Nice house an' all and she's got two bairns, two little lasses, one three and one five. He might think he's fallen on his feet but he'll come to a bad end, you'll see . . . I hear you're going to be married again?'

'I am married.'

'Oh, I'm glad. Is it to the lad next door? I mean, Mr Conway?'

'Yes, it's to Mr Conway.'

'That's good; he was a nice fella. Made a name for himself an' all with his guitar. I once heard him play; he made that thing sing.'

When she became silent and stood, her eyes blinking, her fingers twitching one against the other, Peggy said, 'I . . . I must go else I'll miss my train.'

'All right. Goodbye. Just a minute.'

As Peggy moved away a hand came out and clutched her arm, saying, 'D'you forgive me?'

'Oh yes, don't worry about that; in fact, I never blamed you, Rosie. And I missed you when you left, so don't worry any more.'

When the face crumpled she turned swiftly away and made for the ticket office. Poor soul. How could anyone change so much and in so short a time, because it was only a comparatively few years ago that she had been a plump, pretty, laughing, likeable young woman.

She was saddened by the meeting and wondered if she could do anything for her, but told herself, no, she'd better

299

not. Anyway, no matter what she looked like, apparently she wasn't destitute.

In Newcastle she picked up the altered suit. The morning had turned slightly chilly and a fine rain was beginning to fall, so she decided to go into a restaurant and have a coffee. But the first one that she approached appeared full and when, further along the street, she came to a self-service cafeteria, she went hastily inside.

With a cup of tea in her hand she went to an empty table, and she had almost finished the drink when somebody at a near table exclaimed, 'Look, it's still raining but the sun's coming out.' She turned her head over her shoulder and looked through the window to where the wet road was glistening in the watery sunshine, and as she turned her head back she noticed a family leaving a table and moving towards the doorway. The woman looked young, in her mid-twenties and was smartly dressed, as were the children. The man had his back to her for a moment until he stopped to lift up the smaller of the two girls, and now his head seemed to be on a level with her own. She watched him hug the child to him, then straighten up, and now he stood glaring at her for a moment. She imagined he was going to make a move towards her, but what he did was hitch the child closer to him until its face was almost pressed against his own and then he smiled a smile that widened his full lips but, as she had seen before, did not separate his teeth. The young woman now looked over her shoulder and spoke to him; she was pretty and she looked happy. She began to push up an umbrella while he put his hand down and caught the hand of the elder child that was held up towards him, all the while keeping his gaze fixed on herself. Then something the woman said drew him through the doorway.

She now heard the children's gurgling laughter and she turned her head on her shoulder again and looked through

300

the window. The woman was holding the umbrella over him and the children and she was laughing into his face. Then the umbrella was tilted and she saw the back of them as they moved away out of her sight.

She sat back in her chair, her body trembling. That look on his face. It was as if he had said, 'Look what I've got now; two for the price of one.' And that girl, or that woman, or that wife; had he married her? How long would she be happy when she found out where his true love lay? Would she be like many another woman, keep her mouth shut while her children's lives were marred and scarred forever?

She wanted to go home; no, not home; she wanted tomorrow to come and get away. She wanted Charlie's arms about her. She wanted his love, something good and clean . . .

An hour later she was in his arms in his mother's sitting-room and she was pouring out the incident in the café. And when she ended, 'It'll be the case of Emma over again, only with both of them,' he shook her gently by the shoulders saying, 'You can do nothing about it. Yet, something *is* being done about it; it's coming into the open; the authorities are taking a hand. Look at the cases on television recently. But now you can be sure of one thing; Emma is safe, not only through marriage but through his new interest. He won't try any more tricks.'

'No, he won't try any more tricks, but those two children will likely have to pay for it.'

'Well, you know what my mother's always saying: everything in life has to be paid for, and you've paid for the happiness that's going to be yours in the future. It's been a long time from our schooldays, Peggy, but I've got my childhood sweetheart at last. Do you love me, Mrs Conway?'

'With all my heart, Mr Conway.'

'I can ask for no more then; but I can add one more thing: my heartfelt thanks in that you're free, if not actually from the house, then from its clutch of women.'

THE END